Ben Elves is a native of Norfolk. After spending many years in the Royal Air Force as an armourer and then working as a technician in nanotechnology and as a photographer, he now teaches aviation and mechanical engineering. His first love is motorcycling, followed closely by travel, photography and history. When not working or writing, he is most likely to be found exploring country lanes and winding roads or old ruins somewhere in the world, accompanied by a camera looking for inspiration.

Ben Elves

THIRTY PIECES OF SILVER

AUSTIN MACAULEY PUBLISHERS™

LONDON * CAMBRIDGE * NEW YORK * SHARJAH

A CIP catalogue record for this title is available from the British Library.

ISBN 9781398406278 (Paperback)
ISBN 9781398406285 (Hardback)
ISBN 9781398406292 (ePub e-book)

www.austinmacauley.com

First Published 2021
Austin Macauley Publishers Ltd®
1 Canada Square
Canary Wharf
London
E14 5AA

Foreword

I remember as a young child, around six years of age, secretly rooting through a wardrobe in my parent's house and finding an immense book bound in cream-coloured leather and bearing the inscription 'The Holy Bible' in gilt lettering on the front cover. I opened this gigantic tome and was instantly taken by the fantastic artwork inside; paintings by the great masters of the Tower of Babel, for example, a young man holding the head of a giant by the hair, and a bearded man with long hair who had been nailed to a couple of big planks of wood. My first impression was that this enormous book told a truly horrifying story that I probably shouldn't read as my parents wouldn't think it suitable for a boy of my age. They may have been right about that of course…so me being me, I started to read bits. I was lucky, my mother had invested many hours in my preschool years teaching me to read and write, and I was, therefore, able to do 'joined-up writing' by the time I started my schooling at the age of four.

I wondered what on earth sort of story this was; it seemed at first to be about this big man in the sky who was truly frightening…a nasty man full of spite and hatred and jealousy, a big giant he was; who delighted in making people suffer and seeing people in misery. I hated him. I thought that nobody should be that unpleasant. I put the book away, but the images of the artwork inside stayed in my head…and I revisited the book frequently to look at the pictures again, each time reading a bit more of the stories within. It all seemed to be about war and hate and doing as you are told. Oh, and lots of begetting, whatever that was. And men sleeping with their daughters…which seemed a bit odd. It wasn't long before I realised that this was the book about the god that we were being taught about in school. And yet I saw a huge disparity between what I was being told and what I was reading. At school, we were told that God was our Father and He loved me and everyone else, and that whatever we did, God would always forgive us but send us to hell if we were bad (a bit confusing, I have to say), whereas this book made God out to be someone who wanted everyone to suffer unimaginable horrors and be thankful for it. Nothing was ever good enough for God.

I thought about this a lot and then started noticing the things in the big cream book didn't add up. There were bits in it that said one thing and then contradicted itself. I couldn't understand how there were only four people in the entire world; Adam, Eve, Cain and Abel. Cain then killed his brother Abel and went away. Don't blame him: his mum and dad would have been rather annoyed. Anyway, after a while, he came back because he was rejected by the people…and a huge question jumped out at me shouting, "WHAT PEOPLE? THERE ISN'T ANYONE ELSE!"

After some while and a good amount of secret reading, I decided the book was rubbish, and so was all the stuff I was being taught at school about it all…even some of the Hymns we were expected to sing in morning assembly seemed idiotic, and there was no way I was going to praise that psychotic bastard up in the clouds who was letting people starve in foreign bits of the world.

Other than scoffing at the odd fool who thought God was nice and the Bible was true, I had no real thoughts on religion through my early teenage years and didn't think any more about it until I joined the RAF. Then in training, I had to attend something called 'Padre's Hour' where I was obliged to listen to what I considered to be the biggest pile of logic-defying nonsense I had ever heard. I didn't like the padre – he seemed too full of self-satisfied smugness and thought he had an answer for all questions put to him, so I decided I wanted to catch him out with something he couldn't shrug off as a miracle, or 'God moving in mysterious ways'.

I asked him about the Cain and Abel thing – who were these other people – and got a look of anger fired back at me. *Gotcha!* I thought. He answered my question like a true politician – by not answering it at all and waffling on about something else.

As I grew older and my interest in history became deeper, it dawned on me there was probably an element of truth in the Bible; it was just a case of reading between the lines. *The Bible is a legend*, I thought, *and there is always something true in a legend.*

This book is a step in my journey through my thoughts and conclusions so far regarding Jesus, who he was, and what was really going on. I confess to adding a bit of fiction to the accounts of his life found in the Gospels to fill in the missing bits but I have done this after many years of research; investigating not only the gospels, but trying to put myself into the mindset of the people of the time, their hopes and lives, the events, politics and the society in which they lived, and finding out about their religious views and practices. Human nature has to be taken into account too, for that is the one thing that hasn't really changed. Since Jesus was around, we have had had nearly 2000 years to banish hatred, greed, perversion, violence, bigotry and stupidity, but we haven't managed it yet.

It should be remembered that our own society has changed beyond recognition in the past 60 years, and we cannot look at the story of Jesus without understanding that he and his contemporaries lived in a culture totally alien to ours in both time and geography. People back then had a tough time living on a knife-edge where their existence teetered between disaster, death, persecution and disease on the one hand and a life which was hard and full of suffering on the other…and they knew nothing else, there was no organised welfare structure, and there was no concept of 'human rights', just law. So much in their world was mysterious, unexplained and seemingly illogical. It is no wonder these comparatively backward and ignorant people wanted something to believe in, that there had to be a point to it all, and that one day, things would get better.

The purpose of this book is simple. I wish to offer a story different from the one that has been embellished upon and mistranslated over the centuries and to enable the reader to start asking questions about us as a society and what we believe in, the integrity and motivation of the church and the people within it, and to ask the reader to think freely about faith and religion and what the bible actually says, using common sense and not attributing events of the past to some form of holy magic. For even now, there are many so-called intelligent people who switch off from thinking about what must have been the reality in favour of the comfort of having something nice to believe in, despite how ridiculous it all seems when studied in the cold light of day. At this point, I would like to add a little fact which I find quite entertaining; and that is, that your average Atheist knows almost a third more about the Bible than your average Christian.

Anyway, that's enough of hearing about me…lets now hear the story of Him.

"It has served Us well, this myth of Christ."

Pope Leo X

Introduction

A New Religion

Being a Roman citizen was a source of great pride, as was being a hater of those who practised the new religion of Christianity. Christians – pathetic pacifists who believed in loving numbers, loving secrets and mysteries, loving each other, and loving their enemies too. Would Rome have ever achieved greatness by loving its enemies? No. The only way to treat your enemies was to crush them, show them who was in charge, then show them the advantages of being under Roman authority. Those who can't be persuaded should be persecuted and killed as a lesson to others.

Christians.

Worthless effeminate troublemaking scum.

Paul had been a Christian hater. He had believed in hunting them down, rooting them out and punishing them for their idiotic ideals. That was until he nearly died of exposure in the desert. His mind had played tricks on him. His obsessive hatred had changed under the influence of his thirst-driven delusional hallucinations.

Paul came from the desert a changed man. He realised that instead of persecuting Christians, he could manipulate them. Indeed, Jesus had been a charismatic man, Paul wished he could have met him, and some of the stories surrounding him had already become fantastical – The stuff of legend. Jesus, the failed rebel, had become a hero – his knowledge of medicine had become acts of God, and instead of just being a radical Essene Messiah or Bishop, there was now a belief that he really was the son of God.

Manipulating Christians would be easy. Already in their ignorance, they believed just about anything good or magical said about the man. The more unbelievable the story, the more the fools believed it.

Now is the time, Paul thought, *to get these people organised into a proper religion*. The rewards could be great. It seemed to Paul that wealth and power were just around the corner. He just had to spin a few very good yarns. And so, Paul founded what has become the Catholic Church.

Paul, later known by the apostles as 'The Liar'.

Paul, who was blamed by Emperor Nero for the Great Fire of Rome and had his head hacked off.

Paul the Saint.

Even after 2000 years, Paul's ambition makes a fortune. Thanks to the power struggles and politics of Roman emperors such as Constantine in AD 312, and a few years later by Theodosius – the man who outlawed the majority of the Gospels; their manipulation of people still continues – as does their hypocrisy. Two thousand years of lies, persecution, torture, robbery and murder had paid off. For the Roman Catholic Church is still one of the richest and most powerful organisations in the world. It is also one of the most secretive.

And the last thing they want is for anyone to know who Jesus *really* was…

Chapter 1
Bethlehem

The holy woman lay back in the dry, sweet-smelling straw, a thin sheen of sweat all over her exhausted body. The birth had been easier this time, her first had been sheer agony and the thought of this one had terrified her, and a dark, flea-infested stable hadn't been the best place to give birth either. Being an Essene wasn't easy, and despite being of the old nobility, no one in Bethlehem was prepared to give her and her family a bed for the night. Essenes weren't too popular these days, and they tended to be regarded by the majority as being a bit hard-line – not fitting with the new culture of hedonism that seemed to be slowly but surely pervading Hebrew culture since the arrival of the Romans. They had travelled down from the north by ox-cart to register for the census, and the journey had taken its toll on her, triggering the birth of her new son. She wasn't due for another four weeks.

Rachael, the midwife, smiled at her.

"Good news, my lady, the child is whole and healthy."

Mary smiled with relief and closed her eyes, utterly exhausted.

"Shall I fetch your husband?" Rachael asked.

Mary nodded; she did not have the strength to answer.

Joseph was squatting on the ground outside the stable entertaining his son James when Rachael bent down beside him and whispered.

"My lady wishes you to attend her – you have a beautiful son."

Joseph looked up. "How is the child?" he asked, unable to hide his anxiety.

"As a child should be," she answered – a careworn smile upon her lips.

"And my wife?"

"Tired, and in need of the sight of you and little James," she said.

Joseph stood and lifted James into his arms. He kissed James on the forehead.

"Let us see your new brother," he said.

"Have you chosen a name for the boy?" asked Joseph.

Mary nodded. "Yehoshua – Jesus, I think – our Messiah suggested it last month. He feels it is important to name him so, if the prophecy is to bear fruit."

"Jesus it is then. It is a shame he was born before the registry of the new census. We have enemies, and I would prefer that the Sanhedrin remained unaware of his birth. I fear we will have to go into hiding, for the Sanhedrin have already warned King Herod that you were with child. It is fortunate that they know not our names, or where we live. Yet."

"We should go to Egypt," Mary said, "My cousins will protect us and the children can be educated there. They can learn the old ways and remain free of the corrupt influence of the Temple in Jerusalem. We will have them taught the path of the true Essene."

"We should have them taught the Egyptian knowledge too, engineering, medicine, mending of the mind, philosophy and so on. Perhaps also the way of warfare. I will teach them carpentry and the art of building. We should leave as soon as we are able…or rather, as soon as you are able. I will have Elizabeth informed of our decision. She should, I think, come with us and bring the baby John with her. We must move quickly and in secret back to Galilee, have the baby circumcised then head to Egypt." Joseph stood. "I will summon the three Magi; they wait outside the town. Their rites will take but a few minutes to perform. Are you strong enough to eat yet? You still look very weak."

Mary looked up at her husband. "It is not the hunger for food I have – it is the hunger for change. The boys will be the cause of it. The day of truth and judgement is in sight." She looked down at the baby in her arms and a tear of joy rolled slowly down her left cheek. "It is hard to believe this innocent babe has already so much responsibility, and that our nation's future lies in the palm of his tiny hand."

"Amen to that."

Joseph knelt beside his beloved James. "My boy – you must love your brother like no other. You do not understand why yet, but as you grow together, you will come to understand that the one born alive after you will be a great man. As a child, you must help protect him, and in time, he will protect us all and save us from the corrupt. He will truly set us free."

James looked up at his father. "Pee, pee?" he said.

Joseph smiled and ruffled his hair. "Nice to see you were listening, Son," he said.

***

The journey to north was uneventful. Two-year-old James was fascinated by everything he saw – horses, camels, donkeys – everything. At one stage, they had been passed by a Roman patrol with their polished helmets and shields blazing in the sunshine, red cloaks dusty with the grime of the road as they marched along to the sound of clanking equipment. They looked fearsome and healthy, alert and well-disciplined. When James saw them, his mouth gaped and his eyes widened. He pointed at the men. "Sodgers, Daddy!" he shrieked, jumping up and down. The platoon commander looked over as he marched and smiled at the young boy, raising his fist to his chest to salute him.

James clapped his hands with delight, and Joseph nodded at the man. When the patrol had passed, Joseph halted the ox-wagon. He wiped the sweat from his brow and looked at the muddy smear he had left on his sleeve. The heat today was ferocious, and his hair felt dirty and damp. Joseph's eyes ached from being screwed up against the bright burning sunlight for hours. Flies buzzed around the rear of the ox as it lifted its tail and defecated loudly.

"Mary, we will be home in four hours, we should rest a while. How is the baby?" he asked.

"Travelling has bothered him not at all – he seems suited to the slow rhythm of the road," Mary answered. "Tomorrow, he must be presented at the synagogue, and then I really must rest a day or so. After that, we should journey to south and west for the Nile. We dare not linger too long. The priests and our friends in Qumran will deny our visit if questioned, but it's pointless taking risks unnecessarily. I do not want to be around if Herod's men come looking. I trust God's goodwill to help us, but we must still take care," Mary said.

They drank the warm brackish water from their skins, to wash down their lunch of bread, goat's cheese and grapes, and within the half-hour, they were moving again – Joseph and James on foot, leading the big dusty farting ox, whilst Mary fed her baby on the back of the cart.

By early evening, they were home – Mary's cousin Elizabeth was waiting for them in the central courtyard-cum-garden of their flat-roofed house, nursing her son in the shade of the olive trees. Elizabeth looked radiant and beautiful –

13

motherhood seemed to have brought out the best in her. At 41, she looked no different than she had at 25, other than a few soft lines around her big brown eyes and the corners of her mouth. The signs of a woman who smiled for much of her waking hours. She shone with happiness at the sight of Mary walking towards her with her new baby in her arms. Elizabeth stood, kissed her cousin on the cheek and motioned her to sit beside her.

"This is he?" she asked, looking at the sleeping baby in Mary's arms.

"It is indeed, cousin," Mary replied.

Elizabeth looked down at her own child. "And my John is to be his fellow Messiah," she said proudly. "I fear the honour may be the death of him. But what has been decreed must come to pass."

Mary placed a hand on her cousin's knee. "Worry not, Elizabeth, Jesus will take good care of him. John will be always dear to my Jesus. In the new kingdom, John will be a lord, a Messiah like no other, and he will preside over the church of the new Israel. He will pass laws to ensure the purity of our people, and be known for his wise ways. But, Elizabeth, he must be educated first.

"We must flee to Egypt for a time – I fear Herod the king. He will forever seek to protect his throne, and he must have by now been informed that a new king is among us. He will, in all likelihood, hunt my son down and have him put to the sword along with all who are associated with him. Come with us. John will be as a brother to James and Jesus, the same way you and I are as sisters. We have influence in Egypt, our kinfolk are respected there and the boys will be safe and will gain benefit from the teachings in that land."

"You speak wise words, cousin," Elizabeth said, "Egypt is indeed far further than the reach of Herod's spear-points, but I have a worry that those very spears are already on the march. What if Herod has already issued orders to his soldiers? They would seek for us all and look for our deaths, it is true, but I worry that they may be upon our doorsteps any time now. I heard from the synagogue messengers that Herod has discussed the death of all Essene boys aged two years and younger. Despite his liking for cruelty, I doubt he will go to that extreme. He will take no chances of being usurped but knows that although our people are not strong enough to stand against him, such a move would cause rebellion. It is, as you say, not just Jesus that is in peril but James and John too. Likely, all of us."

Elizabeth's face suddenly became angry. "And the Romans stand back and watch! Caesar Augustus cares not how his lands are controlled, as long as they are controlled. My husband says it suits Rome to see the Hebrew people fighting amongst themselves. He says they are well versed in the policy of 'divide and conquer'. When do we leave?"

Mary looked up at the sky. "The day after tomorrow," she said. "Pray that Herod's men do not reach us before then, else the only journey we make will be to meet God. And we must not meet Him until His work here is done. Fear not. God knows this, and He will ensure our safety."

Joseph walked from the dim coolness of the house into the garden. "It is arranged – Jesus goes to the temple at sunrise for circumcision and we leave for Egypt as planned. The synagogue is sending two warriors with us on our journey to protect us. The priests say Herod's men may be only three days away and are busy spilling blood wherever they find a male child. We are not safe, but God willing we will escape in time. You come with us, Elizabeth?"

Elizabeth nodded. "What choice is there?" she said. "I did not think Herod would kill all the children. It seems that I was wrong."

***

Two days later, they were travelling again and heading south and west towards the land of their forefathers – the land that their people had once ruled and then become slaves in before Moshe led them through the wilderness to their freedom so many centuries ago. James spent a lot of his time with the two guards, both Zealots from villages around Masada – the small city sandwiched between the Dead Sea and the great barren land of En-Gedi. Joseph had made him a wooden sword, a spear and a shield, and the little boy tried his best to be an Essene warrior. James had decided that their two goats were enemy prisoners and shouted at them mercilessly, prodding them every now and then with his spear. It was evident the goats were unlikely to rise in rebellion despite their bleating complaints.

They had been travelling a week when they camped and had a feast to celebrate James's third birthday. The two warriors presented him with a necklace of beads and tried their best to hide their smiles as they declared him their commander, praising him for his commitment to keeping the two goat-prisoners from escaping. James was a man among men they declared – just look at his huge muscles! The feast marked a turning point in the atmosphere for everyone in the past seven days had been very tense. All eyes had been scanning the countryside on the lookout for the pointed helmets of Herod's troops, but now as the distance between themselves and Nazareth grew, the tension lessened. Everyone laughed as James marched around the campfire flexing his arms and showing off his physique as the wood crackled and sent clusters of sparks heavenward to the starry blackness. Even Jesus smiled as his baby-blue eyes gazed at his big brother in the orange glow of the firelight.

Their slow and discreet journey took them to Caesarea, and then down the coast through Jappa, Jamnia, Azotus, and then to Ashkelon where they hired a small boat and its five-man crew to take them on to Egypt. They had finally left both Israel and the last of their fears behind them.

Chapter 2
Egypt

It was the middle of summer, and Joseph was once again waiting anxiously for news of his wife. He had heard her cries as she tried to push the baby out. He hated this eternal wait and felt powerless to aid his beloved during the trauma of childbirth. Joseph was a big man – masculine, broad-chested and muscular, with hardened calluses on his hands which were the mark of his trade. But when his wife was in labour, he felt like a helpless child. At least this baby would not be born in a stable.

Joseph cast his mind back to that night three years ago when his second son was born. His life had changed a lot since then, and all for the better. Joseph had run a successful business back home, building and designing houses and also making furniture. He had 30 men in his employ and ran his affairs in a very hands-on manner. He had left the business in the trusted and capable hands of his foreman and had every confidence that the man would continue to make healthy profits in his absence.

Since arriving in Egypt, he had started another business, again designing houses and making furniture, but not getting involved in any actual construction work other than as an overseer. The money kept rolling in, and in the truth, that afforded quite a comfortable lifestyle.

James was now six years old and was showing a keen interest in learning all he could. The boy had a mind like a sponge, soaking up all he was taught – especially in matters of military and to do with his father's workshop. He was always interested in soaking up more. James had an amazing vitality, and he loved fighting with other boys of his age. He won these fights far more often than not. He was learning to be a warrior and a tradesman – a good one. Joseph knew James had charisma too. He seemed to be able to charm anyone.

Jesus was very different – he had great strength of character already, even though he was only close to being three years old. He always seemed thoughtful, and sometimes, Joseph worried that the boy was just a bit too quiet. Jesus loved to watch his father in the workshop, fashioning things from timber or carving shapes in stone. The boy would frequently lift wood-shavings from the floor and hold them to his nose to smell them.

Joseph's thoughts were interrupted by the squealing of a baby. Praise be – it was over. Without ceremony, he burst into the room to see his wife and new child. Mary looked at him and smiled, eyes tired and bloodshot with the sheer physical effort of the past few hours.

"Husband, the more children we have, the easier it gets. We have another son. You must name him."

Joseph took the bundle from the arms of the Egyptian midwife and looked at the frowning face of his new son. "He is Jude," he said. "James, Jesus, and Jude. I think a daughter would be nice next." He smiled at his wife.

"Is that so?" said Mary, her voice hoarse from her recent exertion. "And perhaps you would like to give birth to her too?"

Elizabeth walked over to him with her arms outstretched. "Joseph, I think it's time for the baby to be washed, and your wife would benefit from sleep. Away with you now and wash yourself too. You have the odour of a dead ox!" Joseph was shooed from the room, and as the door was closed behind him, he lifted his arm and sniffed at his armpit. Elizabeth was right. He smelt truly awful. As he walked across the courtyard to the workshop, he stopped. Hezekiah the priest stood in the shadow of the workshop doorway. "It would seem we both have news," the old man said. "A boy or a girl?"

Joseph grinned. "Another boy – Jude. I settled for the name you suggested."

The old priest smiled. "This is welcome news, Joseph – and how is the new-born child's beautiful mother?"

"She seems well and in good spirit, Father. May I ask what this good news is that you bring?"

"It seems that as God gives, he takes. Jude comes into your world, and King Herod passes out of it. Joseph, Herod is dead, his interminably long 34-year reign of terror is ended, and his three sons rule in his stead. The new king of Galilee, Archelaus, seems to be a very different man to his father. This king holds no fear of the Sanhedrin. He regards them as a council of fools. The power of the Sanhedrin is weakening in Galilee."

Joseph nodded. "And do you know how he thinks of the Romans? Herod made himself very popular with our overlords," he asked.

Hezekiah shrugged. "I know not yet. And it matters not. I must go, Joseph. I have others I must pass this news to, and letters to write." Without further words, the priest turned and shuffled off through the gate. Once outside, he looked back at Joseph and gave a little dance, then laughed and walked away.

***

Later that evening, Joseph sat with his wife and told her of the news from home.

"I think we should stay here in Egypt awhile yet; the boys would benefit from their learnings still," said Joseph. Mary nodded in agreement.

"I worry some about Elizabeth though," she whispered, "she seems unhappy here, and so does John. He and Jesus fight some. Already there seems to be jealousy in John's heart, and animosity grows between them; Jesus has a toy, John wants it. Jesus has a cuddle, John wants one. And so on. He craves any attention Jesus gets."

"They are but little children yet, Mary, no less should be expected of them at their age, and things will change," Joseph said in hushed tones. Personally, he would prefer it if Elizabeth decided to leave and find happiness back in their homeland as he felt that she was living in his pockets half the time, and he was himself finding a growing dislike inside him for her son. He did seem to be quite an odd little fellow with a nasty streak that seemed to fester just beneath his skin. His tantrums were plentiful and unwarranted too, and many a time Joseph had been sorely tempted to slap his backside. Young John was in desperate need of some harsh discipline, and Elizabeth seemed to be both unwilling and incapable of supplying it.

Mary bit her bottom lip. "Joseph, I fear to say what is in my heart for it feels like meanness, but – well, sometimes, I see such a look of hatred in John's eyes when he looks at our second son. It appears almost a form of madness sometimes, and for one so young…well, I confess it disturbs me. And a more stubborn child than John I have yet to meet. He passed three years of age only days ago, and seems as resolute as a Roman emperor!"

Joseph smiled and sat back in his chair. "Perhaps a Roman emperor he will be one day; Rome could do with a fine Hebrew mind running the world. Never would our people see oppression again, eh?"

Mary touched his hand and smiled. "Joseph, sometimes you speak nonsense, as do all men. Sometimes, you speak wisely, but your notion of John ruling Rome? I do not know which that idea is – stupidity or genius. Now please, let me sleep, the baby will wake soon enough for feeding."

Joseph rose from the chair beside the bed and bent down to kiss her on the cheek. He stood and, for a few moments, looked down lovingly at her, then turned and left the room. He had work to do.

***

The following day, young James arose early, breakfasted and headed into the yard for his tutoring. Today's lesson was about God and his many identities in different lands. How he was also the Egyptian God Aten, the One God. How Aten was depicted as the sun, the God of light and, therefore, the God of all life. Within minutes, James was bored silly. Learning about God was the one thing he didn't really care for. As Hezekiah spoke, James's attention wandered. In his mind, he pictured himself fighting great battles against the sunset. He had not noticed his little brother wander over and sit down beside him. And as the morning hours sidled past, he also failed to notice that his tutor was no longer talking to him as he daydreamed but to an attentive Jesus.

***

As the weeks rolled past, Mary was fully occupied caring for Jude, who seemed quite frail compared to his robust brothers. Joseph spent his hours in the workshop making all fashion of things from wood, or drawing plans for new buildings. James and Jesus had lessons, though how much Jesus was learning as a two-year-old was anyone's guess. John appeared in the yard quite frequently now too, for he wasn't going to miss out on lessons if Jesus was having them. The weeks turned into months, and months into years. By the time Jesus was seven years old, he had learnt a great deal. He learnt about God. He learnt about medicine, and what plants could be used to heal certain ailments. He learnt how to speak to people who were troubled. He learnt history and became familiar with the names of many Roman, Greek and Egyptian leaders and generals. He learnt about engineering, mathematics and trigonometry. He also learnt to question what he was taught, and as he grew older, he learnt to think in depth about the things he was taught. He learnt never to assume that because he was told something that it was an undeniable truth. He was taught to draw his own conclusions.

By now, Jude was attending the old priest's lessons too but was finding things like theology hard to grasp. If Jude could see something, he could relate to it. He was finding learning quite difficult, and having a short attention span didn't help. Jude much preferred physical work and having fun. His two older brothers adored him – always smiling, kindly, and slightly mischievous.

Then, three weeks after Jesus' tenth birthday, and only one week after John and Jesus had had a fight in the lane outside the house which resulted in two broken noses, Elizabeth announced to Mary that she wished to return to Galilee.

After a week of preparation and many tears, Mary waved Elizabeth goodbye as her beloved cousin departed with a caravan for the coast to catch a vessel sailing for home. Joseph had mixed feelings – for his own part, he was somewhat glad to see her and her brat of a son leave, but he did not like the sadness which the departure brought to his wife.

It was only four months later when the tragedy occurred. Joseph, whilst repairing tiles on the workshop roof, dislodged one underfoot, slipped and fell.

Joseph felt cold as he lay there in the sun, knowing his neck and skull were broken and feeling his life slip away from him. There was no pain, and he was unaware of the clear liquid and blood running from his ears. He felt a deep sadness and despair draw over him like a cloak of black fog as he thought about never seeing his boys grow to manhood, and he knew he would never again see that wonderful look on his wife's beautiful face as they made love. His vision blurred as he silently wept, unable to wipe the tears from his face with arms he could not move. A few minutes later, he quietly slipped into unconsciousness and made his life's final journey to the land of the dead.

It was Jesus who found his inert body lying in the dust of the yard by the workshop wall. He cried uncontrollably as James calmly walked up behind him and held his shaking shoulders. James had not a single tear in his eyes, he felt just sadness and anger but did not know who to be angry with. It was no one's fault, just a tragic accident. After Joseph's body was lifted and taken for preparation for the funerary rites, Jesus walked into his father's workshop, sat on the dusty floor and lifted a handful of wood-shavings. He knew the smell of freshly cut wood would always remind of the hours he spent watching his father planing, chiselling, smoothing or sawing – fashioning all manner of objects from the timber. As he sat there, feeling lost and alone, Jude walked in.

"Jesus, what are you doing? Why are you in here?" he asked.

"I am remembering Father," he replied quietly. "We will never see him working again. God has him now, and it is not right. God has all the things he wants, for he is God. All I want is my father, and He took him away from me. The one thing I want, God took. Does that sound like a God of love to you? Have I done something to offend God, that he wants to punish me so? Or did you offend him? Or was it James? I don't think so. We do all we can to please him, don't we? Or has Father gone to sit with God as a reward for being a good man? If so, Father's reward is our punishment, and I don't understand it."

Jude looked at his older brother. "God is punishing Mother too, Jesus. It is not just us. Do you think Mother offended God?"

"Mother never offended God," said James evenly from behind them. "But Father is gone, regardless of the reason. We must be brave. We mustn't cry. We must work hard as Father did, harder perhaps."

"Then we must stick together and help Mother," said Jesus, "she will need us. Perhaps this is God's way of testing us."

***

After Joseph's funeral, James spent more and more time with Jesus in the workshop. Despite only being 12 and 10 years old, they had become quite capable and talented carpenters themselves, and Jesus felt in his heart that whenever he was working, his father was working through him. He felt that his hands were being guided by the strong sinewy hands of Joseph as he cut and shaped. James gave up on his tutoring after four months or so to spend more time at work, but when Jesus asked him if he should do the same, James glared at him.

"Don't you dare," he said. "You would dishonour both Mother and Father if you did that. Jesus, you must learn all you can. Make some sense of the world. Being a carpenter or a soldier is all I am fit for, and Jude is no better than I. But you, Brother, you are different. You think about things. You could be a doctor with all you know about medicine already. Or an architect for that matter, you are good with numbers and drawing."

"There is too much for you to do here alone," Jesus said.

"No matter, Jude can help when you are at lessons." James smiled and winked. "And he is easier to boss around than you too."

***

And so Jesus continued with his education and found the more he learnt, the more there was still to learn. He learnt more about politics, astronomy and numerology, the history of his people, he immersed himself in the writings of the prophets and spent hours in the synagogue questioning the priests learning all he could about church law. He learnt all he could of the tribes of Israel and became interested in the different ideals of the Hebrew peoples – surprised at how the way they practised their religion according to the region from whence they came. Jesus was starting to feel that these differences were hypocrisy in some ways and that the church should be united. *If the church were united*, he thought, *then the people would be united too. And if the people were united, then the Hebrew people would become a great nation once again. And a great nation would please God, as that is just what He had intended at the very beginning of the world.* As Jesus thought about this more, he became more convinced that his own Essene beliefs were the correct ones. Obey God's laws, unify the people, and woe to those who stood in the way of God's will. He considered what he knew of the workings of the Sanhedrin, and thought them to be corrupt – self-serving pigs interested in only their own positions of wealth and power. Men are only interested in doing themselves a good turn in the name of the Lord. He thought about the long-gone Hyksos, a powerful and ferocious warrior tribe of the Hebrew people who had united their beliefs and practices, and, as a result, had overthrown Egyptian rule over the Lower Nile and formed a kingdom worthy of that built by the pharaohs of old.

If the children of Israel could defeat the mighty forces of the Egyptian Empire, then they could do the same to the hated Pagan Romans. A revolution was needed.

***

Jesus' 12th birthday soon arrived, and after the evening's celebratory feast, Mary asked him to accompany her on a walk.

"What is wrong, Mother?" asked Jesus, as they walked past the lush green fields in the orange glow of the late evening sun.

"I have been observing you," she said simply. "I have also been hearing a lot about you from Hezekiah and your other tutors, your brothers, and many others who know you. You are quite a remarkable boy, and very nearly, a man. Your father would be proud of you, as I am."

Jesus walked in silence, not knowing what to say.

"I think you are a little frustrated though, confused, and know not who you are," she continued. "So, it is time you were told. Jesus, you have a destiny, as do we all, but yours is different from all men before you. It is for no small reason that you are the way you are. I see plainly that there is much going on in that head of yours, perhaps if you tell me what it is and why you ponder so much, I can explain why. Jesus, what things cause you such great depth of thought?"

"Mother, I do not fully understand all that I feel," he said. "But some things are clear to me. When I learn about our people and God, I feel blasphemous thoughts, and it makes me afraid that I offend God. But I cannot stop them. Am I evil?"

Mary stopped and smiled at him.

"No, my dear son, far from it. But please, tell me what these thoughts are – do you hate God?"

"No, Mother, I do not. But I am beginning to hate the church and those who hold rank in it. They are liars, Mother, and use God's word to their own ends. The church is a church of basemen and their petty desires, and it is not the church of The One God. As in the time of Moses, our people have strayed from the path, and the church is what has led them away from it. The Church even seems to disapprove of science and true knowledge. We are God's chosen people, and yet the priests have us turning our backs to Him. The world is full of sin, and I fear God will smite us all and punish us if we do not return to the old ways. I have thought about Herod and the Romans, and I think God sent them as a warning, they are the beginning of our punishment, and we fail to see it."

Mary placed a hand on his shoulder. "It is time then, I think, to help you understand. There is a prophecy that a man will come to Israel, and bring change to the world. Bring the people closer to God, and this man will come from the land of Egypt yet not be of the land of Egypt. He will know God's intentions and obey God's laws, not the laws of the church, and he will be king of all the Jews. He will topple the false kings of Israel, he will oust the invaders of our land, and he will bring judgement down upon the false priests of the Temple in Jerusalem and build Israel anew. He is a true son of God, and he is you."

Jesus looked at his mother, the enormity of her statement catching him totally off guard.

"Mother…I…I am only 12 years old. What can I do? I am no king. I do not have gold, an army, or anything like the power of a king."

"You must listen to Hezekiah, for he knows who you are and believes in you. He says the proof that you are the *chosen one* is in the way you are. You are to be made a Messiah soon, for you know already more about God's ways than many a priest, it seems. You are gifted."

Jesus' throat was dry. "A Messiah? Me? A Bishop? But, Mother, I cannot be a Bishop in a church I feel is wrong! I…I don't understand. I am a carpenter's son, no Bishop or King," he said hoarsely.

"My dear son, the best way to change a church is to hold rank in it and change it from the inside. This is your destiny, Jesus, and has always been. But you must be careful, you will make enemies. They will be many and powerful. You will sometimes think the world hates you, and as long as you remember that you are a true son of God, you will win through in the end. Have faith."

Jesus felt his stomach rise with fear. "What do I do? How am I supposed to change things?" he asked.

"You will know in your heart. Pray to God, and he will show you and tell you what to do." Mary knelt and put her arms around Jesus, holding her head against his chest. She could hear and feel his heart pounding with anxiety. "I love you, Jesus, and I have faith in you. Do not be scared, for others will help you. Your cousin John for one – he will help prepare the way for you in the hearts of the people, for this is a prophecy too. He will have faith in you and love you also, and it is the same with your brothers. I see in both James and Jude a deep love for you. They hold you close to their hearts and admire you. They look up to you, value your opinion, and you are the voice of reason for them. Soon enough, all the Hebrew peoples will look upon you with the same feelings in their hearts. They will all be as your brothers and sisters, and you will show them the true path to God."

"John?" Jesus asked. "John has always hated me; we fought. Hardly a day passed without…"

"Yes, you fought." His mother interrupted. "This concerned both myself and your dear father for a while, and I have spoken to Hezekiah about this. He told me this was John's way of getting the measure of you – finding out who you really are. As John grows, he will think back and consider his childhood here in Egypt with us, and he will see why he harboured jealousy in his heart. But he will come to terms with his feelings and actions. Understand them. You and he will travel on different roads for many years. On occasion, your paths will cross, of that, there is no doubt. But in time, your destinations will turn out to be the same – as the favoured sons of God. Now come, let us return home and allow you to think upon your destined path."

Jesus walked all the way home beside his mother in silence. His mind was racing. He knew he had to think hard about what he had been told, and he felt that a great weight had been placed on his shoulders.

***

The following morning, after a restless night's sleep, Jesus went into the yard for the day's lessons with Hezekiah.

The sound of wood sawing and the laughter of his brothers in the workshop seemed at odds with his mood.

Hezekiah spoke first. "You seem sombre this day, Jesus," he said. "Your mother has told you your path?"

Jesus nodded, and Hezekiah sat on the ground next to him.

"What your mother told you is true. I have done all I can to educate you, to equip you with the tools you need for your life's journey. I will continue to do so as long as I am able, but I feel the time will soon come when you will be the one to teach me. I see the way you question the teachings of the church and the way you see the world. And now you know your place in that world, I hope everything is much clearer to you. There will be times when you doubt yourself, perhaps even doubt God. This is good and will ensure you always think about your path. But do not fear, you will always have others to turn to – your mother for one. She has absolute faith in you, and you will find in time, that others do too. Now…there is important news I must convey to you. King Archelaus has had the throne taken from him by Caesar Augustus. I hear a tale that the temple in Jerusalem sent word to Rome that the king was a blasphemer and a breaker of Mosaic Law. I would guess that the emperor feared rebellion by his subjects, lacks faith in Archelaus' abilities to maintain control over his kingdom and deposed him. It would appear that his lands now are to become a strictly controlled Roman province. Great changes are upon us, and it could possibly serve our people well. But this news demonstrates the power of the Temple – something not to be underestimated.

I think today would be a good day to forget lessons. Spend time with your mother and brothers, think about who you are. Think about what you are to become. Tomorrow, we will resume your education in a different manner – the time has come for me to educate you in what *you* feel you need to know, not I. This will be my challenge, I feel." The old priest smiled warmly. "I will see you tomorrow."

As Jesus watched Hezekiah walked off through the gate as he had done so many times before, he felt lost. His life was changing very quickly, it seemed. Yet at the same time, he felt a strange kind of elation because he could now justify his thoughts about the church without fear. He realised God would not punish him for his thoughts, for they were God's thoughts also, and his frustration at the world was a mirror of God's own frustration. So now the question was – who is God really? Or what?

Jesus decided to spend the day with his brothers.

"What's this? No lessons today?" asked James when Jesus walked into the workshop.

"No. And if I have a day off, then so should you. Let's go and take a walk along the river," Jesus replied. Jude whooped with delight, happy to be released from his day's work. James nodded and wiped the sweat from his forehead with a rag.

***

It was mid-morning when they sat down on the riverbank, dangling their feet in the cool refreshing water. They watched as the occasional fish broke the surface of the water to catch an insect skating along the surface, sending ripples outward in ever-increasing circles.

"Men are like fish," said Jesus. "Don't you think?"

"How do you mean?" said James.

"See how the little fish live their lives in the water, unaware of what goes on above. They know there is a world above, but they do not concern themselves with what occurs there unless it is within easy reach. They have no clue that we sit watching their movements. And we could dive in and catch them if we wished, and put an end to their lives. But we don't. Why should we? Perhaps we could net them and carry them to a different place, and instead of them living wild, we could keep them in a reservoir or a pond, and they would live in a manner more to our liking."

James furrowed his brow. "I don't understand," he said.

Jesus looked at him. "Men swim around oblivious to God most of the time. They don't care; they just go with the flow of the water – even if the current takes them away from God. But a net could stop them – drag them back against the current and nearer to God. Just like a net could drag those fish nearer to us. I suppose a man who could be a net and bring people nearer to God would be a fisher of men."

"You think too much," said James, throwing a stone into the water.

"No, James, I think enough. It is other people who think too much, but they don't think about the right things. Take priests, for example. They think a lot about God's laws and how they can be applied to make the people obey the church. They think about how God's word can make them rich. They should be thinking about how God's word and laws are not for their good but that of the world. Ask yourselves – why do priests need to live in fabulous palaces and temples in fine clothes and dripping with gold? Manmade churches, not God. What God made was man, and a man's heart is God's temple. Man's heart is what is sacred, not mere buildings of stone. A church should expend its efforts in the service of God and man, not in gaining land and jewels. The Church is no better than the Romans – they just want power and wealth. And like the Romans, they think it is the right thing to build temples of stone, not temples of the heart."

James looked at him steadily. "That is blasphemy," he said, shocked at Jesus' outburst.

"No, it isn't," he said. "Who says that what I say is blasphemous?"

James thought for a moment. "The priests – they would curse a statement like that…"

"Indeed, they would," said Jesus, "and that is exactly my point. Don't you see? The priests would punish me for saying this in the synagogue. But there is no priest here now. God is here now though, and does he punish me? Do you see a bolt of lightning from the sky striking me down? No. This means that the will of the Church is at odds with the will of God."

Jude tugged Jesus' arm. "Why should God bother punishing you if the Church can do it for Him?" he asked.

"Because", replied Jesus, "he can. And the Church no longer works for God. If God doesn't care about an individual – what is the point in praying? Did God not care about Abraham, Moses, David or Noah? He cares about us all, for we are his children. God has punished individuals before, wiped out cities even. Why would he not do it again? This is the way of God, you see – he brings the sword and fire to all who insult him. I tell you this, if the Jewish people do not return to God, they will be punished and persecuted for all time, death will always follow in their shadows."

"What about people who live in distant lands? Those who live there may never have heard of God," said James.

"God will not punish them – it is not their fault if they have not heard the word of God. And some of the faraway people have still the old knowledge of where to build their holy places. These places are the key to God's plan. But He will punish those who have heard His word and have chosen to act in a way that offends Him."

The boys sat in silence for a while, James and Jude pondering the words of their brother. It was Jude who spoke first.

"Jesus, why doesn't God destroy the Church then?" he asked.

"Because He doesn't want it destroyed, He wants it changed," Jesus replied. "It has to be changed by men though. God is a father to us – think about this. If you made a ladder in the workshop, but it was too short, would Father have destroyed it and killed you? No, he wouldn't because it is still a ladder and it could be a good one. What he would have done though, is got James, who has more knowledge than you, to show you how to change it – lengthen it, to make it fit for its purpose."

Jude and James both nodded slowly. "It makes sense," said James.

"The church is just like that ladder," Jesus said. "It does not allow us to climb high enough to reach God. And some of the rungs need to be repaired."

Jesus stood up abruptly. "Shall we walk some more?" he asked.

Jude jumped up. "Let's race!" he shouted.

The boys spent the rest of the day playing along the riverbank. They had a few running races and gave up when James won the first five. They played at fighting, and Jude nearly wet himself laughing when Jesus pushed James into the river. James emerged from the water spluttering and laughing and was met with more howls of laughter from his brothers when he slipped in the mud and landed with a squelch on his backside. He scooped up a handful of the rich sticky mud and hurled it at Jesus, catching him on the left ear. Jude laughed harder, doubling up with delight, so Jesus picked up the helplessly giggling Jude and dumped him face down in the mud next to James. Jude rolled over and sat up, and the three boys roared with laughter.

Eventually, they decided it was time to head home. They had managed to wash most of the filth off themselves in the river, but as a consequence of their day's adventures, they looked quite bedraggled. When they arrived home, Mary saw them laughing in the yard and she hounded them into the bathhouse to scrub themselves clean before mealtime. When this was done, they ate ravenously and Mary watched them eat with a smile on her face. She saw the way James and Jude kept looking at their brother with both love and respect in their eyes. She knew that both brothers would do anything for Jesus, even die for him. She hoped they would never have to.

***

Hezekiah sat hunched over his table, penning a letter by lamplight in the dimness of a sparse room. The letter was to be sent to a close friend in the Sanhedrin in Jerusalem.

'You must prepare, my friend,' he wrote, 'for the prophecy to come to pass. The son of Mary and Joseph is indeed the man we await. Already, his head spins with ideas regarding church affairs and the true intentions of God. He has an intellect that many will find threatening and has an insight into the ways of God that I have never seen before. I can no longer be a teacher to him, merely a guide. The boy Jesus already has a huge place in the hearts of all that know him, and he has the charisma to spare. I predict he will journey to his homeland within the next four years. I await news of the welfare of his cousin John, who must soon be told of the manner of Jesus' home-coming. John has great responsibility too and must be prepared for it. I need you to travel to Galilee, inform the Essene Council that Jesus is to be proclaimed a Messiah before the year is ended. The kings, the Romans and the rest of the Sanhedrin must not know, for when Jesus returns to the land of his people, he must be fit to take the authorities unawares...'

When the letter was finished, he sealed the small parchment scroll with wax and gave it to his manservant, Levi.

"See this is delivered," he said. "Place it only in the hand of Joseph of Aramathea in the Jerusalem Temple. No one else. Travel safely, and I will see you in a few weeks."

Levi nodded and disappeared into the darkness of the night, the scroll tucked neatly into a pocket inside his travelling cloak.

***

"I wish to see some of the great temples, I think. Hezekiah, will you take me?" Jesus asked. "I think it important to see some of the buildings of old."

Hezekiah nodded. He looked at Jesus, now 15 years old and already a man. "May I ask why?"

"Because some of these temples are built in holy places," Jesus said. "I need to see at least one. I need to see the Great Pyramid, Hezekiah, for it marks the centre of the world. I spoke to God about this last night, and he told me this is where his power originates. The rest of the world is planned from there."

Hezekiah looked squarely at Jesus. "You talk directly to God?" he asked.

"Yes," Jesus replied.

"How long have you been doing this?" he asked.

"For three years, although more often of late."

Hezekiah stared at him for a few moments. "We will go tomorrow," he said.

***

As they journeyed to Memphis and onward to Giza, Hezekiah realised that he had as many questions for Jesus, as Jesus did for him. They were now more like intellectual sparring partners than teacher and student.

"Jesus, why do you think the church is wrong in its ways?" Hezekiah asked quietly as they trudged slowly along an ancient stony road, listening to the far-off braying of a donkey carried to them on the hot desert breeze.

"Because the Church has reduced ancient knowledge to mere superstition. Because they spend their time in petty arguments instead of fulfilling God's plan," replied Jesus quietly. "What do you think, Hezekiah?"

"I believe you are probably correct," replied the old priest. "The church turns us from God, not towards Him. They fear knowledge and learning in the masses, for knowledge is power and it would lessen their power over the people. They themselves have little real knowledge of God, but all they need is for people to believe they have more knowledge and understanding than everyone else. Remember, in a world of the blind, the one-eyed man is king."

"The Egyptians had great knowledge though, I fear we are in danger of losing it; their knowledge would benefit all mankind if used correctly," Jesus said. "But they were given this by others, the old ones, who doubtless did not pass on all they knew. How much knowledge is already lost?"

Hezekiah smiled grimly. "I doubt we will ever know. There are clues left behind all over the world, perhaps one day, people will be able to piece them all together and the knowledge will be rediscovered. I fear a great age of ignorance and superstition will descend upon the Earth first, and Man may even destroy himself before the knowledge is regained. We must make war on those who bless ignorance and embrace evil for their own gain – become as evil as them for a time – but only for the greater good. Only after they are gone will men know peace and, with their unity and understanding, will come the second age of knowledge, and that will bring us closer to God."

Jesus walked on in silent contemplation for a while as the distant donkey continued its complaining, its raucous noise making Jesus think of the mindless chanting of those who rattled out their prayers to God without thought of what those prayers actually meant. For many, they were just words to chant at mealtimes and in the synagogue out of habit, just as they had done for years.

"Perhaps the children are the key. A new generation is easier to teach than to try to re-teach the old," he said. "Yes – it is clear to me now. The children must become the army of God. They are not tainted by leaders of the church. Their innocence will be the guiding light to the Lord."

"Look to the horizon, Jesus," said the priest, pointing with his staff, "the Great Pyramid is in sight!"

Jesus looked up, shielding his eyes against the glare of the sun. "And when I have finished here, I think it is time I returned to my homeland to start the work of God the Father," he announced.

Chapter 3

Nazareth

Jesus was 16 years of age by the time he reached his new home – a house just a mile or so from the isolated small village of Nazareth. Located halfway between the western shore of the Sea of Galilee and the coast, Nazareth was the sort of place that seemed thankfully to have been forgotten by the outside world. The dusty main street was lined with only a few small houses, and at the one end was a well – at the other a tiny synagogue. None of the locals could remember the last time they had seen a priest or a Roman soldier, and few of them had travelled more than a few miles from their homes in their entire lives.

The place was perfect for Jesus to use as a base. He knew he was destined for a life travelling the road to spread God's word, but here was a perfect place to return to whenever he needed to feel he was home. He was a saviour with a great destiny, that much he knew, and the future of his people depended upon him and his cousin John. Jesus had been informed by Hezekiah that John had been declared a Messiah in the Essene church just a few months after his own declaration.

Hezekiah had travelled to Nazareth with Jesus and his family but departed for Qumran the day after their arrival in this dusty but beautiful forgotten village. The priest said he had to prepare an introduction for Jesus at the Essene Council, for they were unaware as yet of Jesus' return from Egypt. He left instruction for Jesus and James to follow him in seven days and told them that his manservant, Levi, would accompany them on their journey. Jesus and James were also told not to leave their new house until they were to depart in a week. Jude and Mary were not to mention the presence of Jesus in Nazareth to anyone – the first anyone was to know about Jesus' whereabouts was on his arrival in Qumran. In truth, Nazareth was so small everyone would have known of his presence before he reached a mile's distance of the place. Secrets were impossible to keep in a small town like this. But as it was so isolated, any secrets in the village tended to stay in the village.

The house was a simple building, facing south. It consisted of two surprisingly large rooms – grand by local standards, built of clay bricks and roofed with timber beams which were covered with branches. The floor was hard-packed dried mud, and there were a few simple sticks of furniture within. Each room had a crude square shuttered opening serving as a window, and an equally crude doorway. Outside was a ring of large stones stained black and orange from the heat of past fires. On one side of the building, someone way back in the distant mists of time had attached an awning of striped cloth to act as a shade, but it now hung bleached and tattered – the two supporting timbers dried out and splitting with age and the weather. A few stunted shrubs and an olive tree grew randomly around the place, and there was evidence of the recent visit by a few diarrhoeic goats lying splashed and sun-dried on the ground. At the rear of the house, a six-feet-high wall enclosed an area roughly twice the size of the building, and a second olive tree stood in the middle. The house was a far cry from the beautiful home they had made for themselves in Egypt, but dry, dusty and plain as it was – Jesus instantly liked its simplicity.

Two days after their arrival in Nazareth, Elizabeth arrived unannounced and unexpected. She had a bare minimum of luggage, and it was a mystery to all how she had arrived.

"How did you know we were here? And…how did you get here?" Mary asked.

"Old Hezekiah sent word a few days ago regarding your imminent arrival here," she said. "John does not know you have come; he is in the desert these past three weeks, conversing with God. Mary, is God's work to start soon? John is consumed with passion for the work ahead and has been advised by the Essene Council to await their word before doing anything."

"I don't know yet; I am sure Jesus or Hezekiah will send word. In the meantime, however, I cannot say how pleased I am to see you – the years have been kind to you, Elizabeth, you look no different than you did the day you left Egypt," said Mary.

Elizabeth embraced her warmly and kissed her on the cheek. "Mary, I wish I could say the same for you, cousin dear, but…what has happened to your hair? It was beautiful and black, now it looks so white!"

"My hair changed within a season, Elizabeth. It was the season following Joseph's death. I loved him dearly, and the sorrow I suffered in losing him took a heavy toll on me. My sons helped me through, whether they know it or not. I am so proud of my boys."

"And where are they?" asked Elizabeth.

Mary called the boys into the room where her cousin sat. Elizabeth could not believe how they had grown. James was now 18 years old, stood over six feet tall with broad, muscled shoulders and chest. A thick black beard adorned his square chin, and his long black hair flowed like troubled water halfway down his back. His eyes were dark brown, like those of his father. Jesus at 16, was only slightly smaller but had short hair and was clean-shaven. Like both his mother and brother Jude, he had piercing blue eyes that bored through her, as if he was looking at her very soul. A slight cruel smile adorned his lips, and his left eye was slightly narrowed against the sunlight streaming in through the doorway. She saw his nose was slightly crooked, like that of her son, and remembered the fight Jesus and John had had all those years ago. He had a dangerous look, this Jesus. Jude, 13, stood a handbreadth shorter than Jesus and wore a fading scar across his forehead from a long-forgotten fall during a tree-climbing adventure. Jude wore his usual cheeky smile, and Elizabeth thought that this one would be very popular among the local girls. He looked almost identical to Jesus but kinder, and there was something about him that made her want to wrap her arms around him and hold him safe.

She looked again at Jesus. She could see the intelligence in his eyes, and the smile he wore frightened her a little. He looked like a born killer, she thought, but he had an air of authority about him. *No*, she thought, *this man will not kill. Just a look from him and others will be more than happy to kill for him. Together, James and Jesus would make a formidable pair.*

Jesus broke the silence. "I am pleased to see you again after all these years." He took her hand and kissed it. "How is my dear cousin John?"

Elizabeth was a little taken aback by his reference to her son as 'dear'.

"He is well, Jesus; he is full of fervour for God. He has become a devout and true holy man. He lives up to his title of Messiah."

"And how are you?" asked James.

"Tired," she said, "and feeling dusty from the road."

James leant forward and kissed her cheek. "Then we will see you are refreshed – I will see a bucket of water is prepared for you to wash, and food," he said. James turned and walked back into the house, Jesus and Jude following close behind.

"Mary, you have no boys to be proud of – they are men. And handsome too!" said Elizabeth, giving a wink.

The three brothers left their mother and aunt to talk the evening away, they knew the two women had many things to discuss and much to catch up on.

"Do we travel armed?" James asked Levi later that evening.

"It would be advisable," replied Levi. "There are many dangers on the road, and it is never a safe place to be, but I would suggest we run before we fight and do all we can to travel unnoticed. I know this country well – I will do all I am able to keep us from harm. For a start, it is best to avoid the main roads, for that is where spies, bandits and soldiers tend to lurk."

"Swords and knives then," said Peter. "We shall hide the swords in the cart and carry the knives under our cloaks."

"Levi, do you know if my cousin John travels armed?" asked Jesus.

"I am aware he does not. He believes God is his sword, and if he comes to harm, it is because God wills it," replied Levi.

Jesus looked at Levi for a few moments. "Am I right in making an assumption regarding my cousin?"

Levi looked at him. "That depends on the assumption, Master," he said.

"Would John be regarded by some...or generally perhaps...as a little...eccentric? Possibly, ah, emotional? Let us say, less than sensible?"

"No, Master, your beloved cousin John is just plain mad."

The Temple at Qumran, or 'Damascus' as it was known by some, was a simple building. The Essenes believed that church adornment should be kept to a minimum, and the key to a building's beauty lay in its simple structure and proportion. It was a very spartan view. Jesus stood in the plain whiteness of the temple meeting room in front of the council with James to his left and Hezekiah to his right.

"So, Hezekiah, this is our other Messiah," said Melkhi, one of the council's chief priests.

"His name is Jesus, of the line of David, Father," Hezekiah said.

"And the big fellow beside him?" asked Melkhi.

"His brother James," replied Hezekiah.

Melkhi stood and walked in front of Jesus. He faced him and looked him in the eyes. "Welcome, Christ, we are your friends and allies in the coming struggle. I, Melkhi, stand before you, and recognise you." He turned to James.

"James, brother of the Christ Jesus, I tell you this – you are the one selected many years ago by your father to be your Messiah's companion. To aid him and protect him. You are 'Bar-Abbas' – the chosen son." Melkhi turned to face the rest of the council. "Tonight, we *initiate* the Christ and His Barabbas."

The night's initiation into the Essene Council's inner circle lasted until dawn. As the sun sank over the barren hills to the west, Jesus and James were led into the temple. A small bell was rung, and there was a scraping noise as a large wooden square hatch was dragged open, exposing a beautiful orange patch of sky, allowing the evening light to flood the large bare room. The council stood in a circle around the two *initiates* and all wore plain white robes.

Melkhi performed the ceremonies. As the day's light faded, lamps were lit which flickered and smoked, casting ghostly shadows around the walls, and he sang hymns and spoke verses of rhyme in an unknown tongue that Jesus was later told was the language of the time before Noah. He pressed a knife into the chests of both Jesus and James, drawing blood. He then hung a rope around James' neck and made him swear always to protect his brother, to defend and obey his word, or hang himself. James took his oath, and Jesus swore an oath that he would do the same for God. They were then commanded to lay side by side on their backs under the square hole in the roof and they gazed at the thousands of stars smeared twinkling across the night sky as the priests prayed and chanted.

At dawn, Melkhi stepped outside the temple and held aloft a piece of bread and a jug of wine to be blessed by the rays of the rising sun as he called out yet another prayer. He then re-entered the temple, placed the jug on the floor between the two brothers and broke the bread in two. "This bread is the body of the Essene Council!" he said. "Eat of this as a sign of our brotherhood!"

After the bread was swallowed by the two brothers, Melkhi picked up the jug and poured some of the wine into two cups. He then raised the cups and called out, "This wine is the blood of the Essene Council! Drink of these cups as a sign of your oaths!"

When Jesus and James had taken a small taste of the sweet red wine from the cups, they were refilled and passed around the attending priests who each, in turn, took a small sip from each. Melkhi drank last, and after wiping the rims of the cups with a small white cloth, he handed one to Jesus and the other to James.

"This cup is yours," he said to Jesus. "It is an earthly gift for you that you may use to bless others. It has blessed you on the night of your birth into the council. Keep it with you always – until death. And when you arise to Heaven, God will provide you with another."

Melkhi then repeated what he said to James.

The door to the temple was re-opened as the small bell was rung again and the brothers were then led out into the morning light and escorted through the sprawl of white single-storey buildings along a path and down into the gorge beside which Qumran sat. Birds twittered and sang as the group carefully threaded their way along narrow ledges into the shadows of the ravine. Eventually, they were led into a cave containing hundreds of large clay jars.

"Behold," said Melkhi proudly. "The secrets of Qumran. Our great library. The writings and records of our people dating back since the time before Mathusala. This is our history, and within lay accounts of 'The Wise Ones', records which recount the true messages of God. Confined within these clay vessels are the secrets that the Senhedrin would kill for, only so they could destroy them all. Word of their existence must never travel outside the council – or even this cavern. But now you have taken your oaths before God, their secrets are open to you. If you defend God, you should know him. These documents show the true God."

After they had made their way back up the precarious path from the depths of the gorge, they all retired to the refectory, where they were served breakfast. Melkhi leant across the table towards Jesus and spoke, "The time for change is decided by you. We are here to aid you when and where we can. I offer you one-piece advice before you depart though. It is about your cousin, John. Tread carefully in your dealings with him. He has a fragile mind, and sometimes, his closeness to God is a burden to him. But you should hear him preach! He warns of your coming to the people, he warns that the Pharisees and Sadducees are blasphemers, and he tells them to beware of their future."

"Melkhi, I thank you. We must have patience and ensure our own people become close to us. We must bring our own closer to God before we spread our influence further afield. And the people must be behind us before we tackle the Temple in Jerusalem. I must also form my own council, 12 men, the same as this council, to work with me. I think John would be best advised to do likewise.

Three councils working together and yet separately, and towards the same goal," Jesus said.

After they had eaten, Jesus and James slept for a few hours and then readied themselves to depart for home.

They bade goodbye to the council, and Hezekiah motioned them into the temple for a quiet word as they were about to leave.

"I have a friend who shall call upon you soon – within the month," he said. "He is a friend and can be trusted, even depended upon. Welcome him. He is named Joseph, from Aramathea. He is well placed in the Sanhedrin. Take his council; always have an ear for the news he brings. Joseph is our eyes and ears among the hypocrites and the corrupted false leaders of our nation."

"Thank you, Hezekiah," said Jesus, and he walked out of the temple into the afternoon sunshine.

Only a day away from Qumran, Jesus stopped in his tracks, the donkey he was leading stumbled into the backing of him nearly knocking him to the ground. Jesus had a determined and thoughtful look upon his face and announced to James and Levi that he felt it was time to start speaking to the common people. The donkey brayed, adding its own opinion, and Jesus stroked its head gently.

"I will start to spread the true word of God and Man in the very next village we come to," he said quietly.

"I am no hurry to return home. Until now I have hidden my presence. I will so no longer."

He turned and thanked Levi for his services and requested he returns to Hezekiah to resume his duties. Levi nodded his affirmation and they agreed to head their separate ways when next they reached a community.

After walking for only an hour, James spied the smoke of cooking fires less than a mile distant and off to the right of the road. Twenty minutes' travel saw them in the centre of a small settlement, ten single-storey houses around a central well. Jesus walked up to the well parapet and sat upon the wall. His donkey sniffed around his ear and a young goat approached him hopefully, but as neither man nor beast of burden offered the creature food, it soon lost interest and wandered off bleating like a baby. James took the donkey's halter from Jesus' hand and led it to a rough timber frame a few short yards distant – the remnants of a derelict shed, and he tied the animal to it alongside his own. He stood with Levi, casually watching and waiting to see what Jesus would do next.

A minute or so later, a young woman came out of her small house and, seeing the two men by the old shed and the third by the well, hesitated, and then walked over to them.

"Is it water you need?" she called out to Jesus.

"No, thank you," Jesus replied, "where is everyone?"

"All the men work whilst us women attend a sickbed. An elderly father of our village lies in pain and weak. He sweats greatly with agony."

"I would like to see him – is he injured?" asked Jesus as he stood. James wandered over to stand beside him.

"No, he has no injury. He complains of severe pain down below and cannot stand or sit. He also lives in fear of the need to relieve himself of anything but water. As a consequence, he refuses to eat anything but the smallest mouthful to pacify his hunger," she replied. "He has been this way for ten days and nights."

Jesus turned to James. "Sounds like the old boy has a sore arse-hole and is too embarrassed to tell anyone," he said quietly. "I shall attend him, see what I can do. If I eject all the women from the room, you speak to them whilst I work. Here, around the well will do. I am sure you will think of something to talk about – just make sure they leave myself and the old fellow alone a short while."

Jesus followed the young woman into the small single-roomed house. She led him by the hand to where a grey-haired, bearded man lay on a cot. Jesus could see he was as much distressed by the presence of the dozen or so women fussing around him as he was by his obvious physical discomfort.

He stood silent and motionless in the doorway until he had the attention of everyone in the room.

"I am here to help with this man's ailment. First, I need privacy with the patient. Please all leave and go to the well. My companion wishes to address you all."

The women hesitated for a moment, and then shuffled silently out of the building each with a look of doubt and scepticism etched upon their faces. Jesus pulled closed the shabby cloth door behind them.

"We are strangers, old man. I am Jesus; may I ask your name?"

"Simon," replied the old man cautiously.

"It is my guess," Jesus continued, "that you suffer as much from embarrassment as you do from pain. You need not be embarrassed with me, for I am a man of healing. And as we are total strangers – there is no need to panic. You have a sore behind, am I correct?"

The old man nodded uneasily.

"Are you split from a hard motion, or is it a lump of some sort?" Jesus asked.

The old man swallowed nervously. "It is a large lump," he said. "It weeps at times."

Jesus nodded. "Does it weep pus? Water? And at times a trace of blood? Or would there be liquid shit in it?"

"Water, blood and puss," the man replied in hushed tones.

"You must turn on your side; I will need to see. Do not worry; there is no shame here," Jesus said.

The old man turned over as asked and bared his backside to Jesus, who washed his hands in the water basin at the side of the cot, then knelt to inspect the man's swelling. He saw a monstrous boil right beside the man's rectum, and when he pressed gently at the side of it, Simon winced a little and he could see a tightly curled thick hair coiled up in the centre of the head of it.

"You ride a donkey much?" Jesus asked.

"Usually," said the man, "but not at all of late – the pain is more than I can bear."

"I will have to cause you more pain, Simon, it will hurt like the devil, but it will be short-lived and cure your affliction. After three days, you will be fine. Do you want to be relieved of this pain?" said Jesus.

"Aye, I do. Do what you have to do – please, but make it quick," Simon whispered.

Jesus stood, pulled a sharp short-bladed knife from his leather pouch and held it briefly over the flame of a lit candle in the corner of the room. He allowed the flame to lick the entire length of the blade, making it sooty black. He bent down again, wiped the blade on a small cloth from his pouch and, parting the man's buttocks with his left hand, held the blade over the huge boil. "Ready?" he asked.

Old Simon nodded, biting his bottom lip.

Jesus deftly flicked his wrist, and the sharp blade parted the boil in two. A vile-looking mix of lumpy pus and clear fluid flowed out. Simon was grunting and panting with pain.

"Just a few seconds more," said Jesus, who placed the small knife on the bed, and then squeezed the offending lump until only blood came flowing out. Jesus could see the hair that had caused the infection, so he picked up his knife, and teased the hair out of the incision. He then gripped the hair between thumb and forefinger and pulled. The root came free with a click, and Simon yelped. Jesus stood.

"Simon, I am done. You must wash your behind – cold water will be a relief for you. Add salt to the water if you have any. Wash yourself gently every three or four hours for the next two days and eat plenty of fruit. Also, avoid the donkey," Jesus said.

Simon turned over on his back and grinned. "The pressure is gone…thank you, young man. May I try and stand?"

Jesus extended a hand and helped Simon to his feet. A look of relief washed over the man's face.

"Aaaah – that feels so much better already. How can I thank you?" he asked.

"There is no need for thanks. Do you wish to go outside into the sunlight?"

After scrubbing his hands, Jesus helped Simon walk out of the house and the women surrounding Peter all turned as one, surprise on their faces.

"I am healed it would seem," announced Simon. He was still a little sore but in nowhere near as much pain and discomfort as he had been.

James had been speaking to the women of his brother's ability to heal and how it was a gift from God. He had, of course, twisted the truth a little and also *forgot* to tell them of Jesus' Egyptian education. As a consequence, he had created the impression that his brother was something of a medical prodigy – perhaps even something of a magician. This impression was further compounded by Simon's appearance among them after Jesus had only been attending him for ten minutes.

As the women surrounded him, Jesus shushed them and leant against the well parapet.

"I wish to tell and advise you, as God's people," he said. "Let love and faithfulness never leave you – bind them around your neck and write them on the tablet of your heart. You will then win favour and a good name in the sight of both God and men. Remember, the eyes of the Lord are everywhere, keeping watch on the wicked and the good. I see your good deeds too, in the manner that you cared for your dear Simon in his discomfort. This pleases God. Some may ask how Simon was healed – I say leave the matter be – it remains an issue between only myself, Simon, and God." He looked at each woman, in turn, and said, "Like a gold ring in a pig's snout, is a beautiful woman who shows no discretion and asks that which should not be asked."

42

Jesus walked over to his donkey and declared that it was time for them to leave, and as they walked out of the village towards the road, one of the women, unable to resist her curiosity, asked Simon what Jesus had done to heal him so quickly.

"He just laid his hand on me," said Simon. "And I was healed. It was a miracle."

When eventually they arrived home several days later, Jesus and James found their mother in tears and sat on the ground leaning against the wall.

"Mother, what has happened? What is wrong?" James asked.

"Jude – he has been given a beating. He is in a terrible mess – his face and back are black and purple…" she replied.

James reddened with anger. "What bastards did this to my brother?"

"It was soldiers – they did it for laughs. He went a walk to go have a look at the market in Gabae – James, for the sake of us all, do not do anything hasty," Mary said as James stormed off into the house to see his brother.

Jude lay on his bed – James hardly recognised him. There was a whistling from Jude's nose which had evidently been broken. His eyes were purple and swollen, his jaw was cut, and there were deep red marks around his neck.

"What happened, Brother?" James asked.

"Wrong place, wrong time. I interfered where I shouldn't have. I saw a woman being pushed around by soldiers – I thought that it was only going to get worse for her, so I pushed one of the soldiers off her and got this beating for my trouble. At least, she managed to get away," Jude said hoarsely.

"You were brave. But it could have turned out worse for you. What soldiers were they?"

"I think they were the Roman Prefect's troops. There were four of them. James, are you annoyed with me?"

James smiled. "No – how could I ever be annoyed with you for being gallant? Just be careful in future, eh? I will fetch our brother, see what he can do for that unsightly mess of a face you have."

For the following week, Jesus tended Jude's injuries with ointments and poultices and even managed to straighten his nose a little. Jude's swelling went down, the bruises abated, and his cuts and abrasions started to heal fairly quickly.

The three brothers were sat around the small cooking fire outside the house with their mother one evening when the visitor came. He was dressed in the full regalia of a high-ranking priest of the Temple of Jerusalem. He introduced himself as Joseph, from Aramathea. Jesus welcomed him whilst Mary and James disappeared inside to prepare a meal.

Joseph sat with Jesus and Jude.

"I have news for you, Jesus," he said. "Your cousin John has appeared from his wanderings in the desert. He now preaches and baptises around the Sea of Galilee. He is developing quite a following. The word goes around, and the ears of the temple are burning. John seems to be an angry preacher; he is vehement in his lectures to the people – loudly warning them of the corrupt ways of the Pharisees and the Sadducees. In a very short time, he has managed to earn the disapproval of the Temple.

His ways are not subtle. I heard a word of you too – there is a story you performed a miracle of healing a few miles from Qumran."

Jesus remained silent, thinking of what he had just been told. Joseph looked at the yellowing bruises on Jude's face. "What befell you, young man?" he asked.

Jude told him of his misadventure, expressing his hatred of the soldiers as he spoke.

"Do you wish for revenge?" Joseph asked.

Jude nodded slowly. "It would be nice, but I am not sure it would be right. Perhaps I should be better wishing for justice."

"Jesus, how do you feel about this?" the priest said.

"I think Jude has seen – and been a victim of – an unpleasant side of humanity and needs to be taught how to deal with it. He wishes for revenge, certainly, but he needs to learn how to channel his emotion. He is brave, and this is an asset. Why do you ask me?" Jesus answered.

"I have had a discussion with Hezekiah, and we have an idea that may help our cause in the future. We think it may be of benefit if you had the ability to strike down those who are most dangerous to you. And be able to do it unexpectedly. You need someone you can trust, what better person than your own brother?"

"What is your idea, Joseph?" asked Jesus.

"We think it would help if Jude was introduced to the ways of the Sicarii – the Dagger-men. He is now 13, yes? A good age to start his training."

"I would trust your judgement, but I do not think my mother would approve somehow," Jesus said. "And I for one have no wish to be the one broach the subject to her. You must remember – Jude is her baby!"

Jude snorted and Jesus winked at him.

Joseph nodded. "I think it may be prudent for both Hezekiah and myself to discuss this issue with her, together – privately. We shall move her seeing towards our way of things." He turned to Jude. "What is your opinion, young man? This does, of course, concern you."

Jude shrugged his shoulders. "If my brother thinks it wise, so do I. I would like to work for my brother's cause, I don't care how." Jude smiled at Jesus. "I would be happy for you to know you can rely on me," he said.

Jesus placed his hand on his brother's shoulder. "I will always trust you, Jude."

"Life will not be easy for you, young Jude," said the priest. "You will have to live away from your family for a time."

"I would expect that. When do I leave?" asked Jude.

"Just as soon as your mother approves," Joseph replied.

Within the fortnight, Hezekiah had arrived, lengthy and emotional discussions were had, and Joseph of Aramathea had finally departed with Jude as his mother waved him goodbye with moist eyes and a heavy heart. No one could say when they would hear from him or see him again. Hezekiah had said it maybe two or three years before he returned. Mary was heartbroken as he left but later that afternoon told James she understood why he had to go. She swore she would pray for him every sunrise, noon and sunset. A few days later, Jesus declared that he needed to go amongst the people to preach and heal, and that he wanted James to stay behind to keep their mother company in Jude's absence, but Mary insisted James go with him. Despite the argument, when Jesus departed, James was with him.

"Where are we headed, brother?" James asked.

"Everywhere. Wherever we need to be," Jesus responded.

Chapter 4

John – the Baptist

After 23 months of journeying around Judea, preaching and treating the sick, Jesus and James stood on the peak of a low dusty hill above the Sea of Galilee.

The hot, dry air had no movement, and the midday sun hung high in the deep blue sky, baking the rocks and trees and creating a shimmer over the rocky ground. The turquoise waters below them looked beautifully cool and inviting.

Jesus took a drink of warm brackish water from his waterskin and handed it to his brother. The liquid eased their thirst but could not suppress the hunger that gnawed at their bellies. James raised his hand to shield the sun from his eyes. "I think that is him," he said, pointing with his other hand to a spot on the coast some way off in the distance. "See a man stood in the water? He has a small crowd gathered about him."

Jesus screwed his eyes against the glare and looked to where James was pointing. "Yes, I see them. Let's head down and find out if it is indeed our cousin, eh?"

They picked their way carefully down the hillside, taking care not to slip on the loose rocks which tried to trip them and send them sliding downward. They reached the hot sand of the narrow beach, took off their sandals and walked along the edge of the water. They walked in silence, feeling the sea cool their feet, washing the dust and grit away from between their toes. It felt like heaven after their long walk.

As they approached the crowd, they could hear the voice of John, preaching and ranting.

"Come to me! Be baptised in the waters of new life in the name of Jaweh, Jehova, *The One God*! Fail to do this and you turn your back on the Lord! One man soon comes in the light of God, and he will judge you all with his measuring rod, just as God will judge at the end of days! Ignore the lies of the corrupt ones

– for they run the temples and serve only themselves! Turn your backs to the words of the Pharisees and Sadducees – they will soon feel the wrath of the 'Great Messiah'! They twist the words of God to justify their ways! Who will come to me next for baptism in God's blessed water?"

Jesus pushed his way through the crowd. "I come to you. I ask for your baptism."

John looked at him, head at an angle and his left eye half-closed against the sunlight. "I know you, don't I?" he said.

"If you are indeed John, son of Elizabeth, then yes, you do," Jesus replied.

"I cannot place you. But I know I should…" John said.

"Would you recognise my brother James? If my mother, Mary, were here, would you recognise her? Or our old teacher, Hezekiah?" Jesus asked.

John's jaw dropped. "Jesus? Is it really you?" he whispered.

"It is. Now please, cousin, baptise me."

"It should be me who asks you for baptism," said John, bowing his head.

"John, please, baptise me. I ask you this as you are a Messiah, and I would feel honoured to receive your blessing in the name of God." Jesus walked forward till the water reached halfway up his legs and knelt before his cousin. "Please baptise me, dear cousin," he asked again.

John knelt beside him, placed his right hand at the back of Jesus' head and pushed him facedown into the water. "I baptise you, Jesus! I baptise you in the name of God!" he shouted as he held his cousin's head under the water. "May the Lord's light bless you and guide you!" he screamed and released Jesus' hair from his grip.

Jesus surfaced, gasping for air. He raked back his wet hair from his face and stood. "I thank you, John," he said.

John stood and looked at him with tears in his eyes. "As a boy, I treated you badly. I held jealousy in my heart, and it ate at me – deep inside. Please forgive me," he said quietly.

Jesus placed his hand on John's head. "I have nothing to forgive, but if it eases your conscience, I forgive you anyway. Now I believe it is time for you to baptise my brother; after that, we must talk – just us three."

That evening, Jesus, James and John sat by their campfire on the seashore. The fierce heat of the day had given way to a welcome chill, and all three men had blankets draped over their shoulders. James occasionally prodded the fire with a stick, sending fountains of sparks tumbling and swirling into the air, illuminating the smoke and then fading to nothing.

"John, I hear you have been upsetting people with your preaching. This is good, but keep an ear to the ground. The Temple considers you a blasphemer, as no doubt they will consider me," Jesus said.

John nodded his agreement. "Of this I am aware, but I must do God's work regardless of my own safety. I have people – disciples, who have ears everywhere. Through them, I hear much. Trust me, I am not foolhardy. Zealous – yes, an idiot – no."

"Just keep far from harm's reach, cousin. I know you are no fool. But consider this – Caesar Augustus is now 74 years old or thereabouts. When he dies, the empire of the Romans will no doubt change. Whenever an emperor dies, there is a great power struggle as contenders for his throne vie and plot against each other in their merciless struggle to climb to the top of the dung pile. For a year or two at the least, there will be chaos and confusion in the world. Power will shift from one person to another; there will be changes in who holds what office. Those new to their position will fear those they replace, and the replaced ones will suffer animosity towards their successors. This is the time we should rebel. Between now and then, there is much to organise. I can only pray that God gives us another four or five years to do this. Judea must break free of Rome when they are least able to hold us in chains."

"And what are your plans, Jesus?" asked John.

"I do not wish to tell too much of detail, you never know what may happen, but this I can tell you – I plan to gather men to me, men I can trust. I will gain the trust of the masses – raise a militia. I will create a child army; youngsters who will follow my word to their deaths. I will then discredit the Temple and incite a rebellion. The detail of this stays in my mind, but that is the general plan – subject to change, of course. I tell you this because I want you to do the same – working independently of me. We shall unite together at the rebellion – but not before. United, we stand a chance of expelling the Romans and the priests who blind our people to the truth. Those we cannot expel, we either eliminate or convert," said Jesus.

John looked at him steadily. "As simple as that?" he said.

"No, it will be by no means simple. But I believe it is possible, with God's help," Jesus replied. "Keep preaching, cousin, gain followers, but try not to anger the authorities too much – yet."

"I hear you preach well, Jesus. I also hear you perform miracles of healing," John said.

Jesus smiled. "Indeed, I do. Indeed, I do."

The following morning, Jesus and James prepared to leave, but John asked them to stay with him for a day or so long as he wanted Jesus to preach with him. He said he also wanted to hear Jesus' teachings for himself. Jesus agreed and stayed with John for four days before heading off with his brother back towards Jerusalem. In that time, Jesus realised that John had changed a great deal. They had become good friends, and all of John's former animosity had disappeared entirely. Jesus could see that John was finding that keeping a grip on reality was difficult, and that he was a little unpredictable. Somehow, though, it added to the impression that John was truly in touch with God, and it made him seem more holy. Jesus also noticed that John suffered mood swings, despite the fact that John tried his best to hide it from him.

When Jesus and James left, John took himself off to the hills for a few days and cried.

Jesus only stayed in Jerusalem for a month before heading off again. This time he went alone, insisting James went and stayed at home with their mother. Jesus wanted to go back to Qumran and spend time with the Essene Council and read through some of the ancient scrolls kept hidden in the cave before heading on back to the Sea of Galilee. He had no thoughts or plans of deliberately meeting up with John again in the near future, but if their paths crossed, then that was fine with him. He planned to just see where the road took him for a time and told James to inform his mother that she should not to expect him back much before the following spring. He had a lot of planning to do, he said, and that he wanted to also spend a lot of time studying in Qumran's extensive library.

Jesus actually ended up staying in Qumran for four months, involving himself with study and debate with the council. During his time there, the council's respect for him grew. They enjoyed debating with him and welcomed his fresh approach to argument. He spent many an evening in deep discussion with Hezekiah but was appalled to see how old his friend had become. Hezekiah was becoming frail and thin, but he still had a mind as sharp as a razor.

When Jesus left Qumran, he headed north from the Dead Sea. He enjoyed the loneliness of his journey – broken occasionally when he stopped to speak to travellers he met along the way. As Jesus walked, he surveyed the landscape around him, marvelling at its beauty. He stopped to admire insects searching for food or the birds singing in the trees. *I am in love with this land that God gave us*, he thought.

When he had covered only half the distance to the Sea of Galilee, he changed his mind. He realised that he missed his mother and James. His heart ached to be with them again, and suddenly, the loneliness he felt became oppressive, so he turned from the road to make his way home.

It was mid-morning when Jesus walked into eyeshot of his mother's house, and James was the first to see him.

"Jesus! It is you!" he exclaimed. "By all that's holy, we have been worried sick about you since we heard the news." James grabbed Jesus in a bear hug, overjoyed to see his brother.

"What news?" Jesus asked, when finally, James released him, allowing him to breathe again.

"You haven't heard?" asked James, wide-eyed.

"No, Brother, what have I missed?"

"It is John. He has been arrested…the Temple have laid charges of blasphemy and treason against him and are baying like hounds for his execution…the king holds him in one of his own prison cells in his palace! Brother, I fear they are going to kill him," James said.

Jesus fell to his knees, utterly speechless, with sorrow and fear clutching his heart like a fist of iron.

Jesus, Mary and James sat in the shade of the scruffy awning under the afternoon sun. Jesus had pushed aside his fears, and his emotions had turned from sadness to guilt and anger.

"Why was he arrested, do you know?" he asked.

"King Herod Antipas took his own sister-in-law, Herodias as his wife, and John was outraged when he heard the news. He publicly denounced Antipas as a sinner and a pervert and it seems the king's spies were in the crowd John was addressing. Soldiers came, beat him, and took him away," Mary said.

"But Antipas is already married, is he not? To Phasaelis? What of her? Has she died?" Jesus asked.

"Apparently not; it seems Antipas divorced her only a day or two before," James answered.

Jesus was silent for a minute or two. "This is all my fault," he said. "I should never have left him – I should have stayed to help him preach, to take care of him. I should have counselled him more wisely. I should never have spent so long in Qumran…"

"Brother, this is no doing of yours," said James, "You saw how he was – erratic, unpredictable and outspoken, he brought this on himself. Did you not warm him against being careless with his words?"

Jesus stood and looked at James. "Yes. I did. But I did not drive my warning home hard enough. I should have foreseen this. And now not only is John in mortal danger but so is the future of our faith and our people."

"My dear son, do not blame yourself," Mary said.

"Please excuse me, I have much to do and much to think about," said Jesus quietly, and he walked away into the house.

Later that evening, James saw Jesus gathering up some food in the kitchen. He walked over to him and put his hand on his brother's shoulder. "Going away again?" he asked.

Jesus nodded. "I am. I need space to think – alone."

"Where will you go?" said James.

"Away from here. Away from everywhere and away from everyone. Just for a while. A month, maybe two," Jesus answered.

"Are you sure you need to be alone? Do you want me to keep you company?"

"No, James. I will be needing isolation. I crave it. I need to speak to God; I need His help."

Jesus stood under the baking midday sun. The hot desert blew grit into his eyes and took all moisture from his mouth. His head pounded and ached, and pangs of hunger stabbed at the depths of his stomach. He had run out of water well before nightfall and had not eaten for three days. He knew if he did not find water soon, he was dead. The visions had started this morning. At first, he could recognise his hallucinations for what they were, but now he was starting to lose his grip on reality. He saw images of John who spoke to him calmly and told him not to worry – that his imprisonment was part of God's plan. John then grew to twice his size, his mouth splitting open to reveal rows of yellow, pointed teeth. His face became elongated, and his eyes turned black. "Forget Your God." The apparition said, "Come to me. I will take away your pain and make you happy." Jesus had fallen to his knees and screwed up his eyes against the image in his mind. A high-pitched whine screeched in his ears, which felt like a red-hot dagger in his brain. "You killed your cousin," he heard through the noise.

"Fuck off!" he had screamed hoarsely. "Just fuck off and get out of my head!" He rolled over and lay on his side. "Help me, Father; what must I do?" he whispered, over and over again. After a few minutes, he opened his eyes and all he saw was shimmering sand and rocks baking in the heat. He dragged himself shakily to his feet and started walking again, every step a monstrous effort. After only a hundred yards or so, he heard the faint sound of laughing behind him. He turned, but no one was there. He started walking again and once more heard the mocking laughter – this time very close behind him. Jesus stopped. "You do not scare me, Demon," he said. "What is the worst you can do – kill me? You are weak! You do not even exist except in the minds of man! You are a myth to frighten children and the foolish!" he said.

"Come to me…" a voice whispered in his ear.

"If ever I come to you, it is with a sword in my hand and God in my heart! I will tear your eyes out and slice you open like a fish, you bastard." Jesus turned to face his monster, but all he saw was the empty desert. He smiled to himself.

"And so comes the madness that heat, sun and thirst bring. At last…this is the state of mind I have wished for. Now God will see me, and I, Him," he said aloud.

After an hour or so, he tripped over a rock – splitting his knee on another as he fell. He lay there for a while breathing shallowly – feeling the pain of his injury, and he drifted into sleep. He dreamt of his mother and brothers. He dreamt of his father in the old workshop, and then his father disappeared and the workshop slowly changed into the Great Pyramid of Gisa. As he stared at the pyramid, it too faded and he drifted backwards in time, to the era of Moses, and the great Exodus from Egypt. Moses, the great man who manipulated the fears of his pharaoh – his own adopted father. Jesus could see the two of them talking, the paranoia in the great Egyptian king's eyes as Moses promised him that great plagues would ravage his country if the Hebrew people were not set free from the slavery which had bound them since the Egyptians had conquered them decades before when they regained the northern kingdom. Moses knew about the volcanic eruption in the great Central Sea and knew Egypt would suffer the after-effects.

Jesus travelled back further and saw the northern kingdom of the Nile as it was when the Hyksos – his own forefathers – ruled it by the sword and their unshakeable belief that their God placed them above all others, and then back further and saw the forebears of his great people conquering all the lands around them. Fierce nomadic warriors mercilessly slaying their neighbouring tribes and afterwards giving thanks to their god as they knelt with hands raised, worshipping the sun.

God's voice thundered through his head. "Get up! Set free our people. Bring death down on those who insult me. Let nothing stand in your way – not even your own death. Get up and go into the world, tell mankind that I *am* mankind!" Jesus woke with a start. He felt confusion, yet at the same time, he felt ice-cold clarity and was not too sure if he had been dreaming or not. He lay on the ground wondering when it was that he had lost sight of his destiny. After a few moments, he stood unsteadily on his feet and looked around.

In the distance, he could see a stunted tree wavering in the heat haze. Was that a man he saw standing next to it?

Perhaps he has water.

He walked towards the tree and felt his heart sink as it disappeared, nothing but a mirage. Jesus considered that as he was lost, he may as well keep going in the same direction. It made no difference really. If his destiny was indeed greatness in the eyes of the Lord, then he was now in the Lord's hands and He would see him to safety.

The hours drew on and Jesus realised he was no longer taking notice of which direction he was heading but instead was aimlessly wandering, walking just for the sake of moving from wherever he was to somewhere else. He could have been wandering in circles for all he knew. He tripped and fell again, and when he finally managed to muster the strength to stand, he realised his vision was blurred and dimming. He walked as best as he could for another half an hour, continually tripping and stumbling, as exhaustion from the heat and dehydration weighed him down. His legs went impossibly weak forcing him to sit down heavily. He prayed to God for help before once more drifting off into a fitful sleep – full of voices, dreams and nightmares.

He finally saw things as they were and knew no one would understand. God was in everyone because everyone was God. All the priests who claimed to talk to God were lying – there could be no priests, there could be no temples, for everybody was a temple. How was he to relate this to the people who needed a God to exist to explain the ways of the world? His thoughts wandered further and he realised that Man had lost touch with reality – that Man was becoming detached from the world which had been his cradle. The Spiritualists in Britannia still clung on to the old ways, for they knew that what drove Man was the world itself, the elements, and Man's own nobility. God, Man and the world were all one and the same thing.

He saw that if God was in humanity – that if God was in both Man and Woman, and that the differences between male and female were nothing more than another aspect of the duality of humankind. Good and evil, man and woman, joyous and sorrowful, noble and despicable. He needed to find a way to unite humanity somehow, and then once that was achieved, who knew what greatness humanity could accomplish? He needed to spread the message that God is not who the priests say He is, for He is us.

Jude stopped to look at the bundle of rags 20 yards or so from the road. It looked like a body lying face down in the early morning light. *A robber perhaps*, he thought, *setting a trap for an unwary passer-by*. He pulled a slender ten-inch dagger from his sleeve in readiness for an ambush and went to investigate.

He stood over the body – knife at the ready – and prodded it hard in the kidney with his toe. The body remained motionless. He knelt, and holding the dagger to the prone man's neck with his left hand, he hauled him over onto his back. He could see now that the man was not dead but in a very poor state and quite close to it. His eyelids were flickering, and he was mumbling very quietly. The man's filthy, unshaven face was burned and blistered from the sun's fierce rays, his lips were split open from lack of water and his entire body started to tremble weakly. Suddenly, his eyes opened and he stared at Jude with the intensity usually found only in the insane. Even after four years without seeing him, Jude knew the instant he looked into the man's piercing blue eyes, that the man was his brother. This pile of rags was Jesus.

Chapter 5

Great Change

Gaius Julius Caesar Octavianus – otherwise known as Caesar Augustus, was tired. More tired than he had ever felt before. He was feeling his age, for at 76, he knew he had left his youth well and truly behind. And ruling Rome for 46 of those years had taken its toll on him, although Augustus would say that it was the pressure of his position that kept his mind sharp. He had put all he had into Rome. He had expanded the empire's borders, introduced a firefighting service and even started up a police force in the city. He had created a standing army of 170,000 trained troops in 28 legions supported by auxiliary units throughout all of Rome's territories – each one of around 500 soldiers. He had even created a small regular navy. He had ensured all roads in the empire were kept in a good state of repair, and then he had gone on to institute a postal and courier service run by the army. He also established the Praetorian Guard. He had restored temples, founded charities for veteran soldiers, given money to the poor, re-organised the taxation system and united the Roman Empire – putting an end to the civil wars that seemed a regular occurrence. He had seen to it that new aqueducts were built, mines were opened, and had new laws passed – all for the good of the empire and its citizens.

Little wonder he was tired. He just hoped he would be remembered as a good man and a just ruler.

He knew his remaining time was short though. Nowadays, Augustus felt weak, dizzy, and often he could feel his heartbeat irregularly. He had always seemed healthy and full of vigour, but of late that had all changed. He had ever been aware of his own mortality – he had lost too many friends and family members to be able to forget it, and it was because of this he had decided to visit the place where his father died. Nola.

It was the month of Sextilis, and the warm summer breeze blew through the thin drapes covering the open window and caressed Augustus' face as he lay on the bed beside his wife. His stepson, Tiberius, sat on the side of the bed, feeling his world fall apart. He could see plainly how sick Augustus looked.

"Livia, I am dying," he said.

"Nonsense," she replied, holding him close to her, "there are years ahead of you yet."

"Livia, let us face facts. The senate must be told that Tiberius becomes emperor."

Livia Drusilla looked at him and saw how grey his face had become. They had gone for a gentle walk earlier in the day, and she suspected it had been too much for him. His breathing was shallow, and it sounded as if even speaking was a supreme effort. Deep in her heart, she knew he would not see nightfall. She could not imagine how her life would be without him. He was still a handsome man, and even now he seemed to emanate power. What an emperor he had become – Rome had never known a man like him. He had changed the world. Her eyes started to well with tears, and she turned to place her arm over him. Livia kissed him on the forehead.

"I love you," she whispered.

Caesar Augustus looked at her and smiled. "I love you too, Livia."

Augustus turned his head to Tiberius. "Tiberius, I found Rome of clay – I leave it to you of marble."

Augustus closed his eyes and drifted into sleep for ten minutes. When he woke, he felt fully alert. He looked at Livia and Tiberius, saw his physician by the window and saw the two Praetorians by the door. He drew his breath and smiled. "Well – Did you all like the performance?" he asked and laughed. In his weakness, his laugh sounded almost like a cough. He relaxed, breathed out slowly and never breathed in again.

Rome mourned the loss of the greatest leader it had ever known. Tiberius knew he had a hard act to follow, and it terrified him. He did not want the power he had been granted, and he spent the first few months as emperor trying to plan how he could evade as much of the responsibility of his position as he could. Tiberius had gained a reputation from his military career as being a brilliant general and had become something of a legend along the empire's northern frontier. As a politician, however, he felt out of his depth, as the senate soon found out. As Tiberius ducked and weaved his way around important decisions, time wore on, and the patience of the senators wore out.

Within weeks of coming to power, he received a plea from his army in Germania – the soldiers were owed money, plenty of it. They had been promised a great financial reward by Augustus, for the blood and tears they had shed and spilt in those cold forests of the north, and they had seen none of it. Tiberius ignored the missives he was sent, not knowing how to deal with the problem he had inherited and loathe to send them so much money from the state treasury. He foolishly hoped the issue would die down and go away.

That same year, as one man was granted power he did not want, another man was granted power he had desired for years – and he intended using every opportunity to wield it. Annas, the high priest of the Temple of Jerusalem and president of the Senhedrin, was dismissed from his position, and Yosef Bar Kayafa, known to all as Caiaphas, was elected to replace him. Caiaphas was determined to put Herod Antipas under pressure to execute the man known as John the Baptist. For some reason, despite having been insulted by him, the king seemed loath to kill the maniac preacher and had held the man captive for many months. Caiaphas couldn't understand it, and he certainly was not going to put up with it. This 'John the Baptist' was an insult to the temple, and to make matters worse, he had heard there was another damned Essene preacher wandering around the north performing 'miracles' and generally undermining the authority of his church. As chairman of the high court, he was going to get rid of the two of them. He wasted no time in organising a private audience with Valerius Gratus, the procurator – governor of the Roman Province of Judea, at his villa in Caesarea Philippi. Caiaphas used all his political skills to gain the trust of Gratus, and to ensure that they were allies. Neither man wanted to upset the status quo and Caiaphas left Caesarea safe in the knowledge that he had cemented a firm friendship with Roman authority and thus re-enforced the safety of his own position in the temple, as well as ensured the temple's authority over the people. Now he felt he was in a good position to start purging the country of these renegade preachers and maybe get rid of a few of those troublesome Zealot terrorists which had started plaguing the land as well.

Chapter 6

Men to Trust

James sat alone on the roof, watching the sunset, deep in thought. He often missed his childhood in Egypt and remembered with great fondness his brothers as they had been. Jesus – usually quiet but his best friend. Always there with affection and a smile. Jude – always giggling and laughing. He felt that as children, both of them had looked up to him and valued his opinion as their big brother. Now he felt that he was the one who had to look up to them. He was not bitter or jealous – just sad that the old days had gone, fading into a distant memory. Egypt was a chapter in his life that was well and truly ended, and now, life in Jerusalem was yet another chapter about to draw to a close. Tomorrow they were heading northeast to live in Capernaum on the northern shore of the Sea of Galilee. They were leaving the city behind them with its surrounding landscape of desert scrubland and going to live near the sea surrounded by lush green fields and thick forest. It was the northern end of John's old stomping ground. He thought of John rotting away in prison these past two years and shuddered. He wondered what fate awaited himself, Jesus and Jude.

They were all packed and ready to go. Tonight they were all to sleep here at the house in Jerusalem and the three brothers were going to depart at sunrise. Their mother was staying here for a time, and Elizabeth was to come to live with her in two days. Elizabeth was no longer the beauty she was. The arrest of her only son had aged her unbelievably, and the worry and stress had etched great lines of worry and sadness into her face. Dark circles had settled permanently around her eyes; she looked 20 years older than her real age, and her physical health was suffering as much as her mind. She had written many letters to Antipas begging him to set her son free but had never yet received any answer.

James stood and stretched his arms. He was feeling tired and knew that the following day would be a long one. He turned and saw Jude watching him from the top of the roof-steps.

"What are you thinking, Brother?" Jude asked.

"Nothing really," James answered, "just wondering what the future has in store."

"If we stick together, it does not matter," said Jude. "You know Jesus would lay down his life for us – we should promise to do the same for him if the need arises. I cannot help but feel that hard times are headed our way. We have a lot of hard work before us, made all the harder with John in captivity."

"Then we should sleep while we can, yes?"

Jude walked towards his brother. "Will you lay down your life for our brother?" asked Jude.

James nodded. "Of course, I would."

"Remember that promise," Jude said.

"Are you doubting me, Jude?" asked James, feeling a little offended at the tone in his brother's statement.

"No – I just want to make sure we all know where we stand before we head north. There is danger ahead." Jude grinned. "Don't worry. I trust you, and I believe you."

Jude entered the house, followed by a tall, thin man who appeared to be roughly the same age as Jesus. "Jesus, there is someone I would like you to meet," said Jude. He had been gone all morning having said that he had an errand to run. Jesus and James were sat at the rough wooden table in the kitchen of their new home. They looked up.

"This is Simon – Simon Zelote as he is known. We, ah, worked together for a while," Jude said.

The stranger nodded to the seated brothers and looked directly at Jesus. "Your brother Judas here says you are looking for help," Simon said.

Jesus looked at Jude, and then back to Simon. "That depends on what you mean by 'help'."

"I know who you are. I have come to you from Qumran. My friend – your brother thinks you may need protection. He and I have spent much time together before, and I assure you, I am worthy of your trust," said Simon.

"I cannot pay you, Simon Zelote. I have no wish to be an employer," said Jesus.

"I do not come to you either for commission or coin. I come to you because I have heard of you – heard much about you, and it is the things I hear that has drawn me here to Capernaum."

Simon unexpectedly dropped to one knee in front of Jesus. "Please accept my help, friendship, and service, Lord," he said.

Jesus looked at Jude who gave him a slight nod. He looked down at Simon and placed his hand on his head. "Welcome, Simon of the Zealots, friend and servant of God. A man my dear brother trusts, I also trust."

Simon stood and looked at James. "I have heard much about you too. And I am proud to be in such good company."

James said nothing but just stared at the man with a blank face.

"Tell Jesus what you told me earlier, Simon," said Jude.

Simon sat on an empty chair next to James, who watched him warily. "It so happens that I know your old friend Hezekiah, and when I last spoke to him, he told me there is another who seeks you. He may be here already. His name is Phillip – from Bethsaida, only a couple of miles from here. This Phillip is one who knew your kinsman, John. He was baptised by him in…in Philoteria, I think. Hezekiah met him in Qumran, for he had gone south to seek you out after John spoke of you. This was only a few days before he was arrested. It is my guess that many hereabouts will welcome you, for some have seen you before and the loss of John has come hard to them."

"You are well informed, Simon," said James. "How so?"

"I make it my business to be well informed. A man of my background cannot afford to be otherwise," Simon answered. "As I am sure Judas here will affirm."

Jude nodded his agreement. "As Sicarii, we like to know who is who, and who is connected to who. For many reasons."

Jesus stood. "Perhaps we should let ourselves be found by this Phillip."

Jesus stood on the small wooden pier. A small crowd of about 30 people had gathered around him listening to him speak, whilst James, Jude and Simon stood around about 20 yards away, watching the spectators with interest.

"Repent, for the Kingdom of Heaven is near," Jesus said. "You are all aware that many years ago, the Lord said unto the people, 'Do not commit murder – for those who murder will face Judgement.' But I tell you now, any man who even is angry with his brother will also face Judgement. A man who insults his brother may face the judgement of the Sanhedrin, but if he thinks his brother's a fool, he faces the fires of Hell."

A man stepped forward from the small crowd. "I have a question for you," he said.

"Then ask, dear friend, for no one should be ignorant of the meaning of God's word. There should be no mystery in faith, and I am here to give you understanding," Jesus replied.

"How can you say these words regarding murder when your own brother – a disciple of yours, is of the Sicarii? He is a dagger-man, yes? Surely, he faces Hell? And you also for your complicity in his trade?" he asked.

"In answer to this, I say – and listen well, that I bring not peace but the sword. Do not think I have come to abolish the Law or the word of the prophets! I have come to fulfil them. I tell you the truth – until heaven and earth disappear not the smallest letter, not the least stroke of a pen, will by any means disappear from the Law until everything is accomplished. Anyone who breaks one of the least of the Commandments and teaches others to do the same will be called least in the Kingdom of Heaven, but whoever practices and teaches the Commandments will be called great. I tell you, unless your righteousness surpasses that of the Pharisees and teachers of the Law, you will not enter the Kingdom of Heaven," Jesus replied.

"That does not answer my question," the man said.

"Indeed, it does answer your question. Think about this. Think hard upon what I just said. Obey the word of the Lord and you are saved. I am here to teach the Law – to guide you and teach you that same Law. But that Law and God's word need to be defended, for the word of God should be heard by all for the salvation of the world! And my brother works to do this. If the defence of the Law of God calls for the spilling of the blood of God's enemies so others may learn, then it is not murder – it is the saving of souls and the defence of the Law. You should have gratitude that a man such as my brother is prepared to bloody his hands so that you may not," Jesus answered.

"So…a man who kills so that others may be saved is not guilty of murder?" the man asked.

"It seems, my son, you have learnt this lesson. For the life of one weighs no more than a feather compared to the needs of humanity. There is no task nobler than that which serves mankind, for in serving mankind one serves God himself," Jesus replied.

The crowd eventually dispersed, but the man who had questioned Jesus stayed behind.

"I have searched for you – I was told of you by John, the Baptist. I even journeyed to Qumran to find you. I have many questions for you. Please do not think I doubt your words; I only seek further understanding," he said.

"Then follow me, Phillip, so that you may learn, and in time, teach others."

Phillip's jaw dropped. "How do you know my name?" he asked.

Jesus smiled. "John baptised you, and so you are known to the Lord. As I do the Lord's work, so you are known unto me," Jesus replied.

Philip fell to his knees. "I wish to help you do God's work, though I may not be worthy. I have a need to understand the world, and I need to understand God. I am full of confusion, and I see clearly that you bring clarity and light," he said.

"Then stand with me, and as you walk beside me, listen to what I teach the people."

James, Jude and Simon walked over to them.

"Well, who is hungry?" Jude asked.

They returned to the house, ate and discussed the preachings of John for a time. Philip, it seemed, had been something of a regular attendee of John's lessons.

"Why did John speak of the Pharisees and Saducees the way he did?" asked Phillip.

"This is because they have in some ways changed the Law to both empower and enrich themselves," Jesus answered. "They seek to confuse and add a mystery to God's purpose where there is none. Anyone who does this pushes people away from God and themselves, instead of bringing them closer. I do not know if they do this out of malice, for some I have spoken to genuinely believe they do right and so cannot be called evil, but in truth, they do it for greed, and greed is a symptom of evil. They are perhaps merely misguided and need to be redirected in their ways. But their conviction is so great that it will never be easy to do this. Sadly, many in the Senhedrin are more the politician than the priest. Some are simply businessmen who use the temple for personal gain, and there are others who simply enjoy the power that the priesthood gives them over the people. This is not what being a priest is about. Certainly, they should teach the Law, but it is not their place to turn a profit from it. They are not here to punish – for that is the Lord's great task after Judgement. They are here to defend the people from themselves. They spend too much time in council discussing God's teachings, which is not their task. Their task is to teach the Law, not try to see how it can be translated to suit their own purpose."

"I know a man who would benefit from your teachings," Phillip said. "He has not been blessed with any social skills, but he has been a good friend of mine for many years and lives not far from here. He keeps it quiet, but in some ways, he holds the same opinion of the temple as you. He thinks he is wrong to think the way he does, and it weighs heavy on him. Would you speak with him…please?" Phillip asked.

"Tomorrow we shall speak to him, certainly," said Jesus.

Later that evening, Jude asked Jesus and James to walk with him along the shore.

"I wish to express a concern, brothers," he said as they walked. "I am aware, that we will gain close followers, but I do not think we should entrust them with the knowledge of our eventual purpose for a while. We have to know that they are totally and undeniably trustworthy first, and this will not happen overnight."

James and Jesus were both in agreement.

"Do you truly trust Simon?" James asked Jude.

"Totally, and with my life. I have known him for three years. I know him very well. Which leads me to a suggestion," Jude answered. "Simon and I, both have skills in ascertaining whether a person may or may not be trusted without them ever knowing. Jesus – would you allow us to take responsibility for maintaining a close eye on those who wish to become close to you? We can be your eyes and ears. Think of it as another form of protection."

Jesus thought for a few moments and agreed to the idea.

"Then I must go away for a few hours, I have a task to fulfil tonight. I shall see you tomorrow," said Jude, and he walked away back towards the village.

James turned to his brother. "What Jude says is sense. If he and Simon are to be away at times gathering information though, you need someone who stays by your side to defend you against the unexpected. I wish to be thought of as the man who will do this for you," he said. He hugged Jesus. "I am your big brother, and I will be your bodyguard too. It's a big brother's job."

"Thank you, James. I have always thought of you like that anyway. I know you will always look out for me. You, my beloved brother, are my very own Praetorian guard."

They walked back to the house in silence, both lost in their own thoughts. James was happy that he had regained some of his status as the big brother.

The following morning, Jesus and James rose early, only to discover that Jude had not yet returned from wherever it was he had gone. After a light breakfast, they departed for Bethsaida to meet Phillip's old friend.

They arrived in the small, neat village at mid-morning, and Phillip left them at the wharf while he went off to fetch the friend he had spoken of. He returned half an hour later with a huge man by his side. Plainly, the fellow had muscles to spare underneath his loose tunic. Across the left side of his head, he bore a monstrous scar, and his eyes seemed oddly unfocused.

"Look at the size of him!" James said quietly as they approached. "He could knock out a camel with one punch!"

Jesus smiled. "Indeed, he is almost as big as you dear brother."

"This is Bartholomew," Phillip said, introducing his friend a minute or so later.

"You are Jesus? A Messiah? A Nazarene?" Bartholomew grunted. Jesus nodded in affirmation.

"Mmm. Can anything good come out of Nazareth?"

"Good manners can," said James, plainly insulted by his remark. "Although it seems they haven't reached this far north as yet."

Jesus placed a hand on James' shoulder. "We are here to enlighten, not argue," he said. "Your friend Simon tells me you are troubled by conscience, and he has told me why. You are not wrong to think the way you do – in fact, your views are closer to the truth than you imagine. It would appear that you have a brain between those ears, and you use it the way God intended. I could have a use for you, and in return, I would like to teach you more, so you can better understand your thoughts."

Bartholomew looked at Phillip. "I think this is the man who will change your life forever," Phillip said.

Bartholomew nodded. "I will listen and judge for myself." He turned to Jesus. "You have all day to spare?" he asked.

"I have a lifetime," Jesus answered. "Come, let us walk."

By the following spring, Jesus had gained quite a substantial following. Jude and Simon regularly disappeared for a day or two – sometimes together, sometimes alone. Jesus never questioned their movements, trusting in their intentions.

James remained at Jesus' side all the time, never more than a few feet from him when they were outside, or when Jesus was preaching. Phillip and

Bartholomew roamed the countryside telling of Jesus' teachings and encouraging people to go and listen to him.

People had now started gathering in their hundreds to listen to what this Essene Messiah had to say, impressed by his openness and willingness to answer any questions put to him. It seemed that wherever he went, people already knew of him and he had become quite a popular figure in the area of the Gallilean Sea. He carried out baptisms, ministered to the sick and taught the word of God on the beaches, in villages, in the fields and in the hills.

Jesus and James had journeyed to Taricheae on the western shore of the sea when James was asked by a young woman if he was the brother of the Messiah. At the time, Jesus was tending to a sick child in a fisherman's neat little cottage. James looked at her smiling face which was framed by long, black, silky hair, and felt his heart skip. He had never seen any woman as beautiful in his life. "Er...no...I mean, yes. I...I am James," he stammered.

"And I am Sarah," she said. "It is my nephew your brother tends, in my father's house."

"Then your nephew is in safe hands."

"You have a great confidence in this?" she asked.

"I have seen my brother perform many acts of healing in the past; some could even be called miracles. He is an amazing man."

Sarah looked into his eyes. "I think a man who guards and shows unquestionable respect for such an amazing man, keeps him from harm and teaches his ways without ever putting himself first, is an amazing man also," she said. James felt himself blush, and Sarah laughed. "Come, I have food for you and your brother," she said. She led James into the kitchen and gave him a cloth-wrapped parcel. "Would you object if I stood with you when your brother teaches later this afternoon?" she asked.

"No, not at all, it would please me greatly," he said. His stomach was in knots. "And perhaps I could take a walk with you after?"

"I think perhaps you could," she said with a smile.

That night, Jesus and James camped in the hills above the village. The wood on the fire crackled and sent the occasional shower of tiny sparks into the air as the smoke drifted lazily up into the sky towards the stars. A meteor streaked across the heavens as the two brothers gazed wordlessly upward, marvelling at the beauty of the night.

"You seemed quite taken with your new companion. And very pretty a companion she made for you," Jesus said after a time. "She seemed quite taken with you too. When is the wedding?"

James poked his tongue out at his brother. "Jealous?" he asked, trying to keep a straight face.

Jesus grinned. "You will see her again, do you think?" he asked.

"I would like to, but who knows when next we will travel this way."

Jesus stayed silent for a few minutes. "I think we shall stay around Taricheae for a week or so. There is much I can do here. Do you mind? And I would quite like to meet this girl, she who can reduce a big brute like you to a quivering mess."

When they eventually returned to their house in Capernaum, they found Simon waiting for them. "I have news for you regarding a weakness in the Empire of Rome," he announced. "It seems that the Emperor is by no means the man his predecessor was. He is proving ineffectual and unpopular – he has even made an enemy of a large part of his own army. I hear that the legions on the northern frontier in a place called Germania have risen in open rebellion. This sort of thing has a tendency to spread, I believe, which may help us in time. Dissension among the ranks of the oppressors is an ethereal spirit who could be a friend to us."

Chapter 7

Fishers of Men

It had been become quite a rare thing in the past few weeks for all of them to be together. Mostly, it had been Jude and Simon who had been away for one reason or another, but they had not found the need to leave in the last eight days. They had been finding out about people – discreetly asking questions and finding out background information in the most innocuous ways they could manage. Jesus himself had made quite an impression in the area, becoming something of a celebrity figure, and they had discovered that many were continually talking of his teachings. The words of Jesus were the hot topic for many miles.

Jude and Simon had spoken to Jesus of the information they had gleaned and went as far as suggesting that a few of the local people may well be worth recruiting to their cause. Jesus was happy to take their advice and decided they would all go to meet certain individuals they had found who stood out from the rest.

The first two men they were going to see were brothers. Simon had discovered that these two men had been ardent supporters and followers of John, and that they had been well-trusted friends of his. They were fishermen and had not been shy in expressing great interest in listening further to what Jesus had to say, having first heard of him from John prior to his arrest and imprisonment and then hearing his teachings first-hand several days ago. Jude had information that these men were to be found close at hand, and that they lived in nearby Bethsaida. When Jesus mentioned them to Phillip, he said that he was well acquainted with the pair of them, and in fact, he had known them for years.

Bethsaida – 'House of the Hunt', was a truly ancient town built on a small hill. In times long past, it had been the capital city of the Kingdom of Geshur, and back then, there had been an impressive acropolis surrounded by a massive fortified wall built on the hill's summit. Now the acropolis showed little of its former glory – just a few large ornately carved but weather-beaten stones marked where it once proudly stood before the town had been utterly demolished by King Pileser the Third and his Assyrian army nearly 750 years before.

As Jesus walked through the remains of the main gateway in the tumbled city walls, he could see how after centuries of neglect, the town was slowly starting to rebuild itself. A new temple had been built just a few yards from the remains of the gate, and Jesus could see that a lot of time, effort, expense and skill had gone into its ornate construction. He ambled through the town with his men taking time to look around at the large two-storey houses made from blocks of basalt rock. The houses were very much the same as those in Capernaum – some consisted of a few small rooms in a ring around a central courtyard with just one entrance, others were just a single large room with a single doorway and a window opening. But whilst the houses in Capernaum were packed together in a tight grid pattern, those here were a little larger and spaced much further apart. He had paid no heed to the architecture of the town last time he was here, but now he thought the place beautiful, as the simply built but well-proportioned buildings basked in the warming glow of the morning sun.

There was a gentle slope running descending to the shore from the lower houses of the town, and Jesus looked down to where the water lapped lazily against the silt and sand of the beach about a mile distant. He could see groups of men clustered around small boats which had been dragged bodily from the water and now sat leaning at angles on the shore. Long lines of posts stood perpendicular to the waterline, with nets slung between them to dry as they awaited repair. Jesus drank in the idyllic scene before him for a few moments as a flock of birds skimmed low across the beach and out over the glittering water, gaining height as they flew.

"I think we should head down to the beach, perhaps the men there will know where we can find the two brothers we seek," Jude said.

"It is as good a place to start our search as any," Jesus replied.

They walked down to the shore and approached four fishermen repairing a net which had been stretched out to show where it had been damaged.

"I am looking for Simon Ben-Yonah and his brother, Andrew. Please, do you know where I may find them?" Jesus asked.

The four men turned and one asked who he was, suspicion in his eyes.

"I am Jesus, cousin of John the Baptiser. The men with me are my friends and disciples," he replied.

The man who had just spoken looked at the man at his side and placed a hand upon his shoulder. "We are the Simon and Andrew who you seek. What is it you want of us?" he asked.

"You knew my cousin John – you were followers of his and were trusted by him. I have need of you, and I ask you to give up your fishing for a while. Please, follow me and become fishers of men."

The brother who had not yet spoken stepped forward. "What – just like that?" he asked.

"Yes, just like that," Jesus replied. "You have heard the word of God from John, and I know you have heard of me too. John is my messenger and he warned of my coming. Well, now I have come, and I call you to work for God."

The taller of the two brothers looked him up and down. "I am Simon. If you are truly the Messiah from Nazareth, I am honoured that you ask for our help," he said. "But we are nothing but humble fishermen. I confess, my heart is warmed by the fact that you came looking for us. What makes us so special that you know our names and make effort to seek us out?"

"God and mankind look favourably upon you – it is your virtue and strength of character that makes you special," Jesus replied.

"You speak as if you know us. As if we have been friends of yours for many years."

"You were friends of my cousin, John. Therefore, you are friends of mine," Jesus replied.

Simon laughed. "I don't know what my wife is going to say about this," he said.

"Your wife will say nothing that you cannot bear – you are called to the new Church to serve humanity. She knows all men of faith may be called. It is your time," said James.

"You are not married to her – she has quite a way with words. Possibly because she never stops using them – and usually at the top of her voice. More so when she does not get her own way. If words could be used to wage war, she could defeat all the legions of Rome in less than one passing of the Sun," Simon replied.

Jesus laughed. "Then it seems I am doing you a favour by taking you away from her for a while."

The following week, Jesus announced a desire to hold a meeting with his men. They walked into the hills above Capernaum and sat under the dappled shade of some trees by a small stream which wound its carefree way downwards, skipping and dancing over small rocks which sat in its way.

"It is time to explain some things to you. I will be direct and to the point; there will be no hidden meanings in anything I say," he said. "This is now the time for total honesty. As you know, much in our faith has a double meaning – such as the code of Pesher, where one thing is said, but those with ears to hear become aware of the truth behind those words. Duality is the basis of our way of life. It is the way of Man himself. With this in mind, I wish our group to work always in pairs. Just as the Sun and Moon guide our calendars together, good and evil both inhabit the earth, and humankind exists in the two forms of male and female, so we shall work also – two by two.

"Firstly – Myself and James. I hear that some in distant Qumran regard James as illegitimate as he was born before our parents' *second wedding*. That means to them, I am The David – the rightful king. Others say he is the Legitimate – and he, therefore, is king as regardless of Essene law, the blood of the David runs in his veins. This was hinted at when he was titled Bar-Abbas, 'the Chosen Son', by the priests.

"So James and I are naturally a pair – representing two opposing views in the church. But between us, if we stay side by side, we are the king and this can be without dispute. This is how the two of us are one.

"Jude and Simon have special talents – they are my eyes and ears. As I have two of each, so I have Jude and Simon as a pair. This is how the two men are one.

"Simon Ben-Yonah and his brother, Andrew, are a pair by blood. By their very nature and blood bond, they are one. They are followers of mine for only a few days. Their beliefs have duality, as I know that using twisted words, John both denied me and exulted in me. Much I have found out in recent days, have I not?" Jesus looked directly at the two brothers.

Andrew nodded. "More than once John said you had lost your way and said you were a 'seeker of smooth things'. He said your ideals were disrespectful to God and that you proved it by being baptised by him when you had already been baptised. But at the other times, he said you were the one who would lead us as a nation to the very face of God."

"So why do you now follow me when you could also have denied me?" said Jesus.

"Because John also made prophecies, and none have come to pass when he said they would. And he did not listen to your advice; he offended those he should have appeased. A wise man knows he never twitches the tail of the lion unless he has the spear to fight him. Especially, when he knows the lion has such big, sharp teeth. He languishes in jail now for his foolishness, proving perhaps that you are the wiser man," said Simon.

Jesus looked at Phillip. "You, I will come to later." He sighed and rubbed his forehead.

"When John was arrested, I had just spent a good deal of time in Qumran. Whilst there, I made many friends – Jews from here in our homeland, and some on pilgrimage from the Diaspora – the empire of Rome. Many facts became apparent as I listened to their news which I now need to relate to you. Much of this is politics, and you should understand that there are political alliances everywhere. Some are secret, some not so secret. Lift a stone, and underneath you will find an alliance, a plot, an agenda and struggle for gain or deep divisions in belief.

Firstly, there is a split between the heads of our faith in Qumran.

Some feel friendship with Rome is good, while others feel it marks the loss of our identity as a people. Then some think it is good to support the kings of Herod, whilst others think it is now time to support the line of David. The latter faction is split further, between support for either myself or my beloved older brother.

Now John was a supporter of the Herodian kings, and when he dared speak out against one of them, he was arrested. You must understand – the Herodian supporters are mostly friends of Rome and earn themselves a great deal of money from the Diaspora Jews. These Jews are wealthy and powerful. They are living the good life under the wing of the emperor of Rome. They are happy to pay money to the old land to maintain their position in Heaven as well as their comfort on Earth.

But there are also some in Qumran who do not support Rome and have acquired and set aside some of this money for arms against the Roman invaders and the Herodians to support the ascension of David's Line. Chief amongst these is Simon Magus, who soon enough will be declared the High Priest of Qumran.

The Magus believes in being open regarding his opinions. I admire his honesty and have told him as much, and in return, he supports me. There are also two more brothers, James and Nathaniel of the Diaspora – influential priests of the Egyptian Church who also show me support. Another who works on my behalf is a man named Matthew who works for the Church treasury. There are others, who for now I will not name, as for now, their usefulness and safety depend upon their anonymity. As you see, I have gained supporters in some surprising key positions. Any questions?"

"When did this split happen in Qumran?" asked Andrew.

"Years ago, but few outsiders knew of it. Most at Qumran did not wish to acknowledge the division for many varied reasons – chief among them being for political reasons and out of fear. It all started to bubble to the surface long before my time. You see my grandfather, Jacob-Heli, sided with Herod many years ago during the Zealot uprising. He considered siding with Herod was to be in support of peace, and to him, peace and the avoidance of wholesale loss of life and slaughter was a priority. This was a defining moment, and as he then held the title in Qumran as 'The David', well as you can imagine – it caused great controversy. It resulted in a split in the Church at Qumran which had long supported the Zealots – and still does in varying degrees. As for the issue regarding either support for or defiance against Roman authority…well, that has been around for a long time. Ultimately though, both Rome and the Temple of Jerusalem are the common enemies of the common people, and despite divisions at Qumran, the time fast approaches when we must cement alliances and rise against those who lead our nation astray from the path of God and the path of freedom and greatness."

"So where exactly do you and the rest of us stand in all this? What role is it you play?" asked James.

"Ultimately…Romans expelled and the Herodian powerbase destroyed. Qumran needs a shake-up because the church needs to change and be more progressive. Reform there is long overdue anyway. The times have changed, and the church needs to adapt and change with them to survive."

"And which of us really is the line of the king, Brother?" said James.

"That is not my decision, or yours. That question has an answer in the future, and for now, it matters little," replied Jesus.

"So why did nobody ever tell me that Father was The David, and I am in line for the throne?"

Jesus looked at James and sighed. "Firstly, it is a mistake to think the line of David comes to us through our father, for it is Mother who carries the blood of the old kings, not he. You were not told because neither our parents nor myself believe you are the heir. According to our faith, you can't be. You are illegitimate in the eyes of the Church."

James stood, shocked by the coldness in his brother's words and embarrassed to hear it spoken aloud in front of others. Until now he had no idea of his bloodline, or even that he was to be thought of as a bastard. He felt betrayed by his brother and by his parents for keeping this knowledge from him. "I need time with this…" he said and walked off, feeling that his whole world had been turned upside down.

"Could you not have broken that news to him in a better way? Privately? Can you not see how you have hurt him?" asked Jude.

"As I said, it is time for honesty," replied Jesus. He paused for a moment. "But yes, you are right – I have spoken unwisely and should have put more thought into my words. I have caused my dear brother great offence by thinking only of the broader picture and not of what is at my fingertips. I owe him an apology."

"Yet you did not tell him that I knew about this."

"And I will not. Neither will you or any other. I do not want him to hate you too, Jude," Jesus said quietly.

"And do you want him to hate you?" asked Jude.

Jesus shook his head. "Of course, not. But given the tide of events we are about to be caught up in, he will hate me at some point, I am certain. Perhaps it is better that is now, so we have time to heal the wound I have caused instead of this mess rearing its ugly head at a time when it could destroy all I work towards."

Jesus stood. "In two weeks, I must return to Qumran for *Full Initiation*. I am to be declared The David – king of the Jews, and a senior bishop. One day, I will be the High Priest and hold the rank of 'Arc-Angel'. But now I must speak to my brother and see if I can undo some of the hurt I have just caused."

When Jesus entered their house, James had still not returned. Jude went to the room he and James shared with Jesus and called Jesus to him.

"James has left us – his belongings are gone," he said sadly. "Where do you suppose he will go?"

Jesus leant against the wall and then slowly slid down it to sit on the floor, sorrow and guilt flooding his chest.

"I don't know. Will you look for him – send back word of his whereabouts?" Jesus replied.

"I will leave this minute."

"What have I done?" Jesus screamed at himself as he stared at the empty pallet his brother had peacefully slept upon just a few hours previously.

It took only two days for Jude to return. With him, he carried the news that James had headed straight to Qumran. Jude had travelled quickly and by chance had caught up with James on the road. James had said he wanted to speak to the priests – but would say no more. James had merely grunted when Jude told him that Jesus was sorry for the way he had spoken, and with that, he had carried on his way, a look of confusion and anger upon his face.

"What is done is done, despite my regrets," said Jesus as they sat on a wooden bench in the shade of the house. "I had to tell James what I did; however, I cannot deny you were right – I should have told him in a different manner. I fear I may have made an enemy of my brother. I wish he were here so I could tell him how sorry I am."

"Only time will tell," replied Jude.

"We must not allow this to hold back the reforms I have planned. It is a setback perhaps, but for now, I must look beyond personal matters. We must go among the people and preach – a busy time lies before us."

That afternoon, the group travelled to Magdela only a short distance away. Jesus stood in the town square and publicly named John the Baptist as a false prophet as a crowd gathered around to hear him speak. With his cousin in prison, he knew he had to distance himself from him or risk undermining his cause. He claimed to all that listened that John was a warmonger and had no more compassion for the people than the emperor of Rome – that he wanted bloodshed on the streets and in the fields of Judea. He said that John was supposed to have been his messenger but had fallen under the spell of those who were not true to God's word. People were shocked and spellbound by Jesus' words, and when he had finished blackening the name of his cousin, he changed the subject to the hierarchy of their religion.

"The *Temple* divides the people," he said. "Why are women regarded as less than men? The highest ones in the church are regarded as pure for they take the vow of celibacy. They regard sex as unclean, but did not God command us to go forth and multiply? Marriage is the pairing of man and women to fulfil God's wish, to achieve what nature intended. Any and all who marry, therefore, are doing God's work, and celibacy is against God's wishes. How possibly can a celibate man who defies God's command to be closer to Him than a man who fulfils His wishes? Why should a man be less close to God because he is uncircumcised, or a Gentile? I tell you this – there is no reason at all! We are all God's children, whether baptised by water or wine. A woman is not less pure because she bleeds when the Moon tells her to, for God made her that way and her body follows God's plan. I say all men are equal and all women are equal to men. But then, there are those men who love other men, and women who love women. What offence do they cause in the eyes of God? None! For God made them that way too, and after all – is there no greater pursuit than the pursuit of love?"

Jesus' audience was astonished – the last thing they expected was to hear words such as these from a priest of Qumran. Jesus preached on for fully two hours and answered questions for yet another two. Finally, early evening arrived and the crowd slowly dispersed with just a handful of people staying behind to questions Jesus' doctrines further. Eventually, even they wandered off home until just one young woman remained. She looked to be about 16 years of age and carried an air of natural beauty and grace despite being covered in dust from head to toe. Up until now, she had not spoken, but finally, she walked forward and knelt before Jesus.

"Lord, I see you have disciples, and they are all men. Prove to me you believe what you teach – that men and women are equal in God's eyes. Allow me to be your disciple for I vow to you that can be equal to any man and am fit for the task. I have walked many miles today from my uncle's house – just to speak with you. I would happily walk many more if you would accept me by your side," she said and looked him straight in the eye, holding his gaze.

"And your name?" Jesus asked.

"Mary," she answered, "Lord, I am Mary, originally of the town of Magdela."

Chapter 8

The Mount

"I have news, Brother. Simon passed me a message, and it worries me some," said Jude. "Caiaphas in Jerusalem has secretly declared his support for James as The David. Although why a man such as he would care what goes on among we Essenes is beyond me. I am sure he has his motives."

It had been seven months since James had left. During Jesus' *Initiation* at Qumran, James had kept well out of sight, doing all he could to avoid his brother. Jesus had heard that James was setting himself against him, but this news regarding the political stance of Caiaphas was more or less an open declaration that the two brothers were officially at odds. He doubted that Caiaphas really cared as long as his own power base remained unshaken and suspected that this alleged declaration of support was merely a tactic to divide and conquer, for the Sanhedrin were far better off the way things are. The council of the Jerusalem Temple were also quite open about being pro-Herodian, and therefore, not anti-Roman.

He also had heard that James was to marry – his wife was to be Sarah, the young woman he had been seeing for just over a year. He doubted he would be asked to the wedding ceremony.

"Do not worry, Brother," Jesus said. "this is my problem, and I must deal with it. I do have a concern closer to home though. As you know, Mary and I have become close, and for some reason, Simon bears her some animosity. We have announced our intention to marry, and since then he continually tries to cause an argument with her. With divisions in the church widening and the rift between myself and my brother growing ever wider, we need unity here, and we can ill afford bad feeling amongst ourselves. I cannot figure if it is jealousy that drives his attitude towards her or concern for me," Jesus said.

"I shall speak with him, but I think he worries that you will be distracted from our cause by her, especially as you have known her for so little time."

Jesus and Jude were walking in the hills around Capernaum. Jude had been away for the past month, gathering information for his brother.

"There is much happening, Jesus. The rebellion of the Roman army has been forgotten, and the legions are again strong and united. Germanicus, the general who sorted it all out with generous diplomacy and no small amount of gold, has now become a favourite of Emperor Tiberius.

The Diaspora temples seem to support your claim to be the David, for Simon Magus has been sending letters to the bishops calling for unity behind him in his support for you. It seems his letters have had a good effect too, for 72 bishops have now declared their undying support."

"The news of Rome is not entirely good to hear; however, it would seem Simon the Magus has achieved great success! Excellent. We must now put more pressure on the church for reform. The way to do this is through the support of the people. Jude, I plan to give a sermon. The bigger the crowd, the better. Can you organise the men to publicise it?" Jesus asked.

Jude thought for a moment. "Why don't you ask Simon? It may make him feel more valued – and it would keep him away from Mary for a while."

Jesus smiled. "There is a brain in that head of yours. I will ask him over supper."

***

It was September, the holiest month of the year for Jewish people everywhere and of all sects.

Jesus had spent the past three weeks wandering through the towns and villages surrounding the Sea of Galilee practising medicine wherever he went, and teaching the Word of God. Mary had been with him everywhere, and he had cut his hair and shaved off his beard to show he had turned his back on celibacy. This had been an outward sign of his open rebellion against the laws of the temple and doctrine. He had blessed and baptised whoever had asked him and made no distinction between sex or class.

Now he stood on the top of Karn Hattin, a prominent hill overlooking Capernaum. There were hundreds of people gathered around him – Simon Ben-Yonah had done well in planning and organising this.

He held his hands out to quieten the crowd and looked upward to the sky. The position of the Sun told him it was around midday – a good time for prayer.

"Blessed are the poor in spirit, for theirs is the Kingdom of Heaven!" he shouted. "Blessed are those who mourn, for they will be comforted! Blessed are the meek, for they shall inherit the Earth! Blessed are those that hunger and thirst for righteousness, for they will be filled! Blessed are the merciful, for they will be shown mercy! Blessed are the pure in heart, for they will see God! Blessed are the peacemakers, for they will be called sons of God! Blessed are those who are persecuted because of righteousness, for theirs is the Kingdom of Heaven!" he shouted. The crowd went deathly quiet – some had caught the hidden meaning in what he had said. The reference to the mourners as being those mourning for the loss of John and being re-educated in the way of Jesus was clever and subtle. But the reference to the peacemakers being sons of God was an obvious statement that those who supported Roman rule now ran the church.

"You are the salt of the Earth!" he continued. "But if the salt loses its saltiness, how can it be made salty again? It is no longer good for anything, except to be thrown out and trampled by men." A low murmur rippled through the crowd as the people realised he was inferring that the church had moved away from God and were manipulating their faith, and that it was up to the common people to rise up before they were crushed underfoot forever. Parts of the crowd were fascinated as they caught on to Jesus' hidden meaning in the words he spoke. Others were quietly telling those who had missed Jesus' subtlety what it was he was driving at.

"You! You are the Light of this world! A city on a hill cannot be hidden! Neither do people light a lamp and put it under a bowl. Instead, they put it on a stand, and it gives light to everyone in the house. In the same way, let your light shine before men, that they may see your good deeds and praise your Father in Heaven!"

"Go out and spread my teachings – take no heed of the doctrines and politics of the Temple of Jerusalem. Rebel against the Temple." he was saying, and many in the crowd knew it.

He spoke further of the law – hinting that those who ran the church were more interested in maintaining the status quo, passing laws and meticulously sticking to religious rites and petty rules whilst making a fat profit, than being spiritually close to God.

He spoke of his disapproval of divorce and adultery. He spoke of the nature of murder. He spoke of his belief that people could do God's will in private, and that public worship was not as important as the temple would have them believe. He warned of false prophets being those in the church who stood opposed to his views and finished by telling them that those who caught the meaning of his words were wise and should live by his teaching. The crowd was astonished and made slightly nervous by the way he spoke, for he had told the people to stand in defiance alongside him against the traditionalism of their faith. But he spoke as if he were the voice of a huge movement within their religion. The people had certainly not expected to hear all he had said, especially as a fully initiated Bishop of Qumran.

He finished speaking by announcing that he was open to questions but asked his audience with a warm smile if they would give him time to take water first, as his throat and tongue were dry and parched. For a further four hours, he sat and replied to as many queries about his teachings and opinions as he could, as individuals stepped forward one by one to talk. Some offered him gifts of food or money. The food he accepted but coins he refused, saying that riches and financial wealth were the desire of the temple and should never be the desire of a true son or daughter of God.

After the six o-clock prayers, a tall, handsome man approached him and quietly asked to talk. Jesus nodded and motioned the man to sit beside him. The fellow seemed plainly troubled and after a moment's pause said that he had once been a celibate priest but had made the decision to marry. As a consequence, he had been cast out of both his order and the church. Disgraced and regarded as unclean he was named a 'Leper' – his name was struck from the temple listings, and he was publicly denounced as one who would never find either peace or the pathway to Heaven. In effect, he was cursed and excommunicated. The man, testing Jesus' word, asked if he would be willing to declare him clean again. Jesus in blatant rebellion to the church's view stood, placed his hand on the man's head and loudly announced, so many around him could hear, "I am willing. Be clean. Show yourself to the priests and offer your sacrifice to God as I command and in spite of them. You are a Leper no more!"

Jesus knew this was one act which had now set him along a path from which there was no turning back.

As the crowd dissipated, two men stood alone, triumphant grins upon their faces as they watched Jesus and his friends gather their things.

"Now we have him. For blasphemy. We have him by the balls," said the shorter of the two.

That night in Capernaum, there came a gentle knock at the door, and as Jesus opened it, the young man outside furtively looked around himself and pushed his way inside apologetically. He hurriedly whispered that he was bearing an urgent message from Joseph of Aramathea. Jesus sat the man down as Mary pushed a plate of bread, goat cheese and olives across the table in front of him. She then poured him a cup of wine and the messenger drank thirstily from it before speaking, firstly thanking Mary for her generosity. He sat and relayed his message as he ate, apologising for his bad manners but explaining he had not eaten for nearly two days.

His message was in the form of news. News that Caiaphas had been informing the Roman prefect of events around the country – of what Jesus had been doing of late. News that Caiaphas had sent spies out into the land to observe and listen to Jesus' teachings. News that Caiaphas had also been writing letters to Rome expressing fear of rebellion in the church and among the Essenes and Zealots which could lead to a large-scale nationalist uprising. News that Rome had responded to the letters from Caiaphas and that Emperor Tiberius had appointed his most loyal and capable general, Germanicus, as governor of all the Eastern territories of the Roman Empire. And fresh from campaigning in the empire's northern frontier where he had gained a formidable reputation for his ability to put down rebellions and crush those who disagreed with the will of Rome, it was now known that Germanicus was already making haste to Judea.

Chapter 9

More Men

By mid-November, Germanicus had made sure that the Romans were starting to make their presence felt. Soldiers quickly became a common sight everywhere. Mostly they were local men who had either volunteered for military service for the money or had been forced with threats and beatings. Some had been pressed into service from jails having been given the simple choice of either being in the army or facing slow and excruciatingly painful execution. Foreign faces were to be seen amongst the ranks too. Pale skinned north-westerners with blue eyes, black men from Africa and narrow-faced troops with hawkish eyes from Dacia and Thrace. It was generally known that they had been briefed not to interfere or interact too much with the local populace and to maintain the role of little more than a high-profile visible presence. They were, for now, mostly just a symbol of Roman authority, a show of force.

For their part, the soldiers generally treated people with respect, and it was plain for all to see that Germanicus had adopted the strategy of showing that Rome was a friend, not an enemy. Germanicus also understood that many of his troops had friends and family in the areas they patrolled and had no desire to divide the loyalties of the men under his command. One or two soldiers had stepped out of line and caused minor incidents and offences to the natives, but Germanicus had these men dealt with very harshly and very publicly.

Jesus noticed that at times soldiers would take time to listen to his teachings, some even made so bold as to ask questions of him. He had even been asked by a few to baptise them. He knew some were listening to him on the orders of their superiors to find out if he was stirring sedition or promoting rebellion, but he could also see that others were there out of curiosity for they tended to keep a lower profile. He knew there would be no issue regarding his teaching and talking of ethics and theology, for the Romans had a pantheon of their own gods and very liberal views regarding religion and worship. A policy of non-intervention was clearly in force until such time as the Romans considered it a danger.

Early one evening, a centurion whom Jesus had spotted a few times previously stepped forward and approached him. Resplendent in shining bronze and oiled leather with a bright scarlet horsehair plume on the crest of his helmet, he wore the resolute look of someone who had just made a momentous decision. As he stood in front of Jesus, he removed his helmet, rubbed his chin and asked if Jesus would baptise his entire family. Jesus nodded with a smile, placed his hand upon the soldier's shoulder and said simply, "Of course, why would I not?"

Jesus poured some wine into a cup, blessed him, and poured some of the wine over the soldier's forehead. He handed the soldier a cloth to wipe his face and told him to fetch his family. The centurion grinned and said a grateful "Thank you", then said that Jesus had baptised his manservant the year before. The centurion smiled again as he dried himself off. "I am to tell you," he said in a hushed tone, "you have friends everywhere – even among the legions of the Roman Army. Some of us also have family in the priesthood."

***

As November turned to December – the least holy month of the year, Mary started vomiting when she awoke in the morning. At first, she thought it was due to exhaustion as they had all spent a great deal of time travelling of late – day after day they had wandered around the coast of the Sea of Galilee. But she knew when she had failed to menstruate for the second month in a row that she was pregnant. At 17 years of age, she knew that she was far too young by Essene standards to be expecting a child, and to most, she would be regarded as a harlot, but she didn't care. The things others might say were unimportant to her, and she was delighted to be pregnant. She loved Jesus with all her heart and was overjoyed that she was now carrying his baby. Her love for Jesus was far more important than the opinions of others. How was she going to tell him though? Anxiety entered her heart and her stomach felt light and hot, for she did not know how he would react to the news. She knew he had great plans, and a horrible thought entered her mind – that now she was pregnant, he would think her an encumbrance. But on the other hand, wasn't he always saying that having children was carrying out God's wishes? She knew she had no choice but to tell him, for being pregnant was not something she could hide forever. She just hoped he would not cast her aside, or that he would not send her away.

She need not have worried. Having spent a nervous week deliberating how to break the news, she eventually just casually told him one evening as they walked back to the house in Capernaum after a day in Chorazin. Jesus was delighted. He laughed aloud and kissed her on the forehead. He grabbed her by the hand and pulled her along the road excitedly. "We must tell my brother!" he cried out at least a dozen times. He announced the news to his brother Jude the moment they burst through the door. Jude grinned when he was told.

"And this is news, is it?" asked Jude.

"What do you mean? Of course, it is news! Wonderful news!"

"You had had no clue? Seriously? And you…being skilled in medicine? She has been puking every morning for weeks! We had all guessed a child was on its way three weeks ago!"

Jesus frowned. "Some prophet I am, when I cannot make a prediction based on evidence that is right under my nose," he said sheepishly.

***

The following week Jesus became aware that Simon's mood had changed somewhat over the past few days. He was deeply concerned by this, and knowing that Simon did not get along too well with Mary, he decided to question him. He caught Simon alone one morning sat on the roof of the house gazing out over the sea in a world of his own.

"What ails your mind, Simon?" he asked.

Simon turned, surprised, as he thought he was alone.

"I notice that you are very quiet recently. It is because of the pregnancy, am I right?"

Simon shook his head. "No – I do not have a problem with that," he said.

"So tell me – why are you with us in body but elsewhere in mind and thought?"

Simon sighed. "It is my mother-in-law. She is angry with me for following you. She is a great believer in the teachings of your cousin John and calls you 'The Evil Priest'. She says I am cursed if I follow you, and that you are a demon who has possessed me. She nags my wife, who then nags me. She nags my sons, and I fear she will drive a wedge between me and my family. I have tried explaining your teachings to her, but she just will not listen. I don't know what to do. Her narrow-mindedness is driving me crazy."

"If you do not know what to do, then do nothing. Please let me help. I will speak with her – she can argue and shout if she wishes, I will not take offence. But I will not give up on the woman, so rest your mind. Show me where she lives, and I will do my best to cure her of her ill-feeling."

"Good luck to you," Simon muttered.

Jesus returned late that night after a day of theological discussion with Simon's mother-in-law. In fairness, the woman seemed like quite a nice person, but Simon was right about being narrow-minded. But he had not mentioned that she had the same capacity for thought as a donkey. Their conversation had been little more than a battle of wits, and it did not take Jesus long to realise the woman was completely unarmed. She was also a sucker for a bit of charm. She would always be narrow-minded, he surmised, but at least from now on, she would be narrow-minded in his favour. He smiled. No more nagging for Simon.

***

After a week in Gaderenes, ministering to the sick and unhealthy of the town, Jesus told his party that he wanted them all to head south to Qumran. There were people there he needed to see – one of whom was Hezekiah. He had heard on the grapevine that the old man was very ill and possibly dying. They journeyed to the Dead Sea wrapped tightly in cloaks to defend them against the cold and biting winter winds. Mary mostly travelled on foot like the men, not wishing to subject herself too much to the jolting and jarring of the cart. They arrived at Qumran late in the morning and were led to the 'Queens House' to be quartered, and when they had sorted out their bedding, they walked over to the refectory and had a light lunch. As they were eating, a priest appeared behind Jesus. Jesus turned and his face split into a broad grin.

"Jude!" he said. "So pleased to see you! Come, sit with us." Jesus turned to his companions. "This is Jude, otherwise known as Thaddeus, head of our Church in Egypt; the Therapeutae. He is thought of as a farmer, for he sows the seeds of holiness, and tends to the sheep."

Thaddeus sat on the bench beside Jesus. "Yaakov Ben-Zebdi awaits you all down at the caves, along with 'Thomas' and Yaakov Ben-Alfus."

Jesus sighed. "This is good. We are all here except my brother James. We shall walk to the caves then, and I will introduce everyone to everyone else. This may well be the only time we are all together."

"Jesus – your brother awaits you in the cave also," said Thaddeus.

Jesus was silent for a moment. He looked at Thaddeus. "I look forward to seeing him too."

After they had eaten, Jesus and his group headed through the temple complex, out through the gate by the Novice's Court, and around the outer wall to a pathway which led down the cliff into the Wadi Qumran. They followed the well-worn path cut into the cliff wall, passing small caves cut into the soft sandy rock. After 20 minutes, they entered a large cave and Jesus stopped in his tracks, staring at James – his brother. After a few seconds, James broke the awkwardness. He stepped forward and embraced his brother. "I am well pleased to see you, Jesus. We may stand divided on some of our views, but we are united in others and tied by blood."

"I ask your forgiveness, James. I spoke to you without subtlety nor thought," said Jesus.

"You have it," James replied.

Jesus stepped back. "We should none of us be strangers. I will introduce everyone." He placed his hand on James' shoulder. "This is my brother James. Some say he is rightful king of the line of David." Jesus walked over to Jude and placed a hand upon his shoulder. "This is my other brother – Jude the Sicarii. He is known amongst many as Judas Iscariot. Next is his friend and mine, Simon of the Zealots, who is also Sicarii." He then walked over to Mary. "This is Mary of Magdela, my future wife, and Philip of Bethsaida, and brothers Simon and Andrew Ben Yonah, also of Bethsaida." Jesus then walked over to Thaddeus. "This is Thaddeus, Head of the Egyptian Therapeutae. Next to him stands Yaakov Ben-Zebdi, a priest known as James, and his brother John Ben-Zebdi. Yaakov Ben-Alfus, a veteran of the Roman Army – known as James Alpheus, is stood beside John. Next is Thomas." Jesus walked over to a proud-looking man stood alone wearing armour and with a fearsome sword lashed to his hip – its hilt heavily encrusted with jewels.

"Thomas is not his real name. His real identity will come as a great surprise. He is Herod Phillip, son of Herod the Great and brother to Herod Agrippa, Antipas, and Archelaus."

Andrew looked shocked. "We are in the prestigious company!" he said.

"We are, indeed," said Jesus. "We also appear to be one missing."

"My brother sends his apologies – he is with Simon Magus for the day, accounting," said James Alpheus.

"James' brother Matthew works for the temple treasury," Jesus explained. "He and Simon Magus have money set aside for us – a good deal of it donated by our friend Thomas," Jesus explained. Herod Phillip nodded his head courteously – a faint smile on his lips.

"I will explain what is happening here. I am going to reform the temple and eventually tear it down, renew the line of David to the throne but on an entirely new basis...and unify our people against Rome. Given time the entire Roman Empire will become the Kingdom of Israel – the great Zion, and eventually, through our spirituality and power, we will expand our frontiers until there is no more land left beyond our influence. Then all will be complete and God's work is done. I will become a High Priest and a spiritual guide and lead the people in Spirit. Either I or James will become the overall king and emperor. It will be the people's choice who becomes monarch. We already have money, influence and arms. We are popular among the people of the North. We need now to spread our support to the people further south and west towards the coast, and out into the Diaspora. That done, we gain control here in Qumran. Thomas has his own army at his disposal, which we shall use to police our country. The Roman soldiers here are too few in number to be a real problem – and the Zealots will be more than capable of dealing with them. Our people in the Diaspora will cause unrest to a degree that Tiberius Caesar will not know where to begin restoring order. Germanicus is a problem here in the Eastern Empire, but no man is a problem too great to deal with for the Sicarii."

"You make it sound easy," said Thomas with a grin.

Jesus looked at Thomas, and after a few seconds, pause and smiled. "Thomas, my friend, when you truly know who God is, you will see that everything could be easy if only everyone were enlightened enough to accept God and see where his kingdom lies."

Chapter 10

A Child

In March, Jesus was in Mesada – the stronghold of the Zealots to the west of the wilderness of Judea. He and Simon had journeyed down to rally support among the Nationalists there and he was surprised at how much support he already had. Simon had already been writing to the leaders of the movement, and all along the coast of the Dead Sea, Jesus was being hailed as the saviour of the Jews. The children there were fascinated by his visions of how the new Israel would be and were calling it 'The Kingdom of Heaven'. Jesus felt inspired by their enthusiasm. He looked at the children and wondered how his own child would be. Mary was still not due to give birth for another four months, but he could not get thoughts of his new son out of his mind. The thought of being a father scared him, but despite his fears, he was excited.

Jude was visiting their mother in Jerusalem, and Jesus planned to meet him there soon, then they would journey together to Joppa, on the coast.

Jesus had started advising the people to refuse to pay taxes to the Temple of Jerusalem but instead to pay them to the temple of Qumran. The Sanhedrin were none too pleased with this and had sent out tax collectors who had tried to bully the masses into giving them their tithes. A few people had paid up, but generally, the taxmen were met with insults and threats – especially around Galilee. Some of the tax collectors had disappeared entirely, victims of robbery and murder. Slowly, the church in Jerusalem seemed to be losing its influence and grip over the people, and the Essene church of Qumran was gaining popularity. Jesus knew it would not be long before he had all of Qumran in his hand, but for now, the Senhedrin still posed a danger to his plan. Caiaphas was a very shrewd man and would prove no easy enemy, for he also had powerful connections and a ruthlessly effective spy network. Jesus knew he could not dispose of him by murder because then the Romans would get involved, but eventually, he was sure he would be able to discredit him to a degree that his own church would depose him of the leadership. Either that or the temple would just fade away as an archaic and dusty relic, no longer a part of society. Either way, a weak Sanhedrin without Caiaphas at the helm would mean the eventual collapse of the Temple of Jerusalem. Jesus was not going to publicly condone acts of violence against the temple tax collectors from Jerusalem, but he was quite happy to incite further ill-feeling against them and had started branding them as sinners and unclean, likening them to pigs.

By the end of April, Jesus, Simon and Jude had left Jerusalem having stayed at his mother's house for two weeks, and as planned, they travelled to Joppa, preaching and healing along the way. He found that the people of the south were becoming a little Romanised and they were already slipping from the influence of the church. This was not good, for the Essenes were regarded as somewhat too rigid in their ways and the people here were actually starting to think of their Roman overlords as a good influence. Jesus realised that rebellion was going to require a social revolution driven by the northern half of the country. He was confident that it would not prove too much of a problem and was sure that the Romans could be goaded into making enemies of the masses somehow. Perhaps the Zealots could stir a little trouble – cause a riot or two maybe and then sit back and watch as the soldiers carried out their reparations.

After a week in Joppa, they headed north along the coast to Appolonia, then they headed inland to skirt the Plain of Sharon – a barren and hostile landscape inhabited by few and bereft of water in any quantity. At Narbata, they headed back westward to the coast, avoiding the Roman city of Caesarea, and arrived at Dor. Three days later, they headed north again, towards the peninsula at the foot of Mount Carmel. From there, they struck inland to Nazareth, where Jesus spent a week preaching in the synagogue. Finally, they journeyed back to Capernaum so that Jesus could be present for the birth of his child.

They arrived at the house dusty and exhausted. Jesus was amazed at how beautiful Mary looked. Pregnancy plainly suited her. Her belly was huge, Jesus thought – it was plain to see his son was going to be a big healthy lad.

Thomas had sent a mid-wife from his royal court at Dion to attend Mary, and she had taken complete control of the house. Jesus had no objection to this – his only interest was the welfare of Mary and his son. The mid-wife fussed and cleaned continually and Jesus was at a loss as to where the woman found her energy for she seemed to be active nearly 24 hours per day. She regarded Jesus,

Jude and Simon as an unnecessary presence in the building and ushered them outside into 'the Lord's good clean and healthy fresh air' at every opportunity. Jesus found this quite entertaining, but Jude thought it quite an irritation. Simon just kept out of the way. Then early one afternoon whilst Jesus and Jude were talking in the yard, they heard a cry of pain from inside the house. Mary's time to give birth had come at last. They listened to Mary's cries for three and a half hours – both of them feeling uncomfortable, helpless and anxious, when suddenly, there was silence for a few seconds, broken by the wailing of a baby. The brothers rushed into the shady coolness of the house and were met by the midwife wiping her hands with a cloth at the door.

She smiled at the men. "The son you have impatiently awaited is not the boy you expected," she said.

"What do you mean?" asked Jesus, anxiety making his voice quiver.

The midwife winked at him. "Your son is a little girl," she said.

***

"Have you a name for your daughter yet?" Andrew asked.

"We are naming her Tamar," Jesus replied. "The generosity of people has amazed me," he continued. "Gifts have been pouring in from the local villages."

"That is because you are well respected," said Phillip.

"What is planned next?" asked Andrew.

"I do not wish to travel too far just yet – I think I will wait until after our wedding before travelling again. I may send Mary and the child to Qumran after we are married, she will be well looked after there. However, I will remain open to guests for now."

"That is good," said Jude, "because there are some of John's followers camped above the town wanting to speak with you."

"Tell them they are welcome here," Jesus said.

Joshua, the spokesman for the group of nine men, was a tough-looking man. His face was weather-beaten and deeply tanned, and he had a nervous tick in his left eye. He had the dangerous look of an Egyptian pirate about him, and Jesus guessed he was well used to being feared by his peers. He had been questioning Jesus for over an hour about the differences between his teachings and those of his cousin.

"John the Good Teacher said we should fast when commanded by the writings of the church. Why do you and your men shun this practice?" he asked.

"How can the guests of the bridegroom mourn while he is with them?" Jesus answered. "The time will come when the bridegroom will be taken from them; then they will fast."

Joshua was silent for a moment. "I do not understand the answer to my question," he said.

"Why go without food when there is food aplenty?" said Jesus. "The time will come when there may be no food – so you should eat when you can."

"But isn't that against God's will?" Joshua asked.

"No," Jesus replied. "It is common sense. Why put yourself through hardship when it is unnecessary when hardship can steal upon you uninvited? Life can be hard enough on its own, so there is no point in making it harder. If God wants you to suffer – then you will. If not, it is not your place to suffer from your own choice. In fact, it is just blind stupidity."

"John called you a seeker of smooth things. You give the impression that you do not wish to make life uncomfortable for yourself," Joshua said.

"Do you think that a man who makes life awkward for himself is a wise man? God would consider the man who deliberately trips himself and causes himself discomfort to appease others a clown – fit only to entertain those with a very limited intellect. But if you wish to make yourselves clowns to entertain the priests in Jerusalem whilst they banquet, drink wine aplenty, and festoon themselves with fine clothes and gold – then feel free. I will not stop you. I might laugh though. As I am sure they do," Jesus said with a grin.

"Are you mocking me?" Joshua asked.

"No, I am trying to show you how ridiculous the idea of fasting is."

Eventually, the men left and Jesus felt sorry for them in some ways. They had been staunch in their beliefs, and he had gone some way to destroy that for them. He knew all they felt now was confusion. But out of that confusion would come enlightenment. Give them a few days to think about what he had said and he was sure they would be back for a few more questions, and they would be converted to his way of thinking.

The weeks and months passed by quickly, and before Jesus knew it, it was winter again and he was a married man.

Chapter 11
Witchcraft and Death

February arrived with a messenger bearing a letter from Herod Phillip but signed with the name of Thomas. His 13-year-old daughter was very sick, and he urgently requested Jesus attend her to see if he could help. The girl had been attacked by one of Thomas's soldiers who had drunk himself silly and had raped her. Thomas had been enraged and once the man was caught, he had him tied, castrated, and his amputated genitals were forced up the man's rectum which had been loosened with a knife. "Let the punishment fit the crime," Thomas had declared. The mutilated soldier was then nailed to a tree and flayed to death with a wire-wound leather whip. The following day, the girl had started bleeding from her womb and she had collapsed after the passing of a further four days.

Jesus left immediately, and on his arrival at the grand and ornate home of Thomas, he asked for the assistance of Hannah – the midwife who had delivered his daughter Tamar. Together, Jesus and Hannah examined the petit young girl. Her rape had resulted in an ugly tear in the wall of her vagina and Jesus could see that she needed stitches. Jesus and Hannah worked quickly as the girl had lost a lot of blood and was very weak. They also did not wish to chance the poor girl wakening while they treated her – she had been through enough already, and to have consciousness return to her before they had completed their task would result in further suffering and agony for her. After an hour, they had her stitched as neatly as they could manage, and as a result, the bleeding was stopped. Jesus checked her breathing and pulse, and although both were weak, he knew that her chances of recovery were good. Physically, she would be in good health in a few weeks provided infection did not set in, but her mind would take much longer to heal. Jesus thanked Hannah for her help and left the bedchamber to speak to Thomas.

"Your daughter will recover in time, Phillip," Jesus said.

Herod Phillip nodded. "I cannot thank you enough," he said.

"You owe a good deal of thanks to the midwife Hannah. She was of great help."

Phillip sat on a chair and motioned Jesus to sit beside him. "Hannah delivered the girl – I am sure she was only too glad to assist you. Again, I thank you. Jesus – I caught the man who injured my daughter. I had him killed as unpleasantly as possible. God will punish me for this, I know it. I showed terrible weakness and unforgivable cruelty but could not stop myself. I could not forgive him."

"God will not punish you – you killed an evil man. Stamping out evil in the world will never be an act punishable by the Lord. My dear friend, the things I teach are aspirations for mankind, but every man should know that no matter how hard he tries to be good, there will be times that he will fail. You must accept this and forgive yourself," Jesus said. "I shall stay here for a time, with your permission, to tend to the girl. She will need you also – her father's love will help her."

The following morning, the girl awoke. Hannah had not left her side since helping Jesus tend her injury, and when Thomas' daughter opened her eyes, tears of joy filled her own. Over the next few days, Hannah ensured the girl was gently bathed twice a day and given three good meals between sunrise and sunset. She recovered her strength quickly and after ten days, Jesus bade his farewells and left for Capernaum. What the girl needed now was her family and the strength of her father.

A week passed and Jesus was home. He looked at his own little girl, peacefully sleeping in her basket, and thought of Thomas' daughter. He tried to think what he would do if anything like what she had been through befell his beloved Tamar, and he felt his stomach churn. In honesty, he knew he would feel the same as Thomas and wish an equally horrible death on the perpetrator of such an awful offence.

An invitation awaited him to teach in the new temple at Bethsaida, so having spent the night of his arrival with Mary and his beautiful daughter, he set off early in the morning with Simon and Andrew. They arrived at the temple in time for the midday prayers, and when these were over, he walked to the front of the group of men there and turned to face them. Before he could speak, a man called out from the congregation. "Is it true that you healed the daughter of King Herod Phillip?" Jesus looked at the speaker and saw he was wearing the full regalia of a priest of the Temple of Jerusalem.

"It is true," Jesus answered.

"And is it true that the girl was sleeping like the dead – that she was bleeding as though mortally wounded," the priest asked.

"What business is it of yours?" Jesus responded.

"So it is true. You healed a young woman who had a demon inside her," the priest said with an unpleasant and accusatory tone to his voice. "Could this man be the Son of David?" the man asked mockingly, addressing the congregation. "No. It is only by the power of Beelzebub – the Prince of Demons – that this man drives out other demons!"

Jesus looked at the priest. "Are you really so foolish as to think that – let alone say something so idiotic out loud? Think on this – every kingdom divided against itself will be ruined, and every city or household divided against itself will not stand. If Satan drives out Satan, he is divided against himself. How then can his Kingdom stand? And if I drive out demons by the power of Beelzebub, by whom do your people drive them out? So then, they will be your judges. But if I drive out demons by the Kingdom of God, then the Kingdom of God has come upon you. Do not accuse me of working with Satan for the good of the people, for he who is not with me is against me, and he who does not gather with me scatters. I tell you this, priest – every sin and blasphemy will be forgiven against men, but blasphemy and sin against God and humanity will not be forgiven, either in this age or the age to come. Future generations will judge you in poor light and call you a fool and an idiot." He pointed at the priest and raised his voice. "You – a brood of vipers, how can you who are evil say anything good? Men will have to give account on the day of Judgement for every careless word they have spoken, for by your words, you will be acquitted, and by your words, you shall be condemned!"

"How dare you speak to me with such disrespect?" the priest shouted, his face flushed with rage and insult. "How dare you question me – call me an idiot? Who do you think you are to say that if we are not with you we are against you?"

Jesus stared at him, gritting his teeth with anger. "Because I carry out God's work," he said. "And if you doubt what I do in the name of the Lord and for the benefit of the people, then you deny God, and a man who denies God is my enemy – especially if he purports to be righteous. A man of the Temple, such as yourself, should be much wiser than you have proved yourself to be. I call you idiot because you show yourself idiotic."

The priest was furious but could not think of a thing to say in his defence. He had come here to try and discredit this Jesus and had been made a fool of, succeeding only in discrediting himself in front of others. He turned on his heel and swept out of the synagogue, black cloak flapping behind him and sandals slapping on the stone floor. Jesus smiled at the retreating man's back. He pointed theatrically at the doorway through which the priest had vacated the building.

"When an evil spirit comes out of a man, it goes through arid places seeking rest and does not find it. Then it says: 'I will return to the house I left.' When it arrives, it finds the place unoccupied, swept clean and put in order. Then it goes and takes with it seven other spirits more wicked than itself, and they go in and live there. And the final condition of that man is worse than the first. That is how it will be with his wicked generation." Jesus looked around at the congregation before him. "Are there any other fools present who wish to accuse me of witchcraft?" Silence answered his question, and many just sat shaking their heads. The people of Bethsaida had no wish to accuse Jesus of working with the Devil for many had been beneficiaries if his healing skills and he was also greatly respected. The same applied to the people of Gennesaret, Chorazin, Taricheae, Philoteria and other towns when, over the next few weeks, he preached and taught in their synagogues.

It was late October when, after an absence of five weeks, Jude and Simon arrived in Capernaum. Jesus welcomed them back, and later that evening as he sat nursing his sleepy daughter in his arms, Jude sat beside him.

"I bring news for you, Brother," he said. "I was at Antioch with Simon and one or two other friends."

"Antioch?" Jesus asked, surprised. "What notion took you so far north?"

"We had an appointment with Germanicus – our beloved overlord," Jude replied. Jesus furrowed his eyebrows in confusion.

"I will explain," said Jude. "One of the greatest threats to our plan is the ability of Germanicus to put down rebellions. He is regarded as a master tactician and a brilliant soldier, yes?"

"Yes, I admit this man concerns me some," said Jesus.

"Well, he may concern you no more – our visit to Germanicus was not a social one. We killed him."

Jesus' jaw dropped. "You did what?"

"We poisoned him – and the thing is, Rome will not suspect our involvement in the crime. Roman politics are turbulent these days, politicians are vying for power and every man has his enemies. Germanicus, it seems, has been upsetting Piso – the governor of Syria. Piso is now blamed for the assassination, and it is widely known in Rome that Caesar Tiberius himself is jealous of the popularity of Germanicus. With luck, Roman paranoia will result in accusations of his involvement too."

Jesus was astonished. "Who ordered the killing?" he asked.

"Simon Magus – but I have not told you this," Jude replied.

"Simon Magus? Why?"

"Who knows? Who cares? Think about it, Brother – this makes things easier for us," Jude replied.

"It depends upon who our beloved Tiberius chooses to succeed Germanicus. 'Better the Devil you know'…as the saying goes," said Jesus.

***

John the Baptist sat shivering in his cell. It was not very cold, but for some months, he had found he was unable to keep warm. He was permanently hungry and was now painfully thin. His skin irritated him – sores had started to appear in his armpits, groin and between his buttocks as he was unable to wash, and he knew he smelt terrible. His long hair was matted, as was his beard and his clothing had all but fallen to pieces. He had been imprisoned now for six years, and as he was only allowed the occasional visitor, he spent most of his time talking to God. He was doing just this – sitting cross-legged on the stone floor with his eyes closed when he heard keys clanking back the heavy iron lock mechanism on his cell door and the drawing back of the three heavy bolts. The door opened and John remained sitting, ignoring the disturbance to his prayers.

"Get up, Filth," he heard a gruff voice say. John ignored the voice, used to the insults of his jailors. Suddenly, his head exploded in dazzling white pain and he felt himself fall onto his side.

"I said get up, you piece of shit – so get…fucking…UP!"

John lay on the floor, unable to move for the pain in his head and felt rough hands grab him under the armpits, lifting him from the ground. He opened his eyes and the soldier who had hit him swam into view. The soldier smiled and punched him in the stomach. John was doubled over with pain and saw the foot swing hard at his testicles. The brutal agony shot deep into his gut and he vomited.

"You dirty fucking bastard," the soldier growled. "You fucking splashed me with your breakfast." He pulled a baton from his belt, stepped forward and swung it hard across John's right knee. John screamed with this fresh pain, and the two men holding him up dropped him unceremoniously into his pool of vomit. John was confused and shocked – what was happening? He had never been beaten before – he was a priest, a holy man above such brutality! This couldn't be real! He rolled onto his back and the soldier hit him with the wooden baton across his other knee. John screamed again – the pain was unbearable.

"Stop that fucking noise!" a voice shouted and John felt his head snap back and his face went numb as one of the men kicked him in the mouth. He tasted blood and felt around his mouth with his tongue. There was a gap where his front teeth had been and he felt a sharp pain lance up from his gum into his nose.

"Put him on his cot and then hold the smelly fucker down." ordered the soldier.

The two jailors dragged him across the room by his ankles and manhandled him roughly onto the wooden pallet which had served as his bed. John saw the soldier draw a wicked-looking knife as he was held down. He saw the edge of the blade was heavily notched as he struggled uselessly against the strong arms that held him as the soldier approached, his heart pounding with fear.

John saw the soldier raise his arm and the knife plunged into his stomach. Hot, white pain seared through his guts as the man pulled out the knife and stabbed him again, and again. John screamed, which made the pain worse, and he started to shake violently with shock. The soldier leant forward and grinned. "King Herod Antipas says farewell," he said. John looked up at his assailant and felt the knife slice across his throat, tearing through his skin. He coughed and choked, feeling the blood run down into his lungs as his windpipe was severed. Blood was spurting everywhere as the soldier sawed roughly through his neck. John's vision dimmed, and the last thing he felt through the pain was the knife grating into the bones of his neck.

Chapter 12
Suffer the Children

The news of John the Baptist's murder had caused chaos at Qumran, and many were worried that he had been killed as a reprisal for the assassination of Germanicus. They feared that they were suspected of being behind the general's untimely demise. Simon Magus was trying his best to quash this idea as he wanted no connection between the Essene Church and the death of the great Roman general. His contract with the Sicarii was to remain a secret, and he could not afford speculation that there was any Jewish involvement in the death of Germanicus. He explained to the council that he had heard John was killed on the request of Salome, the step-daughter of Herod Antipas. He knew it to be untrue, but he thought it was a good rumour to start. What he had heard, but he was keeping quiet, was that the soldier who had cut John's head from his neck was not one of Antipas' but a Roman who had been sent from Antioch. Although he doubted the authenticity of the story and preferred to consider it nothing more than a rumour, it had frightening implications.

Simon walked down the path through the Wadi Qumran to the caves. He had been told that Jesus was there with his entire inner circle, and they were seldom all together. This meeting that Jesus had called must be important, he thought.

He coughed as he entered the cave. "I hope you do not resent my presence," he said.

Jesus smiled. "Not at all. You are most welcome – please be seated."

Simon Magus sat on the bench beside Phillip as Jesus stood to address the gathering.

"It is time to stir unrest. The Kingdom of Heaven is, and can no longer be, a distant dream. You are all to go out and purge the towns of thoughts that John was anything other than a lunatic and that Rome is a friend. I want Antipas to be viewed as an unholy pervert who is no less a lunatic than John. All those who are fond of Rome, or supporters of John or Antipas, are to be branded as 'Evil Spirits'. Go out and drive out these evil spirits, heal every disease and sickness in the minds of those who doubt you. Do not waste time or effort going among the Gentiles or Samaritans, as they are staunch followers of mine already. Instead, go among the lost sheep of Israel. Preach the message – 'The Kingdom of Heaven is near!' Whatever town or village you enter, search for a worthy person, one of our supporters, and stay at his house until you leave. I know I am sending you out like sheep amongst wolves, so you must be as shrewd as snakes and appear innocent as doves. Be on your guard against the temple's men – Pharisees, priests and the like, for they will hand you over to the local councils and flog you in their synagogues. As followers of mine, you will no doubt be accused of working with the Devil. You will be brought before governors and kings if you are arrested and be held as witnesses against me, and make no mistake, they will break your bodies if they feel that is what it takes for you to do so. The Sanhedrin wants my blood. I have already been accused of working with Beelzebub and my good friend from Aramathea – Joseph, tells me they fear I bring rebellion and death to their way of life. There are paranoid whisperings in their halls and corridors. They fear the loss of their power and wealth. You must concentrate on indoctrinating the children, for a brother will betray brother to death. Children will rebel against their parents and even have them put to death. All these men will hate you because of me, but those who stand firm beside me will be saved. If you are persecuted or mocked in one place, flee to another, and when the Romans are gone, it will be more bearable for Sodom and Gomorrah on the day of Judgement, than for that town. Whoever acknowledges me before men, I will acknowledge before my Father in Heaven, but whoever disowns me, I will disown. Do not suppose that I come to bring peace to this Earth, I did not come to bring peace but a sword! Remember – I bring not peace but a sword. This is my motto and my promise, for amongst those who refute any enlightenment, I have come to turn a man against his father, a daughter against her mother. If a man believes in our cause, I don't care if that man's enemies are the members of his own household. Bring children to me if that's what is needed, and I will teach them. For children do not doubt the truth, and they are not corrupted by the desires of adults. Go south, spread my word. Go out into the Diaspora. Bring the fear of God to those who have fallen from his light. It is now December – spend a year on the road and return to me in Capernaum."

The meeting had plainly drawn to a close, and after all the men had left, Simon Magus stayed behind to have a private word with Jesus.

"Jesus, I have a warning for you. It is not just the priests of the temple in Jerusalem who wish you harm. Some here at Qumran want you kicked out of the church and excommunicated. These people see you as a rebel and do not know where or when you will stop rebelling."

"I will stop rebelling when we are all of one faith, the Romans are gone, and…"

"And it scares people." Simon interrupted. "I wish for the same – you may rest assured of my full support. I just wanted you to know that not everyone here feels the same way."

Jesus embraced Simon. "Thank you," he said. "And now I think I would like to visit my old friend Hezekiah."

Jesus knew Hezekiah was very close to death. His long battle against illness was drawing to its inevitable conclusion. He lay on his pallet, breathing shallowly, milky eyes staring blankly at the ceiling in his room. His skin was grey and his sparse hair was white. Jesus sat beside his old teacher and held his hand.

"Who is that?" whispered the old man weakly.

"It is me, Teacher. Jesus, the son of Joseph."

The old man smiled. "Ah, I have been waiting for you," he said, and without further comment, his life ebbed away. Hezekiah lay dead, and for the first time since he was a child, Jesus cried his heart out.

After the funeral of Hezekiah, Jesus made his way north with Mary and Tamar. Mary returned to their house in Capernaum, and after a loving farewell, Jesus travelled on to Gischala in the hills to the northwest.

He arrived in the village and, at the first opportunity, spoke to the priest in the synagogue, asking him to arrange classes for the local children. Two days later, Jesus stood before a crowd of around 50 youngsters, all completely fascinated by his words. He told them of Moses leading his people from under the oppression of their Egyptian masters and told them that once again it was coming close to the time to cast off oppression again – except this time the Hebrew people were already in their own land. This time it was the oppressors who had to be the ones to go, and that would result in fight, not flight. Jesus told of the legendary battle between his ancestor David and the giant, Goliath. He told them how the Romans were like the old Babylonians, clever but brutal pagans who held wealth and hedonism with higher esteem than the God that created them. He called on the children to believe in him, and he would make them heroes like David in the years to come.

From Gischala, he went to Capar Ganaeoi, Abelane and Daphne, preaching the same message to the children. Jesus then headed west to Sarepta and down the coast to Tyre and Achzib, preaching and teaching as he went. He then turned inland and headed back home to Capernaum. Once home, he spread the word that people were to bring their children to the town synagogue. Every day, he spent at least three hours teaching the children about their people's history and how one day – with their help, God's plans would come to fruition. By the end of November, two officers from Thomas's army in the east had come to Capernaum and were teaching the children how the Romans fought and training them how to kill. Children everywhere were gathering information and passing messages on to Jesus regarding details of Roman manpower and the movements of soldiers and military supplies.

Late one evening, Jesus sat lost in thought in front of the fire.

"You seem to think a great deal of the children you teach," said Mary.

"Yes, I do. Children are the future. It will be through them that the kingdom I mould will harden and become reality," he said.

"I am glad you like children, dear husband. For we are to have another. I am pregnant again."

Chapter 13
Parables and Pharisees

Jesus sat with his eyes closed, thinking. He sat alone on the beach with nothing but a gentle breeze and the sound of birds greeting each other for company. He wondered if his actions and words were putting Mary's life in danger, and it scared him a little. Since he had been accused of Devil-worship by the priest from Jerusalem and had embarrassed his accuser in public, he guessed it was only a matter of time before the Temple would try to catch him out again. He was actually quite surprised that more effort had not been made to do so since then. Nothing would suit them more than being able to arrest him and try him for blasphemy, and Jesus was not quite ready for that yet. Joseph of Aramathea had sent him letters warning that the Sanhedrin were less than impressed at the way he was preaching. In fact, they were furious. Caiaphas himself had made it known that he wanted Jesus dead, and there were fresh rumours that a letter he had sent to Rome was the trigger for the brutal murder of John. Maybe he should send Mary and Tamar to Qumran? Simon Magus would ensure they were protected there, and she would be beyond the reach of the Senhedrin. He wondered what else Caiaphas had secretly written to Rome about. Yes – Mary would have to go to Qumran for both her own safety and that of the children. He knew he had enemies in Qumran too, but he was certain that his enemies there would never unite against him with the Temple in Jerusalem, for those in Qumran were Essenes, and those in the temple were predominantly Pharisees. The two sects had a long and at times very bitter history of animosity.

He was aware that his brother Jude was now referred to as 'The Beast' in Qumran by those who thought James should be the David as a sign of their disapproval of his link with the Sicarii and his nationalist ideals, whilst the rest knew him as Judas Iscarii or Iscariot. If only he could somehow unite the Essene church. If he and his brother worked together perhaps they could. If they could agree on the issue of who was rightful king, then perhaps…

Jesus sighed. *Perhaps James should be king*, he thought, *and I will be the High Priest. He will be the physical leader, and I will be the spiritual leader. So the Essenes will be united, and they will have the support of the Gentiles of the north, Herod Phillip in the east, and the Zealots in the south-east. With money coming in to Qumran from the Diaspora, it shows we have some support through the empire of Rome too – and outside influence will help. We already have the temple in Egypt allied to us. And Caiaphas must surely know all this. He and his temple now only have real influence over the south-western part of the country. The area under direct Roman control. Beyond that, the temple is fast becoming powerless.*

He opened his eyes and saw that Mary had sat opposite him. He smiled at her.

"You were deep in thought there for a while," she said. "Are you all right?"

"Yes – there is much on my mind at present," he said quietly.

"Well, your time for thinking is over for now – there are people who wish to hear you speak. Look behind you."

Jesus turned and saw about 50 people gathered a hundred yards away. He stood. "Then speak I must," he beckoned for the small crowd to come closer. "I would tell you a tale, a tale of a farmer. It is an old tale." he began. "This farmer went out one day to sow wheat seeds. As he scattered the seeds, some fell along the path at the edge of the field, and the birds came and ate it up. Some fell on rocky ground where there was little soil, where it sprang up quickly. When the sun came up, they scorched and withered because they had no proper roots. Other seed fell among thorns which choked the plants as they tried to grow, and most wheat seeds fell on well-tilled soil where they grew and yielded a crop a 100, 60, or 30 times more than what was sown. He who has ears, let him hear."

There was a pause, and a small man at the front of the crowd shuffled forward a few steps and asked nervously what he meant.

"There are two possible meanings of what I said. Firstly," replied Jesus, "I could mean that when anyone hears the message about the kingdom of God and does not understand it, the evil ones come and snatch away what was sown in his heart and the message dies. This could be the seed that fell on the path. The one who received the seed that fell on the rocky ground is the man who hears the word with joy, but as he has no root, he lasts only a short time. The one who receives the seed in the thorns is the man who hears but worries about his life, and the burden of wealth chokes it and becomes unfruitful. The one who receives the seed that fell on good soil is the man who hears the word and opens his heart and mind so he understands it and lives by it. He produces a crop yielding a 100, or 60, or 30 times what was sown. That is the first possible meaning to what I said." Jesus' face split into a broad grin. "The second meaning could have been something as simple as a poor joke about wheat and ears."

The dawning of realisation spread across the faces of some of the crowd.

"Let us assume I was not making an awful joke, and let us all sit. The Kingdom of Heaven is like a man who sowed good seed in his field. But while he was sleeping, his enemy came and sowed weeds among the wheat. When the wheat sprouted and formed ears, the weeds appeared also. The man's servants came and asked him where the weeds came from as he had sown the good seed. He told them that an enemy did it. So the servants asked if he wanted them to pull the weeds up. The man declined the offer, saying that they could uproot the wheat at the same time. He told them to wait till the harvest and then separate them, burning the weeds and taking the wheat to his barn. The harvest is the Day of Judgement, and the weeds are the evil in the world."

Jesus looked at the expressions on the faces of the people who now sat in front of him. Most looked like they understood his meaning.

"Think then of the Kingdom of Heaven, as being like a mustard seed," he continued, "which a man planted in his field. It is the smallest of seeds, yet grows to be the largest of garden plants, and becomes a tree. The birds of the air come and perch in its branches. The kingdom of heaven is also like yeast that makes bread grow in the oven. It is like a fisherman's net which lifts good fish and bad, and the angels of the lord are the fishermen who separate them, casting the bad back into the sea."

Jesus looked up to the sky. Dark grey clouds were boiling in from the north promising heavy rain. "The weather looks about to turn for the worst. Shall we adjourn to the synagogue?" Jesus stood, and the crowd followed him up the beach to the small temple. Heavy drops of water started to fall sporadically from the sky as they entered the building, and a deep rumble of thunder shook the sky. "It looks as though our timing was just right," Jesus said.

"It is a shame the same could not be said regarding your observation of the Sabbath," said a deep voice from the shadows. Jesus peered into the darkness of the synagogue, and four black-cloaked figures stepped out into the light spilling in from the doorway.

Jesus smiled at them. "Do you Pharisees from Jerusalem always hide in the darkness of synagogues?" he asked. "From whom do you hide? Are you afraid of the light?"

"We shall have less of your disrespect and sarcasm," said the deep-voiced priest. "We have word that you committed blasphemy against the rules of the Sabbath."

"How so?" Jesus asked.

"You and your so-called disciples have been observed picking ears of corn and eating them on the Lord's rest day," the man answered. "This is unlawful."

"This was three months ago – has it taken that long for you to muster the courage to confront me about the matter? Haven't you read what David did when he and his companions were hungry? They entered the house of God and ate the consecrated bread, which was unlawful for them to do, but not unlawful for the priests. Have you not read in the Law that on the Sabbath the priests can desecrate the day and yet are innocent? I tell you that people are greater than the temple, and they are here. They are the sons of Man, and the son of Man is lord of the Sabbath. You priests make one law for the common people and hold another law close to your hearts."

"And why do your disciples then break the tradition of the elders? They are filthy in the eyes of God – they do not wash their hands and feet before they eat!"

Jesus laughed scornfully at the priest. "And why do you break the commandment of God for the sake of your own tradition? God said to honour your mother and father, and that anyone who curses their mother or father must be put to death. And yet you Pharisees say that if a man were to say to his parents that 'whatever help you might otherwise have received from me is a gift devoted to God' is not to 'honour his father' with it. Therefore, you nullify the word of God for the sake of your tradition. You are hypocrites, and Isaiah was right when he made his prophecy about you when he said, 'These people honour me with their lips, but their hearts are far from me. They worship me in vain, their teachings are but rules taught by men.' Hand washing! Corn on the Sabbath! Nonsense! It is not what goes into a man's mouth that makes him unclean but that which comes out of it, followed by his actions."

Jesus heard murmurs behind him – the small crowd seemed unhappy to hear that the priests seemed to deem themselves above the Law. Nine or ten large men pushed their way past Jesus to confront the priests who backed away a couple of steps. "Who are you to come here and accuse this man of committing a crime which you commit freely yourselves? If that isn't blasphemy, it is surely hypocrisy," one of the men said. "Why don't you scuttle back to Jerusalem and stay there? Do you think yourselves as princes above us?"

"Let us not allow this to get ugly," Jesus said sharply. "Our good friends from Jerusalem have plainly misunderstood the Law, they have made a minor mistake, and there is no reason why we should not forgive them for it. Everyone makes mistakes, and now they have been educated, they have an opportunity to correct their ways." He smiled warmly. "It just appears that some make a deliberate habit of making mistakes."

Jesus stepped aside from the door and the crowd behind him parted. "You are free to leave, take care you do not get too wet from the rain," he said.

The four priests looked at each other, surprised at the turn of events and unsure of themselves. They had thought that the people would be less supportive of Jesus and had not even considered the possibility of being treated with such disrespect. Without a word, the priest with the deep voice stepped forward and walked out of the synagogue into the rain – the other three following closely and silently behind.

"I think you may have greatly offended those Pharisee priests with your words," a voice in the crowd said.

"I do not care, they offended me. And by your reaction, I gauge that they offend you too," Jesus replied.

Jesus sat re-reading the letter that Simon Magus had sent.

'Your life is in peril. I have honest word that the Senhedrin now regard you as a mortal threat to the peace and religion of this country. Regard this warning as urgent – for Caiaphas has sent letters to Rome only this week stating you are organising a rebellion. The Sanhedrin are to send forth agents to gather evidence against you as a heretic, and Caiaphas rages at the offence you have caused his priests. He claims you are the Devil and that you have ensnared the hearts and minds of the people with evil magic. Caiaphas sends priests and the temple militia north to Capernaum bent on your arrest and trial, and Rome will not intervene. I beg you to flee with all speed and steer clear of the roads, for I do not know which route they take. You are most welcome here at Qumran. May you travel in safety: Simon.'

The news was not unexpected, and he was grateful to Simon for the warning. Jesus stood and went to the yard where Mary was playing with Tamar.

"I think you should read this," Jesus said, handing the letter to her. She took the letter, read it, and bit her lip.

"What shall we do?" she asked.

Jesus knelt down beside her and kissed her on the forehead. "Well…worrying is pointless, so that is one thing we will not do. I think we should take Simon's advice and get to Qumran as soon as possible. We can be packed up and ready to go in three hours, I think. I don't know how close the Temple men are – they may only be a few hours away, so we have no time to lose. I would guess they will leave Jerusalem and head to Jericho, then follow the River Jordan north from the Dead Sea. Once they reach the Sea of Galilee, I don't know if they will follow the East coast or the west, and we do not wish to meet them on the road. So we should head north to Thella, then head west to Gischala. Then we hook south to Nazareth, Neapolis, then across the hills avoiding Jerusalem, to Qumran. Come, there is no time to lose."

By midday, they were halfway to Thella. They had packed a few possessions into a small cart and hitched it to their donkey. Jesus would not feel safe until they were headed west and felt that at any time they would hear shouted voices echoing up the valley from behind them, calling them to stop. Before they had left Capernaum, Jesus had casually told a few stall-holders in the market that they were going to travel to Abila, southwest of the Galilean Sea and gave no clue that he knew anything about the temple sending men after him. At Thella, they headed west and uphill. The wind grew colder, and they wrapped themselves tightly in their cloaks. Eighteen-months-old Tamar was enjoying the view sat in the cart under a wicker frame, which Mary had covered with a woollen blanket. Her little face poked out of a gap in the covering, and she beamed wide-eyed over the tailboard of the cart at the scenery behind them as it jolted along the rough track.

Jesus continually turned to scan the path for anyone who could be following them, but they were alone on the hillside.

They arrived in Gischala late at night and slept for a few hours in a barn outside the town. They headed off early in the morning, both of them unable to rest easy so close to Capernaum. Two days later, they arrived in Nazareth, and after staying overnight in an inn, they headed off again.

A week later, they arrived filthy and exhausted in Qumran. Simon Magus was relieved to see them safe. He fussed over little Tamar as Mary and Jesus took themselves off to the bathhouse to clean themselves up. Mary returned and took Tamar to bathe her, and Simon led Jesus to the wall at the edge of the compound, overlooking the cliffs.

"My message reached you in time then," Simon said. "I had quite a panic on when I heard the news, for I did not know how old the news was when it reached my ears. What are your plans?"

"I will stay here a day or so, and then I leave. Mary will stay here with my daughter. May I entrust their safe-keeping to you?"

"Of course. I will ensure they are well cared for and protected."

"I thank you," said Jesus.

"When is the baby due?" Simon asked, patting his stomach and grinning.

"Late in June, we think, but we don't know for sure."

"Will you return in time for the birth?"

Jesus nodded. "I plan to, but I cannot make that a promise."

Simon leant against the low wall and looked down into the Wadi. "Jesus, would you do something for me?"

"Yes, Simon, of course. I owe you a great debt for sending us your warning. What do you wish me to do?"

"The 'Five Thousand', the leaders of the uncircumcised married Gentiles are here, and I have some people I need to see on a matter of some importance this afternoon, and my meeting may take some time. Will you look after them? I know you are tired, but…?"

"Of course, I will. Do you wish me to lead them in the six o'clock prayer service?"

"If you could – break bread for them, and afterwards, supply the seven of them with a lavish supper. The kitchen staff have already been informed the Five Thousand will not be leaving until tomorrow daybreak."

After they had eaten, Jesus led the seven Gentile priests down through the Wadi Qumran for a walk in the late evening air.

"Jesus – I hear Caiaphas thinks you an enemy these days. I heard you had something of a confrontation with some of his senior priests," said Mattathias, the most senior of the seven.

"Indeed I did. I have no doubt there will be more confrontations with them in the future. In fact, I very much hope there will be," Jesus answered.

"You are playing a very dangerous game – Caiaphas does not like having his nose tweaked like that – it hurts his pride, and he thinks that anything which can dent his pride is a danger to his church and the very nation itself."

"Pride is a sin," Jesus said and stopped in his tracks. He looked at Mattathias. "And I *am* a danger to his church. I threaten what his church stands for – because it is not God's church. I give you an example. As a member of the 'Five Thousand', you may have your baptism as a baby, yes? This is a baptism in water. And yet your class forbids you to take your second baptism – the baptism of wine. Why? The second baptism takes a man nearer his God – and yet the church in Jerusalem forbids it for Gentiles. God does not forbid it – the Temple does. Yet God creates us all as equals? There is something wrong in this, do you not agree? I should start baptising Gentiles with wine, I think."

Mattathias laughed. "That would create quite a stir – Gentiles baptised with wine. I doubt there is a man alive who would dare do it – even you, Jesus, would not dare commit such a blasphemy."

A look of anger flashed across Jesus' face but was gone as quick as it came. "You doubt me?" he asked quietly. "I believe you have a right to second baptism. And I tell you now – if you dare take it, I will indeed do it for you – here – tonight. And from now on, I will go amongst your people and baptise all who ask for it. I will even forsake the baptism of water completely, why bother with it at all?"

Mattathias looked shocked. "You will turn the water into wine? Without fear of repercussion?"

Jesus smiled and spread his arms. "Dare you do as I do? Will you allow me to baptise you tonight with wine? In spite of the Temple?"

Mattathias nodded. "Baptise me," he said.

Chapter 14

Confrontation

Jesus had arrived back in Qumran just hours before the birth of his son. He appeared at Mary's bedside, covered in dust from his travels, looking tired and haggard. He kissed her on the forehead and knelt beside the bed, holding her hand.

"I thought you were not coming," Mary said. "I have been waiting for you for weeks."

"I am sorry, my love," Jesus whispered. "I have travelled many miles to get here – it took longer than I expected."

Mary's face screwed up with pain as her abdominal muscles went into a tight contraction. The pain eased, and she looked at Jesus with concern on her face.

"You have a starved and hunted look about you – is everything all right? Are you ill? You look ten years older than you did only a few months ago."

Jesus smiled. "I confess I am hungry. I smell like an ancient, wet camel too."

"Go wash yourself. You are too dirty to welcome your child into the world," Mary said. "But be quick."

Jesus walked off to the bathhouse in the starlit night. He ached all over. He had spent the last three nights sleeping rough and had not eaten for two days. He had heard that the Temple militia were looking for him still. Patrols of armoured men were searching the roads around Qumran and had been doing so for some time – waiting for him to return. His latest offences against the temple were his baptisms of wine for the Gentiles. Word had spread amongst the Gentile communities, and they had flocked in their hundreds to him for baptism. The Sanhedrin in Jerusalem were furious at this latest in a series of outrages and had officially laid charges of blasphemy against him for it. Orders had been sent out for his arrest, but he had mostly been able to keep a few steps ahead of those who were on the roads looking for him. Jesus was now a wanted man. A fugitive. He knew he would be safe in Qumran – the temple militia would not dare place a foot inside the walls of the complex, but getting in and out was far from easy. For three days, he had been trying to get into Qumran without being seen and had finally managed it by crawling up the Wadi past the caves under the cover of darkness.

Jesus walked into the bathhouse and stood by the warm pool. He stripped naked and poured oil into his cupped hand. He then rubbed the oil onto his skin until he was covered head to toe, and using a bronze scraper, he started to scrape the now-filthy oil from his body. When he had finished, he rubbed himself down with a cloth and stepped into the beautiful warm water. There was one thing he knew he did respect the Romans for, and that was the introduction of the perfect way to bathe. Jesus sat down in the water and felt his body relax. He leant against the side of the pool and closed his eyes.

After a few moments, he heard careful footsteps behind him. He turned and saw four soldiers stood, swords in hand, grinning at him. "So you thought you would be safe hiding in a fucking bath, did you?" one of them said. "Stand up, you prick. Ha! It is deep shit you are in. We have orders to take you to Jerusalem, living or dead. Try and escape, and I for one will be more than happy to gut you. Four fucking months, I have been out wandering the countryside looking for your worthless bloody hide, and now I have you, I am not letting you out of my sight till you stand before Caiaphas being condemned to death." Two of the soldiers waded into the water and grabbed him by the arms, dragging him from the pool. The fourth soldier bent to pick up Jesus' clothes. "Leave them fucking rags where they lie. He won't be needing no clothes where he is going. He can march into Herod's great temple as naked as the day he was born for all I care," said the first soldier. He walked up to Jesus, extended his short sword and with the flat of the blade, used the tip to lift Jesus' testicles. "These will be the first to go if you give me any trouble. Understand? I will take your balls off without any thought whatsoever."

Jesus shivered with the cold as he was dragged outside, his stomach knotted with fear. He could hear Mary's cries of distress as she struggled to give birth to his child. He felt anger well up inside him from his stomach, his heart started to beat faster, and suddenly, he felt warmer, he felt his eyes start to burn in his head. "How dare you lay your hands on me!" he shouted. He wrenched his arms from the grip of the soldiers and grabbed a sword from the scabbard of one of his captors. Jesus swung the sword in anger, around and around he whirled it as he felt the blade start to glow white-hot with the power of God – surging down his arm into the weapon. He sliced at the nearest soldier, the man's blood steaming and hissing at his fatal neck wound from the intense heat of the sword blade. "Feel the power of God!" he shouted. The other soldiers stood stock still in shock as Jesus pointed his finger at another soldier and a bright flash of light leapt from his fingertip and lanced across the space between them. The man burst into flames and screamed in agony as the skin on his face started to bubble and melt. He turned to use his power to blast the other two soldiers to ashes…

Jesus woke with a start, shivering in the water. He looked around for the soldiers in his dream, a feeling of panic in his stomach. He relaxed as he realised he was alone. Jesus got to his feet and went dizzy. He stood still for a few moments to let the feeling pass and then got out of the water.

***

Mary was asleep as Jesus cradled his new son in his arms. He squatted down on the floor as Tamar looked in wonder at her baby brother for the first time. Her beautiful blue eyes opened wide in wonder. "I kiss the baby?" she asked and leant forward, brushing her lips on the boy's forehead. Jesus looked over at Mary's sleeping form. She looked terrible. This birth had not been an easy one, and she had more pain to face after the baby had been delivered. The boy had torn her badly on his way into the world, and Mary had faced another two hours of painful stitching. He looked down at his son sleeping peacefully in his arms and smiled. He would leave Mary to choose a name for the boy. After the agony she had suffered giving birth to him, he felt it was only right she name him. Jesus stood. "Come, Tamar, let's go and show your brother around, shall we?"

Over the course of the next month, Mary started to regain her strength. She had decided to name her new baby after his father. He was officially named Jesus Justus, and Mary felt her heart swell with pride as his name was written in the scroll which listed the names of all his forebears, all the way back to King David and beyond. She had given birth to a prince. One day, she thought, her son could be a king. She told her husband of her thoughts, but Jesus just shook his head. "He will be no king. Not unless my brother James fails to have a son. Two girls he has now – the odds are that the next child will be a boy."

Mary drew breath to argue, but before she could speak, the door burst open. "Where is this new nephew of mine?" boomed a voice from beneath a dusty cloak. The figure at the door pulled the hood back from its head to reveal the grinning face of Jude. Jesus jumped up and walked to his brother, arms outstretched. "How are you, you handsome devil?" Jesus asked.

"Very well, now I am here," Jude said. "Show me this new son of yours – and who is this stunning young woman?" he said pointing at Tamar. Tamar giggled and went shy. She looked at the stranger, instantly liking him but feeling a bit confused as he looked so much like her daddy.

Jesus looked down at his daughter. "This is Uncle Jude," he said. "He is my brother." Jude bent down, took Tamar's little hand and kissed it. Tamar giggled again.

"Uncajude got a scratchy face, Daddy," she said.

That evening as Jesus, Mary, Tamar and Jude sat eating, Jesus asked Jude about his travels. Tamar sat as close as she could get to the now washed and much fresher smelling Jude and kept leaning her head against his arm. She had fallen in love with her uncle.

"It has been interesting," Jude said, placing an arm around Tamar. "I have had quite a bit of fun."

"How so?" asked Jesus.

"Well, it would seem that many people cannot tell the difference between us. During the first couple of months, when I was mistaken for you, I denied it and said who I was, but when I started hearing tales that there were temple soldiers out looking for you from Jerusalem, I thought it would be a good idea to stop denying it. There are tales of you travelling a hundred or so miles or so in a day as a consequence." Jude laughed aloud, waking up the baby. "Oops – sorry. Anyway, I have had temple soldiers following me for months. I would disappear for a while, turn up somewhere else after a few days – preach good and loud for a few hours as if I were you, then clear out fast as I could. I even managed to get in a half-hour sermon in Jerusalem, just 300 yards from the temple itself before having to disappear! I cut it a bit fine, I admit, and nearly got caught, but I later heard that you were heard preaching in Galilee the same day!"

Jesus laughed. "I cannot see how you could be mistaken for me – I am far better looking than you," he said.

"Well, that is what is strange – people who claimed to have seen you before said that your looks had improved once they had seen me."

"Have you news of the others?" Jesus asked.

"Oh, yes, Thomas is on his way home from who knows where, and everyone else is lying low in Capernaum – or thereabouts. They are going to wait for you there." Jude looked at the baby in Mary's arms. "No one knows about this little one though, so that changes things for you, doesn't it? Take my advice, brother – keep his existence a secret. He could be used as a tool to get to you."

"Good point," said Jesus. "Anyway, with all these travels, have any beautiful and available young ladies caught your eye?"

Jude shook his head. "Brother, I do not have the time to court – I keep myself far too busy. Of course, there are many maidens that would love to spend time in my company, but as I am pretending to be you, I just have to explain that I am married." Jude laughed. "You see you just do not understand the sacrifices I am prepared to make on your behalf."

Jesus grinned. "Perhaps with you so busy, I should endeavour to find you a wife!"

Tamar jiggled up and down excitedly. "Can I marry Uncle Jude, Daddy? He is handsome!"

***

The following morning, Simon Magus called to visit them.

"You have visitors from Jerusalem," he said.

"Who might these visitors be?" Jesus asked.

"Priests from the temple. They have asked that you be handed over to them for questioning. I told them that they could question you if you were happy to entertain them, but that there would be no handing over of anyone. They seemed to accept this, although with bad grace. Do you wish to speak to them? Or would you rather I say you are no longer here?"

Jesus stood. "I will speak to them. I fancy a battle of wits today – it is just a shame that I have to do battle with men who are only very lightly armed, eh?"

"I think I will come too, just in case they get a little uptight," said Jude.

"Then don't let them see you – this game you have played in pretending to be me need not end yet."

Jesus recognised the men from Jerusalem immediately. They were the same four men that had confronted him in the synagogue in Capernaum. They sat side by side on a bench facing the door as Jesus and Simon Magus approached. The men stood and bowed slightly to Simon, then one looked at Jesus, and sat down again.

"I am told you asked to see me," Jesus said.

"We would have preferred that you would have come to see us," said the man who had been spokesman at their last meeting.

"So you could arrest me perhaps? Have me imprisoned for pointing out that you are, in fact, the wrongdoers in the eyes of God and his people, and not I?"

"You are a blasphemer. You do not believe in the ways of our church."

Jesus laughed. "And neither does Caesar Tiberius. Tell me, when is it you plan to arrest him? He must be terrified at the prospect of standing trial before you. Oh, sorry, I was forgetting, he has a huge army and lots of money, so you would be too scared to try."

"You think you are funny?"

"No," Jesus replied. "I think I see things as they are. It is the world you perceive and your politics that are funny. What did you want to say to me anyway? I am sure you have not travelled so far from your home comforts just to trade petty insults."

The man stood. "You are breaking the rules of our faith. Aside from the fact that you openly insult us, officials of the temple, we hear you do not fast when you should, you do not wash your hands when you should…"

"Haven't we had this argument before?" Jesus interrupted. "I believe we did. And I believe you lost that argument. Have you anything new?"

"You have baptised Gentiles with wine. That is an unbelievable insult to God."

Jesus turned his back to the four priests. "Are you afraid that if Gentiles drink the wine for communion, that there will not be enough to fill your own fat bellies?" he said and walked out of the room.

"You are a dead man when we catch you!" the priest shouted.

Simon Magus sighed. "Have you considered that perhaps now is the time for some reform in the Temple thinking?" he asked.

The leader of the four priests glared at him. "Do not think for one moment that you are safe, Magus. After today's refusal to hand that renegade over to us, you will be considered as guilty as he is. We would think nothing of having you flayed alive. I personally would rejoice at the sight of you being gutted and your innards being your outwards."

After spending the autumn and winter in Qumran, Jesus decided it was time for him to leave. He felt he may as well be in the Temple prison, as to be trapped where he was. He also knew that although the Temple would not dare to force their way into Qumran for now, things might change. Jude insisted on going with him. Mary and the children would have to stay in the safety of the complex. Word was that Qumran was now ringed with both Roman and the temple's troops, but Jude was confident they could make their escape. "I go for a casual stroll nearly every night," he joked, "and they have not caught me yet."

Poor little Tamar was heartbroken when her father told her they were leaving, and she cried herself to sleep that night at the thought of neither her beloved Uncle Jude nor her father not being around.

The pre-dawn morning of their breakout from Qumran was cold. Jude said it was good that there was a chill in the air, for it would dull the wits of the soldiers and make them not over fond of the idea of patrolling too far from their campfires. Together, Jesus and Jude walked down the cliff path in the darkness to the caves and then scrambled down the loose stones to the small river at the bottom of the Wadi. They waded through the cold water until Jude said it was safe to leave the shelter of the gulley. By the time the sun rose, they were six miles from Qumran and had not seen any trace of soldiers other than a few drifts of smoke from distant campfires in the early morning light. They headed east to Jamnia on the coast and then travelled by boat north to Tyre. This far north they knew there was little chance of running into the militia from the temple, and so Jude left for Capernaum with a message to meet up in Sidon three weeks later.

The three weeks passed quickly with Jesus spending his time studying and teaching in the synagogues.

It was late in the evening as Jesus was meditating, sat cross-legged on the floor of the synagogue, when Jude shook his shoulder, making Jesus start.

"Keeping yourself busy with some sleeping, yes?" Jude asked.

Jesus stood stiffly. "It is my foot that has gone to sleep," he replied.

Behind Jude, stood the two Simon's, Phillip, Andrew, and the two James's, Matthew and Thomas – dressed as a simple peasant.

"Thaddeus sends his apologies," said Andrew, "He has had to go back to Egypt on what he said were matters of great financial importance."

"I am greatly relieved to see you all," said Jesus. "How did your travels go?"

"Well enough, I think," said Andrew, "we all met some hostility in the south as expected, but even down there, we found some support. It would seem the general population are starting to feel isolated by the Temple – their friendship with Rome is hurting the pride of the people, for they think it an insult for our nation to be servile to an empire run by pagan, cultureless penis-worshippers. The only people who are happy with the way things are, are a select few who have more wealth than scruples."

"Your brother James is making an honest attempt to show a united front with you and uses his name of Bar-Abbas lightly, almost as a mockery of himself. He shows great humility," Thomas added. "I think he is trying to compensate for what he feels was a betrayal of you – he preaches with vehemence. Your bother loves you."

Jesus nodded slowly. "I know."

"What do you plan next, Brother?" Jude asked.

"I plan to see you all well fed within the hour," Jesus replied with a smile. "And in a day or two, we turn our backs to the sea, leave this sweet coastal air behind us and head south to skirt around the lower end of Mount Lebanon and strike out for Daphne. Then we head down to return to the Sea of Galilee. I plan to meet with the leaders of the 'Four Thousand' – the uncircumcised celibate Gentiles. I wish to baptise them with wine to bring them closer to God, our Father, and further from the Sanhedrin. I will speak with them as I spoke with the leaders of 'Five Thousand'. Then I must meet with my brother James, for he and I have much to discuss and scars to heal. But for now, let us go fill our bellies and fart like cattle!"

Having met with 'Four Thousand', Jesus led his men to Magadan, and then on towards the Roman city of Caesarea Philippi, just southwest of Mount Hermon. For many years, the dry desolate area around the city had been given religious importance and a strong association with the old Pagan god Pan. But more recently, a great white temple had been built for the Hebrew faith. Jesus had no intention of actually going into the city, as he was aware there was a small but efficient military presence there, but he did want to give the locals a quick sermon before dashing off. He knew he would be pushing his luck if he hung around the area too long. After a day talking to groups of only five or six people, Jesus felt uneasy – having the uncomfortable feeling they were being watched. And so an hour before dusk, he led his party away up the rocky hillside above the town to find a place to camp out of sight.

As the last vestiges of light fled from the sky, they found a cave which would offer them some protection from the night-time cold. They wrapped themselves in their blankets and wished they dared light a fire to warm them.

As the light returned in the early hours of the morning, they rose, chilled to the bone, and skirting the city headed south towards the Sea of Galilee.

Within a few days, they arrived back in Capernaum, weary, footsore and hungry. After purchasing food, they headed north for a few miles to make camp, eat and rest.

As they sat around their campfire warming themselves, Jesus, who had been quite solemn and deep in thought, suddenly stood up.

"Tell me, who do the people say the son of man is?" he said.

"Well, some say John the Baptist." Judas volunteered. "And some Elijah, and others would suggest Jeremiah or perhaps one of the prophets."

Jesus nodded. "And what would you, my faithful followers, say?" he asked.

Simon cleared his throat. "I would say that it is you," he said quietly. "You are the son of the living God."

Jesus looked at him for a moment. "Blessed are you – because no one told you this. What you know of me, was revealed to you by God. You are my rock – and on the likes of you shall be built a new order. Yes, you are the rock, and so I shall call you such from now on. Simon, I rename you, Peter." Jesus paused and looked at the men earnestly. "But none of you must proclaim me as Christ. There is danger in this, and I am in reality no greater in the eyes of God than any of you. Understand this – we are all sons of Man and, therefore, sons of God. Do not think that God has favourites among his children. That is why my new order of faith shall rest on the shoulders of the likes of you, Peter, because you assume no greatness, and do not presume to give yourself a higher station than others."

Chapter 15

Revelations

The following morning, Jesus went for a short walk before the others wakened and returned as they commenced their breakfast. He sat down amongst them around the smouldering remains of their campfire.

"It is, I think, the time to act," he said. "I must go to Jerusalem and face the chief priests and teachers of the Law. I am aware that this is a big gamble – but I must do this to afford me the opportunity to face them in front of the masses. I must discredit them with philosophical and theological argument. I am ready for them. But know that I face arrest, beatings and violence at their hands. It may come to pass that I will be killed, but I think it unlikely they will risk my murder in public. I am more than equal to any argument they may put forward in any subject, including the basis for their accusations of my so-called blasphemy and witchcraft."

"You can't do this!" exclaimed Peter. "Not yet – you cannot face them undefended – they will kill you!"

Jesus glared at him. "I must. You are too greatly concerned with my safety and not enough with our cause. This is all about God, and the bigger picture. If I die, I will be a martyr, don't you see? Others will follow in my shadow, using my name to unite them. But I won't die – the priests in Jerusalem have neither the stomach nor the balls to kill me."

Jesus stood and stretched out his arms. "Any of you who follow me must be prepared to sacrifice his way of life and face hardship to do so. My way means life, so to turn away from me is to turn away from life as it should be in its true meaning. Follow me, and you may die, but in death, you will discover true life. Contemplate this," he said and strode from the campfire.

Later that morning, Jesus asked Judas to walk with him.

"My brother, you are my most dedicated follower and the man I trust above all others," he said, once they were out of earshot of the others. "Come, let us find a place to sit where I can speak to you in earnest. There is much I need to tell you, which may cause you confusion, but will I hope to clarify the question of God, and my purpose," he said.

"You honour me, Brother," replied Judas, and neither spoke again for several minutes until they saw a stunted tree and sat beneath it in the dappled shade.

"Jude, there are things which I must entrust to you which I learnt years ago. I tell you this because I need you to trust in me with all your heart, for I will ask a great and terrible thing of you. And if things go badly wrong, you will be an outcast and your name will be cursed throughout the land, now and for all time. My wife, however, will take my place as leader of my new order," Jesus said quietly.

Judas nodded. "What do you wish of me?" he asked.

Jesus sighed slowly. "Alas! I cannot tell you this yet, the time is not yet right. But you must promise me you will do as I ask. I know this is not fair on you, but your part in this has importance beyond measure. And it is never to be discussed with anyone."

Judas looked at his brother with utmost sincerity and said, "Brother, I am your sword, your shield, and trust that I am your servant too. I would lay down my life for you, and would suffer the curses of mankind for the rest of the time in your name."

Tears welled in Jesus' eyes, and he placed his arm around his younger brother's shoulders. "Now I must rip your faith in God to pieces and tell you the real truth," he whispered.

Jesus removed his arm from around his brother, drew his knees up to his chest, and focussed his eyes on a small bush just a few yards in front of him.

"Judas, you know I teach that there should be no mysteries concerning God, and that wherever we go, God is with us. You know I think there should be no priests to stand between anyone and God, and you also know that I believe that no man should be separated from God by his class or caste. There is a very good reason for this." Jesus paused and looked his brother straight in the eyes. "Judas, the truth is, there is no God as an entity, just holiness in ourselves. We are God because only we can imagine he exists. God is a state of spirituality within ourselves, which, when we realise this, it changes us – we are reborn, and thus we become the children of God – the children of our new selves."

Judas looked at Jesus, totally speechless.

Jesus smiled warmly. "Isn't it obvious? That's why I want rid of the priesthoods – who are they to lie and command us to do things in the name of a God that only exists in us when we realise that God actually *is* us! The priests are the blind, and they strive to put out the eyes of those who wish to see. Is it not written that God created Man in His own image? What do you think that means?"

Judas nodded slowly, unsure of what to say.

"I will tell you the real history of the mythical God, which has for so long stopped people from seeing the real God.

Many centuries ago, in a time before the time of the ancients, the world was a cold place, covered in snow, and with mountains of ice. There were people, however, who lived beyond the reach of the snow, and they were wise, and they were enlightened as to the true nature of man. They unlocked many secrets of our world and had the wit to steer clear of mysticism. Their teachers defined themselves by wearing white robes, and they had long hair and unshaven faces. They went out into the world as the ice melted and the world warmed under the influence of the sun, to teach the new peoples the secrets they had unlocked, but sadly, their teachings were misunderstood. The memory of them remains, but sadly, their knowledge does not. They left a legacy of architecture and mathematics, medicine and science – much of which was regarded as magic by those who could not understand.

They spoke of the one thing that has breathed life into the world, but people forgot what that was and gave it a mystical meaning in a search for something that is not there – which is meaning."

"What is it that breathes life into the world?" Judas asked.

"It is obvious – it is the Sun," he replied. "Eventually, people forgot what was taught and, as is the way of men, there were those who wanted power over others. They claimed they knew the secrets of God, and some even invented new ones. New gods who they could blame for things they could not understand themselves.

"But although much has been forgotten of the old knowledge, their teachings have left a trail through history for us all to see if we choose to look. Is it not written that God himself claimed to be the God of Light? Ask yourself, what is our god of light, what is it that brings light to the world?

"There is evidence of this knowledge in Egypt.

"There was a great king, a pharaoh, who was influenced by our ancestors – the Hyksos. They believed in one God, and this pharaoh was enlightened by them. He called this god the Aten and is depicted as the sun disc. Sadly, he was overthrown, and his nation reverted to the ways of previous generations.

To put it bluntly, God is just a name for our own enlightenment regarding morality and self-awareness. Everything else, such as Hell and Heaven is pure myth. And some of our rituals and tenets are no more than advice to help us live well. As an example, we are forbidden to eat the meat from the pig – which is no more than good advice given to prevent us from catching diseases from their flesh."

"But I thought you wanted to overthrow the Temple to become the leader of the church," Judas said, suddenly feeling he no longer understood his brother's aims.

Jesus grinned broadly. "Yes, that is what everyone thinks, and what they must continue to think for a while at least. The people of the world are not yet ready to understand the real truth – it must be a slow process to teach them the reality. My real goal is to overthrow those who lead the temple and become its leader so I can tear it down to its very foundations…and create a new faith and new awareness. I cannot create the new faith beforehand, as I will surely be murdered as a blasphemer, and our people – in fact, the rest of the world, will be condemned to ignorance and mysticism forever.

"Think hard on what I teach, Brother, and you will see that I speak with different meanings, let those who have eyes see the truth, and let those who have ears hear it."

"It is a very dangerous game you play," Judas warned.

Jesus nodded in agreement. "It is a game we all must play for the very future of mankind," he said. "And only you know this, and you must never speak of it to anyone. My aim is not to make life easy for mankind but to allow mankind to achieve its full potential. And you, beloved brother, have an unbelievably important role to play in the future of the world."

***

The days passed with discussions of morality and the sometimes-idiotic rules of the Temple, which gave Jesus' men time to come to terms with what he planned in Jerusalem. This suited Jesus perfectly, as it gave him time to refine his plan in his own mind. Then one morning, he asked Peter, Bartholomew and James to walk with him and Judas. They stopped at the same tree where he had spoken to his brother a few days previously, and Jesus gestured them to sit around its base. Judas had been told by Jesus what he was going to say, and Judas knew to remain silent.

"Peter, I have an important task for you. The time for action is close by, and a duty befalls you," Jesus said. "You are to be the rock on which my new faith is built; my wife will be the leader of the new church under my guidance, and you must be her strength. I give you this task, as I know you would not want it and, therefore, will not abuse the position you will find yourself in.

"James, I wish you to remain by my side, for together we can unite the temple in Qumran. You are my big brother, and I know I can always trust you.

"And Bartholomew, I give you a task too. Go out into the world and preach my new faith…never stop, and never let yourself be imprisoned for your faith. And this I say to all three of you – let no man tell you that you are wrong, and no matter what the future holds, promise me you will never think badly of my younger brother, for he has a rocky path ahead of him and will suffer because of it. Find a place in your hearts to accept his destiny."

"What is it that Jude has to face?" James asked.

"He faces the curse of very black immortality," Jesus replied.

Later that day, Jesus announced that he wanted to visit Galilee once more, and he wanted all of them to be together again to talk and be at peace with each other.

As a group they travelled to Capernaum, having all met up near Ammathus on the western shore of the Sea.

It was just outside Capernaum when they stumbled upon a grisly sight. It was Peter who first saw the lump sticking out of the ground in the middle of a dusty well-trampled area to the side of the road, strewn with small rocks. Peter walked up to the lump and fell to his knees beside it. The others approached, and when they saw the blood-matted hair and smashed skull, they fell silent. Thaddeus stumbled off to the edge of the clearing, leaning against a tree he vomited, unable to move.

Phillip turned away – face ashen white, hands shaking and tears streaming down his face.

Peter looked up to Jesus who stood beside him with an expression of pure fury on his face.

"The poor woman has been stoned to death," Peter said, his voice a hoarse whisper.

Jesus looked at the head sticking out of the ground. The young woman had been tightly wrapped in a white sheet and then been buried upright up to her neck. He knew what would have happened next. Unable to move or defend herself, the group of people responsible would have stepped back and thrown the surrounding small rocks at her head. A horrific, painful and slow way to die. Taking perhaps an hour, her face would have been cut to pieces, her eyes burst, nose and cheekbones fractured. Who knows whether she died choking on her own blood as it flowed down her throat, or when someone finally decided enough was enough and went up to her with a much larger rock, dropping it squarely on her head a half dozen times until they were satisfied that she was either dead or close enough to it to ensure she would never recover.

"This is an insult to Man and God," Jesus said quietly. He turned away. "And another example of the so-called piety of our religious leaders. May the sanctimonious bastards be stripped of their position and cast out in the wilderness where they belong." He walked away, a half dozen paces, and turned. "Please, will some of you bury this poor soul in a civilised fashion?" he asked.

Jesus walked over to Philip, who had returned to the roadside and was sat down with his face buried in his dusty robe, sobbing uncontrollably. Jesus sat next to him and placed an arm around his shoulder.

"Talk to me, Philip," he said. "Tell me why this has reduced you to such tears."

Phillip looked up at Jesus and shook his head. "I cannot say – you would hate me," he whispered shakily.

"You know me well enough to know I would not hate you. Please tell me, my friend, unburden yourself of your sorrow. There is nothing you can say that would damage the love I have in my heart for you."

Fresh tears flowed from Philip's eyes. "I am ashamed of my past! I am not a good man, within me lies the stain of an evil which I can never wash away," he cried.

"Then share it with me, Philip, and together we can make sense of it and shine light into the darkness tormenting your soul."

Phillip sobbed for a few minutes more and then drew a steady breath.

"When I was small, I did what we have just seen to another boy. I had put this to the back of my mind, but seeing that poor woman has dragged out the memories and my guilt."

Jesus said nothing, hoping his silence would create a gap that Philip would find a need to fill with his story. After a few moments, Philip spoke again.

"I was perhaps eight years old. I had a fight with a boy a year older, and I was scared, terrified because he was so much bigger than me. He had mocked me for months because my family was wealthier than his. This particular day, he spat at me, and I lost my temper, and I punched him. I regretted it immediately because I thought he would beat me to a pulp. So I went at him again in a frenzy. We fell to the floor, and I saw a rock within reach of my hand." Philip sniffed and squeezed his eyes shut against the enormity of his emotions. "I smashed it into the side of his head again and again, terrified that he would knock me senseless if I stopped. When I realised he wasn't moving, I ran away to my home and hid for hours. I later found out that he had been discovered by his sister, still unconscious and bleeding. They were a poor family and could not afford a physician. The boy's face was cut to shreds by my precious rock, and I had even burst his eye. He cannot hear ever again with his left ear…and is half-blind because of me. He cannot speak properly and has difficulty remembering things. He has stayed the child he was back then. Because my family had more money than his. Because I lost my temper. I am no better than those fuckers who did that to that poor woman over there," he said nodding his head in the direction of the scene of the stoning.

Jesus sighed. "Philip, it is merely the misjudgement of youth that lead to what happened. Don't chastise yourself so much. Forgive yourself for what you did, but use the memory as a lesson you can teach others about restraint and what can lead a person to violence. Your experience has value, for it means you know full well how guilt works, and the best teacher is always one who has experience."

"How do I forgive myself?" Philip asked.

Jesus looked at him earnestly. "That is for you to decide, for it is your burden, and only by working on it yourself can you ease its weight. But perhaps you could start by facing the result of the acts of others and help to bury the woman we have found."

Philip stood. "Thank you," he whispered. "A trouble shared truly is a trouble halved."

***

The September sun had just dipped below the highest roofs of Rome when Lygdus raised the alarm. Nero Claudius Drusus lay lifeless on the heated tile floor in his villa. Beside him, a smashed goblet lay in a pool of wine. Lygdus – Drusus' cupbearer, later claimed that he had returned to his master's scroll table having been sent to fetch a fresh amphora of wine when he spied his master lying motionless on the floor. He did not, however, raise the alarm until he had despatched a message to Drusus' rival Sejanus which said simply, "The lock is broken, the door lies open."

For Sejanus, it was a very convenient death for Drusus held Tribunica Potestas – Tribunician power. This was reserved only for the emperor – his father, or the emperor's successor. And Sejanus was hungry for power.

Drusus had been a very tempestuous man – prone to violent outbursts and well known for his cruelty yet at the same time very committed to Rome and Roman ways. He had also proved himself quite capable both in the theatres of war and of politics. He loved gladiatorial games and all knew he loved his wine even more. It came, therefore, as no surprise to many that the 36-year-old Drusus now lay without dignity in a pool of drink, wearing vomit-spattered robes next to a table covered in puke-smeared maps.

He was accorded all the customary honours of a high-ranking Roman at his funeral, and his father stared on with a glassy look in his eye as the legions marched past saluting both the emperor and his only legitimate heir…the now dead Drusus.

Beside and two paces behind Emperor Tiberius stood Livilla – widow to Drusus. A casual observer would have seen the bleak look upon her noble face, giving no hint to the secret she held within her breast. It had been she who had procured the poison which Lygdus had used to lace his master's wine. Soon she hoped, she would marry Sejanus, her secret lover, and be wife to an emperor who would have not only the power of the Roman Empire to delight her with but who also had something big and proud and hard between his legs to keep her happy. Unlike that floppy useless thing that her husband had, thanks to his almost permanent drunkenness. Inwardly, she smiled, remembering that nervous feeling she had as she handed over the gold coins to the two hooded Jews and shakily took the small vial of poison in exchange. She had loved the sheer mystery of these two shadowy men whom she had understood to be Sicarii. She had no idea that Simon and Jude had charged her 18 times the value of the odourless poison she held tightly in her grasp, but neither would she have cared. Very little in her life that did not involve her parting her thighs had ever made her heartbeat so fast.

Chapter 16
Spreading the Word

Jesus lay in his bed, considering the work of the past two years. He smiled to himself, knowing that it was not just he who had gone to great lengths in the nine seasons since the group had stumbled upon the bloody roadside mess that had once been a young woman full of the joys of life and love.

Phillip had found some strange kind of inner strength and had talked about his traumatic time as a child quite openly and on several occasions since his tears. It seemed for a while to help him finally come to terms with his past actions, and he seemed driven to atone for his past. And then one evening, a boy had come running to Jesus bearing a message that Phillip was badly hurt.

When Jesus walked into the small barn that the young boy's father owned, he saw Phillip lying on a bed of straw, struggling for breath and with nasty deep friction burn around his neck. The rope that had caused it to lay on the ground beside him. All Phillip could say was "Sorry" over and over again in a whisper between his deep sobs of despair.

The boy's father, a man of huge stature, stood from where he was squatting beside Phillip and looked at Jesus with compassion in his eyes.

"I heard a bit of a commotion in the shed here," he said quietly. "I thought it a bit suspicious and burst in only to find your friend here swinging from that length of rope. Kicking and struggling he was, and going a horrible colour with his tongue sticking out. Lucky, I had my knife on me and was able to cut him down. I dunno how long he was a-hanging like, but it's going to be a few days before he can go around without something to protect his neck…right bloody sore that looks…don't think it was done very quickly that. I reckon he was up there for a good few minutes. Well, I have chucked a fair bit of wine down his throat, so he is a bit pissed now. He will need watching if he nods off, what with his breathing being the way it is, so you are welcome to the barn for as long as it takes. Right…stuff to do, can't hang around…oh…excuse the pun – no offence intended." And off he strode.

Jesus had tended Phillip for a week, never letting him out of his sight. And from the depths of his despair, Phillip had risen – determined to change the way he thought. His self-inflicted brush with death had scared him greatly, and he felt terribly ashamed for his failed attempt at suicide. Jesus spent many hours talking with Phillip, and finally, he seemed to accept that he had no right to cause others sadness by his action in the barn. He became Phillip the Apologist for a good few days and then, one morning, he awoke as a different person.

Jesus just smiled. "Born again," he said with a grin and Phillip from then on referred to the scarring left around his neck as 'the mark of a humble idiot'.

Matthew too had achieved something quite extraordinary. Twice now he had persuaded James Ben Alfas to take a wash. When asked how he managed it, he just winked and said he too had discovered the art of performing miracles and wouldn't be pressed further.

Jesus had also become a party to a secret when he had discovered Thaddeus and Simon asleep peacefully and naked, locked together in a loving embrace by their dying campfire underneath the stars by a riverbank. He had guessed there was more than friendship between them several weeks before and smiled when he saw them looking so natural in each other's arms. *The world is a harsh place*, Jesus thought to himself, *love is where we find it and is a comfort that everyone needs.*

Jesus actually thought they complimented each other well, and that they made excellent companions. Both were quiet and thoughtful men, but whereas Simon had a hard manly edge to his character, Thaddeus seemed quite vulnerable and almost a bit feminine at times. Jesus considered Simon's past and saw that his journey from orphan to the Sicarii, then his allegiance to the Zealot movement prior to becoming part of his small band of men was not just a search for meaning but also a search for a bond with other men. Probably also a search for a place where he could be his true self, and that seemed to include expressing his sexuality.

In fact, it seemed to Jesus that all his immediate followers had come a long way since they had banded together.

Bartholomew was gaining control of his fiery temper and becoming much calmer in general. His headaches from his old skull injury were becoming less and less frequent and his strange dreams seemed to cause him less distress these days too. In fact, Bartholomew tried to view his dreams as coded messages which should be contemplated and translated and he often liked to discuss them with the others in a bid to understand them and himself.

Andrew seemed to have finally come to terms with the death of his wife, which was now eight years ago and just a year before he had met Jesus. His general anger at the world at the unfairness of losing his wife had abated, and after many a discussion with Jesus, they realised they had similar feelings to each other, for Jesus still had deeply embedded emotions regarding the death of his father and how he had failed to see the randomness of death to be no more than fate and not the work of an all-powerful God. Andrew and his wife had been married a mere 14 months and the two had been sweethearts since childhood. Jesus knew from what Peter had told him that they had been overwhelmingly in love with each other and would have travelled to the ends of the earth to make each other happy. They seemed to live in a state of bliss with their only need being the need to be together. Peter had said that when Andrew found out he was to be a father, he considered his life to be complete. Then, one full month before the child was to be born, Andrew's beloved sweetheart started her labour. There were complications beyond his understanding, and the midwife could do nothing. Before he knew it, Andrew was having to bury his wife and still-born daughter, his entire world ripped apart. His brother Peter watched on feeling helpless and unable to assuage Andrews's grief which slowly turned to anger at the world and the perceived acts of a spiteful God. And so Andrew had come to live with his brother, and then Jesus had entered his life and intrigued him. Now he felt he was starting to see God not as an all-powerful entity but as an all-powerful aspect of humanity. He was starting to see that there was a huge overall misunderstanding regarding what life was about. God did not test people's lives – it was life itself that was the test to humankind.

Jesus rose from his bed and stretched. He felt he was getting old before his time. He was now 30 years of age and felt he had been travelling from one place to another all his life. He was starting to feel that the grime and dust of the roads were flowing in his blood, and that the land of his forebears was now an integral part of his body. He was always tired, and even when he lay down, his mind would keep turning like a waterwheel, forever creaking and placing fresh buckets of thought into the channel of his consciousness. He knew he understood what it meant to be human, and that he understood what needed to be done to free humanity from the bondage of greed, power and religion which stopped people

129

from being what they could and should be. His problem was both working out how best to do it and persuading others to follow. The church for their part seemed to be working hard against the truth, and…and…Jesus slumped into a chair, his mind spinning. Tears welled in his eyes and he felt overcome with hopelessness. How was he to free mankind from the bondage of lies and deception? Would he ever see his work come to fruition? Was he strong enough to continue? How could he stop people from believing the outlandish excrement spouted by priests and get them to see the reality? He knew that people could believe anything if it were presented well and gave them comfort from their earthly troubles – so how could he get the world to understand that if they would only open their eyes, the truth would be even more comforting? Religion just gave false hope, whereas reality gave people the tools to deal with their problems and not mask them with fear, blame and the promise of something better once they died. Provided they did what the temple told them, of course. He knew his own views had changed drastically since he was a young boy, but now he felt that the burning desire within himself to help others become as enlightened as he was had become all-consuming.

Jesus stood and walked over to the big bowl of cool water by the window, plunged his hands in and scooped the water into his face.

"The key lies within the fresh minds of the children", he said aloud, "and using the temple's arguments and laws against itself." He shook his head and scraped his long hair backwards, closing his eyes and lifting his face to the heat of the sun rays beaming in through the window. "The key lies within the fresh minds of the children and using the temple's arguments and laws against itself," he said again. How many times had he said that to himself over the past years? It had been a mantra he had imprinted in his mind and repeated nearly every day since…since when? He didn't know. It seemed he had said it forever. He had said it to himself, he had said it to his followers, he had said it to his mother, he had said it to his wife, he was fairly certain he had even said it to the Sun and the Moon and the birds in the sky.

Jesus shivered and was then suddenly bent double with a cramp in his stomach. He fell to his knees on the floor, his mouth filling with saliva. His bowels and stomach heaved, and he knew he was in need of a bucket…and fast.

"Oh no, I don't have time for the shits," he whispered weakly and closed his eyes again, waiting for the inevitable to happen and in too much pain to move from the floor.

Three weeks later, Jesus was once again on the road, dirty, dusty and sweaty. He was feeling invigorated again after his stomach upset and bout of fever. He no longer felt quite as old or exhausted and was again feeling positive about his goals. He was a few pounds lighter and still felt a bit weak, but he knew that within another couple of days, he would be back to his old self. Mary had confined him to bed for ten days and then restricted him to the house for a further week. During that week of virtual house arrest, he had heard plenty of news to cheer him.

Throughout the Diaspora a network of safe houses had been set up where his teachings were being preached and in Hebrew communities throughout the Roman Empire and beyond there were classes being held to teach the children new ways to think and, from what he had heard, there were even emissaries of his new order landing on the shores of that mystical island on the edge of the world that the Romans called Britannia. Jesus thought it would be a wonderful place to visit, for he had heard its peoples were a very spiritual group of kingdoms and the rain washed and misty land was full of ancient magic and the secrets of the 'Old Ones'. Perhaps he would go there some time.

He had heard from numerous sources that his teachings were popular, and he was gaining quite an underground following. His confidence was growing. He had heard from Masada on the edge of Lake Asphaltitus that the militant Zealots were fast learning the ways of the Roman military war machine, and that they too wanted to see an end to the corrupt ways of the temple in Jerusalem. They wanted the Romans gone also and saw the teachings of Jesus as a means to unite the people against the tyranny of Rome and the House of Herod – the line of false puppet kings. Knowing he had a huge secret network of supporters and yet much more simple folk on his side as well as a small but fearsome army of Zealots, Jesus considered it was time to antagonise the Senhadrin more – to show people how backward and power-hungry these high-ranking priests were and to unveil their draconian and evil methodology. He had to expose the true extent of their lies, thieving, and torture. The world needed enlightening, and he was confident the time to act was not too far away. Jesus felt excited and yet at the same time terrified by the prospect. He not only feared the inevitable confrontation itself, but at times, he feared that he would not have the courage to face his chosen destiny. He was afraid that when the time came to change the world, he would be a coward.

And so Jesus was now entering Thecoa – between Jerusalem and Hebron, and just a couple of days from Qumran where he had left his wife and children in the safe hands of Simon Magus. He planned on making his presence felt nearer to Jerusalem and publicly talking to the people there would do the trick.

The following morning, Jesus was woken early by a gentle tap on the shoulder.

"You have a visitor," said Judas quietly. Jesus sat up on his sleeping mat and rubbed his eyes. His back felt stiff and sore, and he considered it might be time to consider stopping sleeping on the ground next to campfires.

"Bring our visitor over, Brother…and could you do me the favour of fetching us a drink? My mouth feels akin to a camel's foot."

Judas beckoned a young fair-skinned man over and walked over to their pack-donkey for a water-skin.

Jesus motioned to the man to sit and smiled. "Excuse my appearance if you will," he said, "I have barely wakened." In response, the young man smiled awkwardly and muttered an apology for disturbing him at this early hour. Jesus shook his head. "No, no, it is I who must apologise. I should have risen earlier, but alas! I fear I have been a little lazy today, whereas you have evidently not by your effort to seek word with me. Now, what may I do for you?"

The young man looked nervously about himself. "Err, well I do not really know if I should be here at all," he said quietly.

Jesus tilted his head and looked at him. "Why ever not?" he asked.

The man looked about himself and leant forward. "Well, err, I am not one of you," he whispered.

"I don't understand what you mean," said Jesus.

"Well, I am a Roman."

Jesus laughed. "Well, that much is plain to see, for fair hair and skin is not much of a disguise in these parts. Do not worry, you are in no danger here."

The man smiled and Judas appeared with two cups filled with water. Jesus took them, thanked his brother and offered one cup to the young Roman. They drank, and the Roman said, "I have heard much of what you teach. I have found myself drawn to what you believe. About how people can all get along. And how we hold good and evil in our own hearts. But I am confused about where I can apply this in my life."

"How does this confuse you?" Jesus asked.

"Well," the young man replied, "As I said, I am a Roman – born and raised with Roman ideals and Roman gods. I fear the gods and yet at the same time cannot help but trust in what you teach."

Jesus nodded. "If you have fear for your gods, then you are blind to the reality of humanity. You have, in fact, been blind since birth – through no fault of your own. Your eyes were put out by the society in which you grew up. Your Roman gods are a fiction. An invention of simple folk trying to explain and put meaning to a world they could not understand. It is no more than that. You need not fear that any god is greater than what is in a man, for if that is the case, would Jupiter himself not have streaked like a fiery ball from the sky and struck down Hannibal? If he had, it would have meant the saving of the lives of countless thousands of Romans. Jupiter did not appear, and in the end, Hannibal went away of his own accord – but only after he had brought Rome to its knees by sheer force of will. Tell me, have you ever seen anything as remarkable achieved by a god, as that which has been achieved by a man?"

The Roman shook his head. "When I look, all I see are the result of the deeds of man but on a magnificent world made by the gods. The world is here, therefore, the gods must exist to have made it because Man did not."

Jesus shook his head. "You see it all wrong…the world was already here, and Man invented the gods – all of them, to justify its existence. Don't you see? There are greater powers than any god, and they are called the stars. They are what made the world. And the world has a life of its own regardless of what you believe. There is no God to fear but the one in your heart. And the one in your heart is you. Think hard about this for everything any person suffers, is either an act of the world's life force or the result of an act of another person. No God will punish you for knowing this deep inside yourself although many would tell you otherwise. Just question why anyone might try to convince you to the contrary, and you will see clearly enough that it is said purely to have power over you by controlling what and how you think."

The young Roman stood and smiled. "I have to say you make perfect sense. It fits with the Greek theories of logic; it fits with what I feel deep down. I am sorry, it seems I have just been plagued by fears of childhood stories."

Jesus looked up at him and smiled. "You were blinded by foolish fears and tales born from ignorance, and now you can see," he said. "And now it is your duty to give others the gift of sight."

As the Roman walked away deep in thought, Judas knelt beside his brother. "More visitors are on the way," he said quietly. "I think these ones you should speak to at a healthy distance from here. I don't think it wise to be seen openly plotting with these fellows, they are a rough bunch."

Jesus looked beyond Judas to a large body of men still a couple of hundred yards away but approaching purposefully. He smiled. "Our Zealots have arrived just as requested."

***

Two hours later, Jesus sat on a hillside with his new visitors.

"Firstly, I must thank you for coming today. I trust you had an easy journey from Masada?" he said. There were general murmuring and nodding of heads as a response. He smiled. "Secondly, I would like to apologise for leading you out here without first breaking bread with you, nor even sharing wine or water. But quite simply, I do not think it sensible that a casual observer should witness this meeting. I suspect that there are more than casual observers about, for I am quite certain I am being watched by agents of the Senhadrin. I know I can trust all of you, as I know that all 72 of you have been sure-minded in your beliefs since birth. This I know to be true because my very good friend Simon has told me it is so – and I trust him completely. I am also aware you have no idea what it is you have volunteered for."

"Cutting the cocks from the priests in Jerusalem might be nice," said a gruff voice somewhere within the huddled group of tough-looking men, to which there came laughter as a response from the rest. Jesus laughed too. "A deserved fate some might say," he said, "but sadly, for you that is not the plan." Several of the men moaned in mock disappointment.

Jesus stood, whilst the 72 Zealot warriors remained seated on the ground around him.

"Within the year, I plan to turn our homeland upside down, give it a good shake and let all the shit fall out into a pile. That shit will comprise of a stinking rabble of Pharisees, Sadducees, the Temple priests and a good quantity of Romans. That shit may be then swept away in whatever manner seems pertinent at the time. There will doubtless be blood. Violence, I fear, will be a necessary evil, but the result will be a free people. Free from Rome, and free from the corruption of the Temple. Without a doubt, the Temple has to go first, for they are the toads and vermin that have a grip on our people's minds and purses.

The Romans will initially be slow to respond, and by the time they do, all these lands will be up in arms against them. I will be the one to lead the assault on the priesthood of Jerusalem. I will show the people just what they are, and the people will be so enraged they themselves will take them down. The people, however, must feel they are an army. They must be of one singular mind. This is where you figure in the grand scheme of things. I have spent many years wandering these lands gaining support for my beliefs, telling people the true nature of the Temple and undermining the grip that the Temple holds on our society. I have told the masses of the true nature of God. The task I give to you is to sweep through the towns and villages in pairs, assess who may be a problem and stir things up a little. I don't mean kill them but talk to other villagers about them, start some rumours about them, that sort of thing. Just to discredit them enough to make it difficult for them to have any influence on general opinion. I have spread the word of peace, and yet as I said, violence will surely follow at some point. So please follow my example and to not be threatening. When you enter a house, always say 'peace to this house', when you enter a town and are welcomed, eat what is set before you, be friendly, ensure the people know you support me. But if you enter a town and are not welcomed, go into its streets and say 'even the dust of your town that sticks to our feet we wipe off against you. Be sure of this, the Kingdom of God is near'. And then tell the people of the other villages in the area that their neighbours are not to be trusted. And remember, tell the people that whoever listens to you, listens also to me. Finally, do not be shy in letting the people know you are military men, for it will do them no harm to learn that we are not a defenceless movement like so many before. Remember we are inciting a rebellion, so do not place yourselves in a situation where you could be arrested for it and always behave in a dignified manner. And thank you, one and all, for volunteering for this task. I place my trust in you."

Chapter 17

Authority

Lucius Aelius Sejanus had come a long way. Tiberius, unaware of the man's role in the murder of his son, had elevated Sejanus to greater and greater positions of authority. Throughout the city of Rome, Tiberius had statues of Sejanus erected, but then, Tiberius was a fool. Sejanus wanted Tiberius dead, and Tiberius did not see it. Tiberius hated his position and his power, and Sejanus was like a ravenous wolf, eager to seize position and power at the first available opportunity, and all the time he plotted to gain it.

Finally, having slowly delegated as much of his power as possible, the time came when Tiberius had had enough. In the winter which fell three years after the death of Drusus, he removed himself from Rome altogether. With the blessing of Tiberius, Sejanus stepped in to fill the void with almost all the power of the emperor, merely lacking the title. The Praetorian Guard consisting of nine thousand troops, of which he was the commander, gave weight to his authority and efficiently isolated Tiberius and cut off his communication with Rome. Tiberius did not care; he moved to the island of Capri to relax and enjoy his retirement, not giving further concern about the issues of state. His passion for sexual perversion was far greater interest to him than any matters concerning the running of the empire.

Tiberius' villa was beautiful, secluded, luxurious, and huge. The perfect spot to do as he wanted. He even appointed a distant cousin as 'Master of the Imperial Pleasures', whose sole job was to find beautiful young men, women and children for the retired emperor to degrade and fuck. He thought that having a child sucking at his manhood was surely a greater pleasure than attending meetings of the Senate, especially if he was watching another child being raped at the same time. Of course, some of the children's parents complained, so it was wonderful that his villa was perched atop a convenient cliff. The thought of acts such as sodomising a little girl whilst watching her grief-stricken parents being whipped and then thrown to their deaths from the cliff onto the jagged rocks below aroused his depraved mind immensely – especially if the girl could see her parent's fate at the same time. So he made sure he did that frequently. He liked watching the gang-rapes too, especially if the victims died during the process. Of course, there were days when Tiberius wasn't in the mood for sex himself, but watching an event of mutilation or two of a beautiful young lady or athletically built young man often entertained and allayed any boredom.

Back in Rome, the Senate struggled to run the empire, increasingly being forced to refer to Sejanus for advice, for the Senate could make very few decisions without empirical approval, and Sejanus made all the decisions on the emperor's behalf. Of course, Sejanus, in his rise to power, had trodden on a few toes and, given his arrogant and grasping personality, had made not only a reasonable fortune but quite a few enemies. Some of those enemies posed both a challenge and a threat to his position. They would have to go. It would do no harm if some those fiercely loyal to Tiberius met a sticky end too…

Of course, he couldn't move too quickly, so he drew up a list of all those that could pose a danger to his regime, and all of their families too. He also wrote down estimations of their wealth. When the purges came, Sejanus was going to take no chances. The only thing to do would be to kill not only his enemies but eradicate their entire bloodlines too. Seizing their assets for his own use would further increase his wealth and power. Given the colossal size of the empire, not all the problems that Sejanus had were local to Rome. Winter was drawing to an end when Sejanus flew into a rage upon hearing the news that the taxes due from Judea were far less than expected.

"What the fuck is going on in that dusty hell-hole?" he screamed. "Those Jewish bastards not paying their fucking taxes? Oh, I will get the gold out of the smelly pious liars. They have plenty of riches for their fucking temples, but none for their rulers!" He spun around, his face purple with rage, and pointed to an armoured Equestrian in his 30s. "YOU!" he shouted, "You are now the prefect of Judea! Get your calloused arse onto a ship headed east, install yourself in the middle of the bastards, take control from whatever weak witted idiot it is who is failing to collect taxes there now, send the useless piece of shit back here to Rome, and get me my fucking money. Don't just run amok – all swords, spears and shouting, use some bloody savvy because I don't want a fucking rebellion on my hands. That is the last thing I need. Fuck this up, and I will have you nailed to a tree with your cock cut off and stuffed up your arse. MOVE IT!" Then man nodded curtly and swept out of the room. Sejanus turned to the officer of the guard, standing next to him. "What was that prick's name? His face is familiar, but I can't place him."

"Err, Pontius something-or-other Pilate, Sir," he answered.

It was early spring when Pontius something-or-other Pilate installed himself in the Roman villa of the Prefect of Judea in Caesarea. Valerius Gratus, the man he replaced, paled when Pilate told him he was ordered back to Rome to answer for the lack of money sent to the senate to fill the state coffers.

Pilate was not impressed by what he saw. His 500 Roman troops were well equipped, disciplined and motivated, but 1500 locally recruited troops in Caesarean Militia were quite a different matter. When he marched with them to Jerusalem to inspect the other 1500 troops of the militia, he was furious. The troops of the Jerusalem Garrison were acting as a law unto themselves and using the name of Rome as their authority. Pilate decided he would show them who was really in charge, so he promoted some of his Roman troops to officer status and placed them in charge of the militia. The original officers of the militia he had whipped and sold into slavery along with their families. His next step was to march his Romans in full battle kit straight into the Temple of Jerusalem and demand three years of back-taxes. The Sanhedrin were furious, but he had the owed monies presented to him in less than two hours.

Pilate immediately returned to his new villa, having left orders for a new training regime to be used on the militia to bring them up to scratch, and promptly dispatched 200 of his Roman troops to collect taxes in areas they had neglected to maraud under the leadership of his predecessor. This seemed to be mainly smaller temples, but there seemed to be a large amount of very wealthy merchants around who had not paid tribute in many a year. On his march to Jerusalem and back, he had time to talk with his troops and found that general opinion amongst the men was that they were happy to see a man of apparent action in charge again, for Gratus had become somewhat complacent and seemed almost to fear the priests of the Jewish Temple in Jerusalem. Pilate also found out the local population seemed to fear the priests more than the Romans. He was determined that would change. It also seemed the Roman jails were full to capacity and beyond. Pilate decided that a good few public executions would solve those last two issues. Hanging up a few people who had been lashed to death around the place would certainly show the locals who were in charge, that justice was being done and that law was being upheld. Pilate allowed himself a wry smile. Judea might be a hot and dusty shithole of a place, but it could prove to be an interesting place to administer.

***

Pilate stood under the summer sun and wiped the sweat from his forehead. He smiled grimly, admiring the handiwork of his troops. In front of him was the blood-spattered chopping stool with a pile of 32 severed hands lying on the ground next to it. Thieves' hands. The 32 thieves had been lined up, and Pilate had picked them out in random order, so none knew who was next. They then had a rope tied tightly around their wrists and were dragged to the chopping stool whilst the remainder watched, knowing this would be their fate soon enough. Several had pissed themselves with fear where they stood, and the air was thick with the sickly smell of the pitch bubbling away in a large pot over a fire a couple of yards from the stool. The victim was then forced to his knees at the end of the stool and a soldier pulled the rope taught, pulling the victim's arm straight along the length of the thick wood with his or her hand palm downwards. Next, Pilate would read aloud the charges slowly and announce the punishment. "Mutilation and removal of the right hand!" A soldier would step forward and hold the poor wretch's hand still, raise his hammer and smash the victim's fingers to a pulp, one by one. The screams were horrible. When the fingers were no more than a bloody mess, there was one more hefty blow to the centre of the back of the hand to smash the bigger bones. Many had passed out by this point with the sheer agony, so the hammer-wielding soldier would throw a bucket of water over the hapless victim to waken him from his stupor. There was no point in chopping the hand from someone who was unconscious and could not fully appreciate his punishment. The soldier would then pick up his hand axe and chop through the wrist just above the rope, hopefully detaching the hand in less than three attempts. This was not that easy, for Pilate had ordered that the axe was not to be very sharp. The victim was then dragged over to the pitch bucket and his stump immersed eight inches or so into the boiling hot sticky goo to seal the wound. Here again, the victim usually passed out. Finally, he was dragged by his feet to the corner of the yard and deftly kicked in the crotch. Punishment over, he was free to go – no longer the concern of Roman justice. Then another was chosen and the whole process repeated. Today this had taken a full morning, and

Pilate was thirsty. *Time for wine and food*, he thought, for this afternoon there were four rapists and a child killer to deal with. He smiled at the thought of the rapists being tied naked to a saltire cross and having their genitals burned off with red hot irons, then being cut loose and having a thick wooden peg hammered into their anuses. They were then released, but the odds were that if the punishment did not kill them there and then, they would be unlikely to survive until the following dawn. *Let the punishment fit the crime*, he thought – *the Jews should like that...an eye for an eye and all that.*

The child killer was a member of his own militia, a nasty piece of work by all accounts, mean-spirited and unpopular. His fate was to be flayed to death. Eighteen of the militia had eagerly volunteered for the task, so Pilate had said they could all take it in turns, three strokes with the whip each until he breathed no more. But he had also said that any one of them that killed him before sundown would be sold to the local Ludus to be trained as a gladiator.

The punishments of the day were lifting Pilate's spirits. The letter he had received the day before had put him a foul mood. For here he was trying to bring a population into line the Roman way, and now he was in trouble for doing just that. Caiaphas, that pompous fat fucker in Jerusalem in charge of the Temple council, had written a sharp letter of complaint to Sejanus saying he had 'offended their religious sensibilities' and was in danger of 'causing civil unrest with his offensive campaign of persecution'. The fat cunt was just pissed off because he had to pay tax. Oh, how he would love to see that man up with this afternoons rapists. He would offend his religious sensibilities all right.

So now Pilate was on thin ice and in an impossible situation. Carry out Rome's will without upsetting the local government. Two ideals that were polar opposites. Pilate was a soldier – get the job done he had been told, and that's what he had been doing. And now he had to appease the fucking priests as well! This was politics, and he hated it. It was vastly different when he had served in Gaul, Thrace and Germania – brutality and war was the only agenda...subdue the locals and crush anyone that showed any signs of rebellion. Still, at least he had his wife Claudia to help. Now there was a woman who could think for herself. They made a good team, he thought. Claudia was his best advisor, and he needed her wise words now more than ever. His father had been convinced that Pilate had married beneath himself, Claudia being from the family of a mere merchant, but she had proved herself to be a superb wife. She was kind, passionate, understanding, supportive and damned good at dealing with people…including himself. What Roman could wish for a better wife? She had this wondrous way of disarming people with that beautiful smile of hers…and he knew that smile would have him twisted around her little finger.

***

Jesus was in a buoyant mood. Only a few days before his 72 Zealots had returned and briefed him on the general opinion and feelings of the population. It seemed that his ideals were popular and the Temple was not. He had mixed feelings regarding the unexpected replacement of the Roman Prefect. This new fellow seemed to be good at his job; cruel, violent but fair. He had shoved himself in the faces of the Temple council backed up by his troops, all resplendent in polished and oiled armour, armed to the teeth and proudly parading their standards and emblems of Roman rule. He had demanded his overdue taxes, and the Sanhedrin had spinelessly shaken with fright and handed it over. So it seemed that even the Romans didn't like the temple priests and their self-serving ways. Jesus could not see Pilate getting himself involved in his plan to overthrow the temple. And by the time Pilate realised what was happening, it would be too late, for Jesus' rebellion would at first appear to only be against the Temple and hopefully he would not realise that it would continue on until the Romans were themselves fighting for control of Judea. Then the next step would be to cause civil unrest throughout the Diaspora, with Jews throughout the empire causing unrest. Rome would soon think that holding on to Judea was far more trouble than it was worth.

So now he was on his way to Jerusalem to antagonise the Temple further. There was a prophecy that the true king would enter the city on a donkey and he was going to play up to it. The word had been spread about his arrival on Sunday morning, and he had been promised that there would be crowds waiting for him to give him a welcome fit for a Roman conqueror. That was planned for Sunday, the day after tomorrow.

Sunday came and the crowds roared. Jesus sat on a beautiful grey donkey that Simon and Thaddeus had purchased the day before in the nearby village of Bethpage, and his brother Jude the Sicarii led it by its halter. His other 11 apostles followed close behind whilst his wife and children walked by his side. Behind them were 22 of the 72 Zealots, discreetly hiding their swords under their dusty robes and ready to fight if things turned ugly. They now acted as Jesus'

Praetorian Guard but covertly. The other 50 were mingling with the crowd – working in pairs, watching and cheering, keeping the spirit of the crowd high and keeping an eye out to quell any trouble.

"*Hosannah* to the Son of David!" the crowd shouted as they waved palm leaves to greet him and welcome him to their city. Many of the palms were thrown onto the ground to act as a carpet for the parade along with flowers and sweet-smelling herbs. Once through the city gates, he dismounted from the donkey, and he was immediately surrounded by the Zealots from the crowd. He walked away from the procession and strode to the temple, the Zealots clearing a path for him through the crowd and shouting, "Blessed is he who comes in the name of the Lord!"

Once at the gates to the Temple grounds, he turned and waved to the crowds who were still cheering and waving palm leaves. He turned and strode through the gates with two of the Zealots, the others remaining outside. The main temple courtyard was a marketplace run by the Temple, littered with the tables of moneylenders and stalls with men selling religious artefacts, doves (some of which were white-powdered pigeons) and jewellery. He marched over to the nearest trader – a moneylender in his late 20s, and kicked his table over scattering coins and parchments, pens and ink, over the ground. The man stood up with outrage on his face, and Jesus looked at him with hatred.

"What the fu…!" he started to shout but was instantly silenced with a punch in his mouth by one of the Zealots. The traders all turned and stared as one as the two Zealots drew their swords and flanked Jesus as he strode to the next table a kicked that over too.

"Remove yourselves from this house of reflection!" he shouted. "This is supposed to be the house of God, not a trading post for the parasites of the people!" He picked up a stool and threw it crashing through a bird-sellers stall. "Thieves the lot of you! Robbers! Cheats and liars!"

Several men grouped together. They looked at each other for confirmation of their own courage and approached Jesus menacingly with anger on their faces.

"Do you wish to see the result of my wrath?" Jesus screamed at them. There was a shout behind them, and two of the traders turned to see a dozen Zealots with their swords drawn stood behind them, smiling happily. The men suddenly looked nervous.

"I didn't think so," Jesus said. "Smash everything!" he shouted, and he and the Zealots set to work kicking over tables and stalls, kicking the backsides of the traders, the Zealots shouting, "*Hosannah* in the highest!"

When all was chaos, men grovelling around picking up coins, records, and frenziedly trying to keep out of the way of kicks at the same time, Jesus shouted, "To the son of David" and strode out – breathless and sweating with his exertions. Minutes later, his entire group were reunited and on their way out of the city to spend the night just a couple of miles away in the town of Bethany.

Jesus smiled to his wife and said, "Well, that has certainly stirred things up a bit…tomorrow could be interesting."

***

The following morning, Jesus was back in the grounds of the Jerusalem Temple bright and early with a dozen of his Zealots for protection. They stood away at a discreet distance but on the alert. He had been talking to a crowd of about 30 people when six of the senior priests strode out from the temple itself.

"What authority do you have to preach in these holy grounds?" one bellowed. Jesus smiled and showed his palm to the nearest Zealot, indicating there was no need for his intervention.

"Who gave you the authority to speak here? Answer me!" the man bellowed again as he walked angrily towards Jesus with a puffed-up chest, full of his own self-importance and a touch of trapped wind from a large breakfast consumed an hour and a half before. When he stood before Jesus, rocking on the balls of his feet with arms folded and looking as indignant as he could, Jesus answered him.

"In return, I ask you one question. If you answer me, I will tell you by what authority I speak. John, my cousin now beheaded, his baptism; where did it come from? Was it from Heaven? Or from men?"

The bellower paused for a moment, then answered, "If I say it is from Heaven, you will ask why we did not believe him. If I say it is from man, I predict you will claim we are afraid of the people, for they will hold that he was a prophet. It is a trick question."

"So is it that you do not know? Or are afraid to answer?"

The priest looked confused; he had lost the momentum of his bluster and the gathering crowd around Jesus were eying him intently, waiting for wise words to tumble from between the man's wobbling lips.

"I am not prepared to say," he said. "It is none of your business; it is a matter for the temple." He drew himself up, feeling less than clever but trying to regain his superiority.

Jesus smiled innocently. "Then neither will I tell you by what authority I speak; you can work it out yourselves with your mighty intellects."

There was a sniggering from the crowd, and the priest reddened with anger and embarrassment as he and his group turned on their heels and retreated to the temple.

"Fat prick," someone in the crowd said, just loud enough for the priest to hear, evident in the way he quickened his pace.

"Now, where was I before I was so rudely interrupted? Ah, yes, I was about to tell you the *Parable of the Wedding Banquet*...I finished the *Parable of the Two Sons*, did I not?"

Chapter 18
Words

Caiaphas, on returning to Jerusalem from a few days in the coastal town of Joppa, was furious. He had cut his visit short and made his way back as fast as he could when he had received the message telling him of Jesus' antics in the temple grounds. The marketplace had been overturned and closed, which meant his percentage of the profits had now dried up. Traders afraid to trade? That just was not acceptable. And then to cap it all, the man had the damned cheek to return the following day and sit in those self-same grounds and teach! What is more, he had made a fool out of Nahum, one of the most senior members of the Sanhedrin in front of a crowd of peasants! So now it was not just that damned Roman prefect trying to weaken the power of the temple but some crazy self-proclaimed prophet too! And where the hell were the temple guards when all this was going on? How on earth could a half-mad arrogant nomad just wander into the temple unchallenged with a crowd of armed men, wreck the place, and just walk away? And where the hell was he now? Worryingly, what was he up to?

Caiaphas sat at the senior council table and glared evilly at the other members. He knew they were nervous, and he was damned well going to milk this for all it was worth.

"Has nobody anything to say? Have all your tongues dried up like the tits on a Babylonian grandmother?" There were some nervous throat-clearing noises as his answer.

"So it falls to me to solve this issue, does it?" he asked, to no one in particular. Again, no answer.

"Then here is what we shall do. The Pharisees are not unpopular with the common people, am I correct? So as this Jesus fellow has made us look impotent in front of the Hoi Polloi, we must get the Pharisees to show him as a heretic. We must also push him into a position where we can get him to say something which will allow us to arrest him for heresy and then we can have the troublemaking fool executed. It doesn't matter what the exact charge is – heresy, witchcraft, even treason if possible. And we have to get the great unwashed back on our side. Is that clear?"

There was a general murmuring and nodding of heads from the council.

"Right," said Caiaphas. "Bloody well, get to it…or do I have to sort that out as well?"

***

"…then the king told the attendants to tie him hand and foot and throw him outside into the darkness, where there will be weeping and gnashing of teeth, for many are invited but few are chosen," Jesus said. He was stood in front of a gathering of some 90 people, aware that some were watching him intently. Those holding him under close scrutiny seemed to be somewhat better dressed than the majority, and Jesus guessed there might be more to these fellows than they would wish to be known.

One of them spoke up with a question. "Teacher, we know you are a man of integrity and that you teach the way of God in accordance with the truth. You are not swayed by men as you pay no attention to who they are. Tell us then, is it right to pay taxes to Caesar in Rome? What is your opinion?"

Jesus smiled to himself. An open question to invite him to be accused of rebellion and sedition perhaps? What a fumbling attempt to try and test him that was. He stared at the man levelly as if weighing him up. He allowed the awkward silence to continue for several seconds, the man starting to feel uncomfortable under his gaze. "You hypocrite," Jesus said quietly, "why are you trying to trap me? Show me the coins used to pay tax. Anyone?" A man stepped forward and handed him a coin. Jesus held it up for all to see held between his forefinger and thumb. "A Denarius," he declared. "Whose portrait is stamped into a Denarius?"

"Caesar," said a few in the assembled crowd.

Jesus beckoned the owner of the coin to him, placed it in the man's hand, and smiled warmly. "Give to Caesar what is Caesar's, and to God what is God's."

Another spoke up with a question. "Teacher, Moses told us that if a man dies without having children, his brother must marry the widow and have children for him. There were seven brothers amongst us, and the oldest married and died, and since he had no children, the next oldest married her. The same thing happened again, and the third married her. He too died. And this went on until all seven brothers married her and died. Then after many years, the woman died. So…come the Resurrection, whose wife will she be of the seven, since all of them married her?"

Jesus smiled again. "I would hazard a guess that none of the seven would want her. Would they not think it odd that she married seven brothers and they all promptly died, resulting in her gaining any inheritance due? Sounds a bit suspicious to me. She was either a murderess or a damnably awful cook." There was sniggering amongst the crowd and the man who asked the question reddened. With that, another stepped forward, a portly looking man who looked like the happy victim of far too many fine meals and exuding an air of wealth and status. "Teacher, which is the greatest commandment of the Law?" he asked. Without pause, Jesus responded, "Love the Lord, your God, with all your heart and with all your soul and with all your mind. This is the first and the greatest commandment. The second is very much like it. Love your neighbour as yourself. All the law and the prophets hang on these two commandments. Now let me ask a question of you. Who is the Christ? Who is he the son of?"

"He is the son of David," the man replied.

"Really?" said Jesus. "Strange that David calls him Lord and Father. How can a man be his own grandfather?"

The man looked at his friends, unable to respond and feeling foolish. He turned and walked away with his comrades. Jesus scanned the remaining crowd before him. He smiled. "And so the Pharisees walk away, unable to speak sense within the boundaries of their own dogma. Remember this, for the teachers of the law and the Pharisees sit in a position of leadership, dictating thought and behaviour like Moses on the throne. For now, you must obey them and do everything they tell you. But never do as they do, for they are the last to practice what they preach. Like all church leaders, they tie up heavy loads and put them on men's shoulders but would not lift a finger to help. Everything they do is done for men to see. They make themselves look grand in their finery, they adore being at the place of honour at banquets. They are hypocrites, for they shut the door of spirituality in men's faces. Spirituality is about free thought, and religious leaders prevent and hate the very idea of it. I predict that these snakes, this brood of vipers, will pursue and flog and kill any of the wise or righteous who show them to be the parasites and tyrants that they really are. I wish to gather you – their children together, as a hen gathers her chicks under her wings. And so they will see their houses are desolate. And so they will understand they will see not their children again until they too can say they believe the truth.

Pay lip-service to these false princes of God. But give your minds to free thought."

***

Caiaphas was furious...again. "You mean you could not get this man to commit to anything? You are supposed to be educated people! Surely, that damned witch did not put a spell on your tongues and turn you into imbeciles. How could you let him outwit you with words?"

The portly Pharisee who had questioned Jesus on the matter of Law looked Caiaphas up and down with a look of anger.

"Well, I did not see you stood beside us questioning this Jesus. Maybe you should have been, for then we would have seen the wisest man in the known world blinding him with his superior wit and intellect. Perhaps it would be more efficient if you did your own dirty work in the future. From what I saw, this Jesus actually spoke a little sense. He has a thinking man's head upon his shoulders."

Caiaphas completely lost his temper, picked up a goblet of wine and threw it at the Pharisee, missing him by an arm's length. "You blaspheming turd!" he screamed. "You are subject to the law of the temple – and I Am The Temple! I should see you executed, stoned to death for your cursed cheek! And I swear I will see the skin ripped from this bastard Jesus before I am done. And every one of his followers too! Nobody undermines my power! Not even the fucking Romans!"

***

Jesus sat in the darkened room alone with his younger brother, the only source of light was an oil lamp – its feeble light flickering between them on a table and casting eerie shadows in the gloom.

"Judas, the time has arrived for you to carry out the task I requested of you."

"Speak, Brother, and I am the agent of your will," Judas replied.

"You are one of my closest friends as well as my dear brother. But I need you to accuse me of heresy to the chief priests of the temple. Make it so they have evidence to arrest me and put me on trial. Make it known your relationship

148

to me, and that will add credence to your claims. Nobody knows that I ask you to do this, and therefore, you will be seen as a traitor, so go into hiding until I have overturned the temple. I will set the record straight afterwards," Jesus said quietly.

Judas was astonished. "Why do you wish for arrest?" he asked – his voice hoarse with the gravity of his mission.

"Because my trial will cause outrage. I will make fools of the priests, and better still, they will make fools of themselves. They will show the temple in its true light, and finally, through my wisdom, words and argument, they will prove themselves to be the worthless thieves that they really are. I will start age of enlightenment, and the nation will turn its back on the outdated idea of organised religion," said Jesus.

"This is a dangerous game, dear brother, but I will do it. I believe in you. The people believe in you. When do I do what you request?" Judas asked, his face suddenly looking to Jesus as if it had aged ten years.

"Tonight would be as good a time as any," Jesus said.

***

They sat around their leader – the man they respected and admired. All 12 of them listened intently to what Jesus had to say.

"I have caused a headache for the Temple. I would say they will look for a way to discredit me, accuse me of all manner of things and you by association. For a short while life, may get tougher. There will be those in the temple who could cause you harm and distress, so, from now on, always keep one eye over your shoulder. There is a chance that I may be seized, and if that happens, I will get word to you to start the rebellion against our so-called religious leaders. I have a feeling this may be the last time we are all together for a while, so let us enjoy our meal."

Jesus looked at his younger brother and gave him a barely perceptible nod. Judas coughed and excused himself from the table, claiming that nature had a call that needed answering.

"And Peter, if any accuse you of being my associate, you must deny it. It doesn't matter how many times you are asked if I am in custody, I need you all free to start the rebellion, so deny me."

"Even if I have to die with you, my lord, I will never disown you," said Peter, as Judas closed the door behind himself and set off with a heavy heart to the temple to accuse his brother of blasphemy.

Chapter 19
Dark Deed

The younger brother of Jesus stood before the Temple, his mouth dry and his stomach churning. Even though he had been told to do this, he felt that it was wrong. Jude felt as if a heavy cloud of doom was darkening his soul, and he had a horrible feeling that something would go wrong – that too much was being left to chance. That something blindly obvious had been overlooked. He had no concern for his own life, but he was worried sick about the risks to his brother. He took a deep breath and walked hesitantly to the main entrance doors to the temple. Two guards stood resplendent in the gold-plated armour flanking the huge wooden doors, their round shields held loosely in their left hands and long bronze-tipped spears in their right, with short swords hanging at their belts. Judas unconsciously felt under his cloak and felt the security of the worn handle of his Sicari – the short and razor-sharp dagger tucked in his belt at his own waist. He quickly glanced over the two guards, immediately working out that the one on the right was probably the greatest threat if it came to a fight. But he was not here to fight. He was here to speak, and not to these two thugs. He walked up to the right-hand guard.

"Caiaphas..." he said, "I need to speak with Caiaphas. It is a matter of import, please see me to him."

The guard looked at him with disdain. "Fuck off," he said simply.

Jude sighed. "Look, I know you are here to guard the door, but this pertains to serious matters which are important on both sides of it."

The guard shrugged. "If you say so," he said, "Right...follow me." And with that, he walked through the gigantic doorway with Jude close behind.

"And what may I do for you at this unsocial hour?" Caiaphas asked.

Jude bowed before the temple leader. "It is more a question of what I may do for you, Oh Holy One!"

"Speak plainly."

"I understand that you desire the man Jesus to be removed from your sphere of influence, much as a thorn removed from one's foot," said Jude in a low voice. He had an irrational urge to pull his dagger and thrust it into the fat priest's eye as hard as he could. The man had an aura of ill-feeling and spite around him, and Jude felt uncomfortable under his gaze.

"Hmm…tell me more," said Caiaphas sulkily.

"I put myself at great risk coming to you; will you make it worth my while?"

"You are that sort of man, are you? Well, if it is money you want, I doubt your motives are good; therefore, I doubt that anything you say or information you give is good either," Caiaphas replied.

"I only want money so I can run. There will be those who want my hide if you take Jesus. I want distance between me and this place, and that has a cost. I will have to start a new life. Far from here."

"So what is your motive?" Caiaphas asked.

"The man is full of shit. I worry that he corrupts the minds of the people with his ridiculous blasphemy. But I worry about my safety too."

"Is that why you come to me hooded and with your face half-covered?"

"Indeed, the man has spies everywhere, and I dare not be recognised, for I am regarded as one of his faithful. He trusts me, and so do the others; they would kill me if they knew I was here."

"So they are murderers too? You may answer, I give you my word, you shall walk away from here safe and wealthier than you came in if you can swear you will get the man to a place where we can grab him. Along with this, you must promise to testify against him in a court of law. We will protect you from harm until after you testify, and then you can disappear to wherever it is you can afford to go."

Jude nodded. "There is a garden called Gethsemene; it is the garden of the oil press at the foot of the Mount of Olives. I am sure you know of it; tomorrow at midnight I shall persuade to be Jesus there. Will you recognise the man?" he asked.

Caiaphas smiled. "I have a good enough idea what he looks like, but to be sure, I shall look for one man kissing another on the cheek. One will be you, and the other shall be him."

***

152

Jude walked from the temple, casting an eye around to see if he was being observed. He had a sick feeling in his stomach, and the 30 silver coins weighed heavy in his purse. Jude was sweating; he had been unusually nervous during his meeting with Caiaphas, and he felt it was the most difficult thing he had ever done. Right or wrong, it was done now anyway. He thought of the irony of his next act; telling Jesus that the dark deed he had been sent to do was done and giving him the money that Caiaphas had handed over before he had swept from the room. Could it really be that the destiny of so many, possibly the future of the world, came down to just 30 silver coins? It seemed impossible.

Chapter 20

Twist of Fate

It was a beautiful balmy evening; there was a faint smell of impending rain in the air and the occasional cloud sailed slowly in front of the Moon. Jesus and Judas walked side by side ahead of the others, talking in hushed tones so that they would not be overheard.

"Are you scared, Brother?" Judas asked.

"No, my heart is full of anticipation and desire to face our people's oppressors," Jesus lied. In truth, his heart was pounding in his chest, and he was suffering from a nauseous feeling in the pit of his stomach. He was having doubts about his decision to have himself arrested, driven by the fact that he felt events were now beyond his control. "Jude, I must thank you for your part in this. In fact, to merely thank you seems somehow inadequate. You have shown me the greatest love by doing what you have done, and I know how heavily it must weigh upon your heart. But please, do not let it bring you down; everything will work out as planned; have confidence in me. Never spend a moment in regret, for you have fulfilled my wish in organising my arrest." Jesus grinned. "And asking for payment was a clever touch. The money will be useful, and it amuses me that the Temple has, in fact, paid in gold for their own downfall."

"I cannot deny I am worried for you, the Temple Guards are not known for being gentle and tender to those in their custody," Judas said, lines of concern etched across his face.

Jesus nodded. "I can handle a beating. A few punches and kicks will do me no great harm. They come for me at midnight you say?"

"Yes, Brother, we have a couple of hours to wait," Judas replied.

"When the time comes, my capture must be peaceable. You must make sure the others do not resist, get them to run. There are many ways out of the garden, and many pathways. It is only myself that is to be taken."

They walked through the entrance to the garden, one of several gateways without any gate and flanked by pairs of rough-hewn stones standing taller than a man. This was one of the side entrances, the main one being more grandiose with finely chiselled and decorated pillars. The garden was truly a place of beauty, a civic park with the fine scents of flowers and herbs which offered a fine respite from the smells of sweat, excrement and the multitude of other odours emanating from the kitchens and houses of the streets nearby. Har HaZeitim; the Mount of Olives rose impressively to their right, and ahead stood an avenue of aged olive trees. They strolled a few more minutes until they came to the small lake, where Jesus decided to sit. He motioned for Judas to sit beside him, and a few moments later, they were joined by their brother James, Peter and Thaddeus. The rest settled down at the bases of some nearby trees, and Jesus turned to them. "A wonderful evening, is it not?" he said.

"Indeed it is," said Thaddeus, "What brought on you sudden desire to come here?"

Jesus leant back onto his elbows and sighed. "Look at the sky, Thaddeus, and the stars. Do you not ever take a walk at night to relax and look at the heavens? It is pure peace. Look up, pick a star and stare at it. And wonder what it would be like to spread out your arms and rise from the ground. Imagine what it would be like to fly."

Thaddeus lay on his back and stared upward. "Do you think one day somebody will learn to fly? Perhaps make a chariot with great wings?"

"It is said that many hundreds of years ago, in a far off land many thousands of miles to the west across a monstrous ocean, that the people have already done it. They learnt the secret of the air and then forgot it," Jesus whispered. "They themselves were taught the secret by other people from another far off land, across another vast ocean. But they are all dead now, and the land is gone. Or so it is said anyway. The Magi have stories about it."

Jesus closed his eyes and sighed, and there was the muted sound of the men laughing quietly beneath the trees. *They have no idea what will shortly happen*, he thought. *Unfair, but necessary*. This had to appear unplanned so he could seem entirely innocent and just another victim of the Temple's fear and spite. It would make them hate Caiaphas and his cronies all the more. "I think I will stroll alone with my thoughts for a little while," he said, rising to his feet and stretching.

"Is it solitude you require? I will walk with you if you wish, act as a bodyguard," Judas said.

Jesus shook his head. "No, I won't be too long. Relax and enjoy the company of friends." He wandered off around the shore of the lake, past some thorny shrubs to a large rock, climbed up onto it and sat. He looked around, saw he was out of sight of his companions and started to shake. His head started to pound, and he felt desperate for a drink, for his mouth felt as dry as the stone he was sat upon. Jesus felt a horrible rising panic; starting deep in his bowels and rising into his chest. He realised this was pure fear. What if the soldiers hacked him down with their swords here in the garden? What if he was thrown into a cell and forgotten, just left to rot – never given the chance for the great confrontation upon which his entire plan hinged? What if he was poisoned in custody? Jesus suddenly felt this was not the good idea that it seemed just a few days ago – that he had not thought this through properly, and he had grown vastly overconfident. His plan now seemed utterly ridiculous. How could he hope for a fair and public trial? He had gone out of his way to antagonise the Sanhedrin and was now handing himself to them on a plate. Why on Earth should he expect them to play by the rules when he himself had deliberately flouted them? No – this was a terrible idea and an awful plan destined to fail. There were too many things that could go wrong. He would have to stop it. They should all disappear for a while, and he could rethink. He should go to Qumran and get some advice. Or maybe not. What was he going to do?

His mind went into a spin, too many things to think about and the fear inside clouding his brain and confusing all thought. His stomach suddenly heaved, and he vomited – sweat dripping from his entire body. Fear. He couldn't think. He wanted to run. Stupidity. He had been a fucking idiot to plan this. He wiped his mouth, the sour taste of his stomach on his lips. He needed to get away. He needed time to rethink. He knew he could not back out now. He knew he had no choice but to back out. He couldn't let the others know his fear.

Deep breaths. Calm down. Go to the others and casually say they were heading off.

Jude. What would he say to him? He felt distracted. More deep breaths. Stand up. His hands were shaking. His breath must stink from the puke.

Calm down for fuck's sake.

He ran his hands through his hair. What to say to his younger brother? Something would come to him. It did not matter yet. Just get the hell out of this trap he had set for himself. More deep breaths.

They would leave. No problem. Plan again. Breathe.

He squatted and scooped water into his face from the lake. He stood. He looked again at his hands. Barely shaking.

Good. Appear calm. Decision made. Leave Gethsemane. Leave Jerusalem. Deep breath again and walk back calmly.

How long did they have before the guards arrived? Ages surely.

Walk calmly. Weak legs. Just walk. No need to appear in a rush.

Jesus walked around the lake and over to Judas.

"I need a word," he said quietly.

Jude and Jesus took a few paces away from the others and turned to face each other. Jesus leant in to whisper in his brother's ear.

"Jude, we must leave, I think…"

"THAT'S THE KISS! THAT'S HIM!" came the shout from the hedgerow behind Jesus, and suddenly, there were armoured temple guards everywhere. Shouts of alarm came from under the trees as Jesus was shoved to the ground and kicked in his lower back. He shouted out in pain and received a kick to his crotch as a response. The pain shot up into his stomach, and he vomited for the second time that night. Judas was grabbed from both sides by his upper arms by two guards and punched hard in the face by a third.

"RUN!" he shouted to the others as James came at the guard kicking Jesus like a maddened bull. Another guard tried to block James by swinging his shield into him, but James was not to be stopped. He hit the shield square on, and the guard was knocked from his feet. James launched himself at the guard beating Jesus, and the two men went tumbling into a hedge. Jesus tried to stand, but another guard kicked him in the ribs and he went sprawling again. Judas was still shouting between getting punched in the stomach, ribs and face. "RUN! RUN! FOR FUCK'S SAKE RUN!"

Simon leapt at a guard, seemingly from nowhere. The guard was huge and almost caught Simon mid-air. The two men went down, the guard dropping his spear. He wrapped his heavily muscled arms around Simon's chest and squeezed as hard as he could. Simon felt one of his ribs crack and hissed in pain. One arm was pinned to his side, but the other was free. He shoved the thumb of his free hand into the guard's mouth and pulled out, digging his fingernails into the man's cheek, trying to tear the man's mouth, then lunged forward and bit the man's other cheek as hard as he could. He felt the flesh give under the fierce grip of his teeth and the metallic taste of blood filled his mouth. The guard screamed with pain and released his crushing bear-hug, but Simon did not release his jaw and the two men fell to the ground. His ear felt like it had burst, and suddenly, he was on his side, knocked off the guard by another who had kicked him in the side of the head. Simon still had a piece of a man's cheek in his mouth, which he spat out.

Jesus finally managed to stand up, turned and saw Judas being dragged to the ground. His immediate reaction was to help his brother, but before he had taken three paces, his head was rocked by a massive blow from a shield and his world went dark as he lost consciousness. James appeared with a sword in his hand which he had taken from the guard he had disabled. He saw Judas struggling on the ground and charged over to help. A guard turned and saw James, but too late. James swung the sword in a downward arc and the soldier threw up his sword to fend off the blow. In James's fury, he seemed to have gained the strength of two men; his sword crashed against that belonging to the guard, partially knocking it out of the way. Brute force and rage making up for his complete lack of skill with a weapon. James felt the sword glance off the man's helmet at a shallow angle, taking off his ear and slamming into the armour over his collarbone, putting a dent in it and breaking the bone beneath. Immediately, he was hit in the upper arm by the edge of a shield from a guard behind him. He lost all feeling other than pain, and his nerveless fingers dropped the sword. He swung his left fist at his assailant, but the man had his shield up again and the blow went squarely into it. He felt something break in his hand and pain went shooting up this arm too. Within a second, he was swamped by armoured bodies and shoved the ground virtually unable to defend himself. He was roughly turned over and his hands forced behind his back and deftly tied. He heard a grunt beside him and saw Simon was lying next to him, face covered in blood and pure fury in his eyes. He raised his head and saw Jude being tied up under the weight of five men. There did not seem to be any struggle from him. He looked to his other side, but there was no sign of Jesus. What had happened to him? Where was he? "Simon, where is Jesus?"

Simon shook his head and was grabbed by two guards and lifted to his feet. Next came James, who was grabbed roughly and lifted, rope burning painfully into his left wrist. He still had no feeling in his right arm and hand. He looked around for Jesus, but there was no sign of him. In fact, there was no sign of any of their companions – just himself, Simon and Judas who was now stood also. He looked around at the guards and saw three of them were having injuries tended to. Everything seemed to have calmed down a little, some of the guards talking quietly to each other and throwing glances at the three of them. Jude seemed to get more glances than himself and Simon, and something from their demeanour gave him the impression it was Jude they wanted, himself and Simon seemed to be merely additions to their prize. What the hell was this about?

Peter fell to the ground amongst the bushes, exhausted. He couldn't believe what had happened. With the fighting going on he had managed to grab the inert form of Jesus and drag him out of the fray, before hoisting him to his shoulder and running as fast as he could. All had been chaos in the darkness. Some of them had run; most it seemed. He saw what looked like James jump into the thick of the fight, and someone else too, but he couldn't tell who it was. He felt he was on his own, and he was scared. He looked at the battered face of Jesus, who was still out for the count. He had to get him to safety.

Eight men surrounded Jude and marched him off into the night with the injured guards following behind. James and Simon looked at each other quizzically; both were confused about what had just happened. Why was Jude so important? What had he done? Two guards grabbed Simon and led him away too but in a different direction which left just himself and the remaining three guards looking at each other. After a couple of minutes, his arms were seized and he was led off after Simon. Once out of the garden, James was escorted to the Roman barracks, untied and thrown into a cell, without a word being spoken to him.

Caiaphas looked up from the paperwork on his desk. Malchus, commander of the arrest squad stood before him, head bandaged and drying blood crusting down the side of his neck. His arm was tied in a sling, and he looked awful. "What happened to you?" he asked.

"I was attacked by a madman. The bastard took my ear off with a sword and broke my collarbone. But he will suffer for it. He is languishing in a Roman jail now with another, charged with rioting, and hopefully, with your influence, awaiting execution."

"And the witch; Jesus?"

"We got him – your man walked over to him and kissed him on the cheek, just like you said. He is in a cell in the guard's barracks. The man that plotted with you got knocked out in the fracas, and I saw someone drag him away. Had my hands full at the time, or I would have taken him too. If we had him, we could ensure he was available for trial as he promised. So I apologise for that." Caiaphas waved his apology away. "Not a problem."

"Is there anything else you require from me tonight, Lord?" Malchus asked, "Only I am very sore and need wine and a bed to lie in."

Caiaphas shook his head. "No – you have done well; you deserve a rest. See the surgeon tomorrow and take three weeks off to heal. And I will see the coin in your pocket tomorrow, for the task you have done."

Malchus nodded curtly, turned and walked from the room, missing the smug smile which spread evilly across Caiaphas's face.

Simon was exhausted and in pain. Running had been hard with what he knew was at least one broken rib. He had slipped the razor-sharp knife down his sleeve, sliced through the ropes which had tied his wrists with one flick of his fingers, and bolted – catching the guards completely by surprise. He didn't have much of a head start but did have the advantage of being unencumbered by armour. He ran, and as soon as he was in the shadows, he climbed painfully up onto a roof and doubled back, hearing the shouts of his captors grow fainter as he put distance between them and himself. He gasped for breath and felt a sharp pain as he sucked air over a broken tooth. He would have to pull that out later. He had to find the others first.

Jude lay on the cold stone floor, hands still tied, and snorting bloody snot from his nose. His right eye was half closed and bruised, and his left elbow hurt badly from when he had been thrown into the cell, landing on it heavily. He hoped it was not broken. He understood why he had been arrested, Caiaphas would want to make sure he held his end of the bargain and would want him at the trial of his brother, but he was determined he would say nothing. He wondered where Jesus was – he must have been taken away first and was probably in a cell somewhere else. He hadn't seen or heard James or Simon either, so he guessed he was being kept separate from them, as he was only a witness. The bastards could have at least untied him though. Jude lay there, trying to listen for sounds which would help him establish what was happening but could hear nothing other the moaning from somebody echoing down the stonework tunnel outside the barred door of his cell. He looked about the gloom but could see virtually nothing other than different depths of the shadow cast from an eerie light coming in from a small barred aperture several feet above his head. He hoped Jesus, James and Simon were all right and had no clue if anybody else had been arrested. He shifted position on the floor and felt his hands tingle as his circulation altered, pumping much-needed blood into his fingers. It was a welcome feeling but uncomfortable. He heard hearty laughter from somewhere outside the little window and briefly wondered what the joke could have been. Jude looked at the window – no sign of dawn, and yet he felt he had already been in this cell for hours, all sense of time was distorted. There was a fit of coughing from the other end of the tunnel, followed by snoring. So there were two people down here with him at least. He wriggled to his knees and stood, gingerly walking to the bars of the door, checking with each pace that he wasn't going to bang his shins into some unknown and invisible obstacle. Perhaps there was some other person in the cell with him that he hadn't seen when he had first been launched bodily into it, but he doubted that; he felt somehow he would instinctively know when he was alone, and his instinct told him just that. He leant his forehead against the bars.

"Jesus, is that you?" he said into the darkness. There was no reply. "James? Simon?" Nothing, the snoring continued rhythmically and without interruption. He listened at the bars for another minute or two, then leant against the stonework by the bars. His elbow still hurt, so he flexed his arms. No, it didn't feel broken but was probably badly bruised. Jude slid down the wall to sit, starting to feel cold. There was more laughter outside, this time a little closer, and a few seconds later, there was a voice.

"Oi, you in there, scum, bet you could do with a drink, eh?" There was laughter behind the source of the voice.

"Get this wine into you," the voice said, and there was the sound of water splashing on the cell floor from the window. The laughter continued.

"Well, it was wine when I drank it; it's something else now." The man guffawed at his priceless joke. "Let me know if you get hungry. I have a shit brewing nicely – I would be happy for you to eat it." He guffawed some more and Judas remained silent; pointless rising to it, pointless antagonising his captors. The man wandered off, bored now he had just shared his incredible wit with his comrades.

Two hundred years later, and still with no sign of the approaching dawn there was a loud bang as a heavy wooden door was thrown open, followed by gruff shouting.

Jude started, surprised by the sudden and unexpected noise, and realised he had been drifting off into a doze. The flickering light of torches cast shadows down the walls of the tunnel, and Jude braced himself for whatever was to befall him next. There was a crashing of a barred door being thrown open and more shouting, the sound of a fight, the crashing of the barred door again, laughter and the wooden door was slammed shut with the rattling of keys. The tunnel returned to its previous state of darkness. The snoring had been replaced with the sound of a man crying in pain. An eternity passed, the crying abated, and Jude fell into a fitful sleep.

Jude was woken by his bladder telling him to urinate and pain in his neck and hands from the awkward position he had slept in. The early morning light illuminated his cell, having struggled through the small window from the outside world. He looked about himself and saw the wooden sleeping pallet under the window. *It would have been nice to have slept on that*, Judas thought, until he realised that if he had, he would have been the recipient of the flow of piss that last night's comedian had gifted to him. Well, now he was going to have to be the victim of his own piss as his hands were still tied behind his back and he had no way of directing his stream. He would have to forget any dignity and just piss where he stood. He walked over to the wall furthest from the pallet, stood legs apart and relieved himself. He felt disgusting, the hot urine flooding down his left leg, but he was without a choice in the matter. He couldn't hold it in forever, and there was no saying how long he was going to be down here for. He walked back over to the barred door, feeling the wet in his lower clothing go cold. He knew it would stink in a couple of hours. Looking around himself, he studied the cell. It looked quite skilfully built. Good stonework. And large. The window was about 18 inches tall, and a foot wide, with two hefty metal bars running top to bottom, and three more ran horizontally. There was no way anyone was squeezing their way through there. Below the window was a row of eight metal rings separated by about two feet from each other and bolted securely to the wall about four feet from the floor. Previous residents had scratched names and small pictures into the stonework but not very deeply. He wondered what had been used to make the marks. Jude looked at the barred door. Six feet wide, wide enough to allow two armed guards through side by side. Vertical bars twice the thickness of his thumb stood less than a foot apart, and a heavy metal block held the lock that secured the bolt that secured the door firmly shut. The metal bars looked worn by the grip of many hands, surprising as the place did not look that old. Perhaps these bars graced another dungeon in the past before being installed here. He listened out for the sounds of the other two people he had heard during the night, but there was only silence.

Jude's stomach growled, complaining that it was empty, and he wondered if he would get some food any time soon. He didn't expect any, but he closed his eyes and thought of fresh bread. It wasn't the first time he had been hungry, and he was sure it would not be the last. He thought of his brothers and Simon and wondered what had happened to them. Maybe they were getting fed this very minute.

His thoughts were interrupted by the sound of the wooden door being opened and armoured men walking along the tunnel. Three guards appeared in front of the cell door, and the largest produced a key from a pouch slung over his shoulder. "Step back to the wall," he commanded. Judas did as ordered, and the man unlocked the door, swinging it open. He stayed at the doorway and the other two entered. One drew his short sword, and the other drew a knife. The one with the sword raised his weapon and held the point against Judas's neck, whilst the other walked up to his side, leant in behind him and cut the ropes which bound his hands. The knife-wielder stepped back and the man with the sword spoke.

"One wrong move, just one attempt to escape, even the slightest sign of disobedience, and I cut you a second mouth under your jaw. Understand?"

Jude nodded slowly, wary of the blade at his jugular.

The other guard slid his knife into his scabbard and took Jude by the left arm, leading him out of the cell. The key-holder pulled his sword and Jude was escorted from his prison, up a flight of stairs onto the sunlight and across a courtyard into the Great Temple of Jerusalem itself.

Jude stood before a huge decorated table on a dais, with seven senior priests sat in thrones on its far side. The one in the middle he recognised as Caiaphas. All were clothed in fabulously rich robes topped by idiotic hats and wore golden chains of office along with expressions of vast superiority. Jude was flanked by two guards in shining armour without shields but clutching evil-looking spears in their right hands. Other, less well-dressed priests stood in a semi-circle around him, silent and emanating resentment and ill-feeling. Jude had never seen so many priests and was surprised that there could be so many who could be prepared to be such shameless parasites to society.

Caiaphas cleared his throat and stood.

"In front of me is stood a deceiver," he announced. There were general murmurings of disapproval from the priests.

He looked at Jude. "Do you claim to be a god?"

Jude looked confused. "Err…no, of course, not."

"Have you ever claimed to be a god?"

"*A* god? I thought you were supposed to think there was only one?"

"Don't get clever with me, Turd."

"I have never claimed to be any such thing," Judas answered, wondering where this line of questioning was headed and what its purpose was.

"Do you confess to performing magic?"

"No."

"Why will you not confess?"

"Because I haven't done it."

"Do you admit to raising the dead and curing the blind?"

"I haven't done that either," said Jude.

"Last night when you were arrested, you tried to kill one of my guards, yes?"

"No, I just stood there getting punched and kicked. Then I was pushed over and got sat on."

"And on your way to the cells, you did try to punch a guard and knock him to the ground, did you not? This was an attempt to escape."

"Difficult, what with both my hands tied behind my back, Your Honour."

A look of anger flashed across the High Priest's face and he was silent for a few seconds. "I have a man who says he heard you say that you could destroy the temple of God and rebuild it in three days. How do you answer that?"

Judas looked around at the vast room and shook his head. "I could do some of the carpentry if you like," he suggested.

Caiaphas swept around the table, walked up to Jude and spat in his face.

"A funny fucker you are, eh?" he said quietly with venom in his voice. He stepped away from Jude and turned his back on him, raising his hands to the air. "Oh Lord, this man stands before us as a witch, trying to divert his lawful questioning by the employment of ridicule, trying to make us; your servants; appear as fools!"

You really do not need my help for that, you fat pompous prick! thought Jude but prudently kept that thought to himself.

Caiaphas rounded on him and pointed an accusing finger. "Are you Jesus, the Living Christ?" he asked, the reality of what this was about suddenly dawning on Jude.

"No, I am not," he said.

"Do you claim to be the son of God?" he shouted.

Jude looked at him directly for a couple of seconds before replying. "If God is my Father, which is as you teach us, then yes, I am a son of God according to your logic."

Caiaphas fell to his knees. "HEAR HIS UNHOLY ANSWER!" he screamed to the ceiling and then started pulling violently at his clothes, trying to tear the cloth. "It is blasphemy, Oh, Lord!" he wailed.

Judas almost laughed aloud at the turn of events, realising they thought him to be his brother, at their incompetence and at the man's ridiculous theatrics, but the other priests seemed to be drinking it all in, lapping it up like thirsty dogs at a spring well. Caiaphas stood and addressed his audience, regaining the composure he had pretended to have lost.

"You have heard his blasphemy," he said solemnly, "What do you think?"

The six High Priests still at the colossal table stood, and as one said, "He is worthy of death!"

"Guards, hold this heretic still," Caiaphas ordered, and Jude was gripped by his upper arms. The High Priest strode up to Jude and slapped him across the face. Judas laughed at him. "I would expect a slap like that of a girl, from a fat man who dresses like one," he said, his disdain for the great blubbery oaf getting the better of his tongue. Caiaphas smiled and pulled a shout leather strop from his robe, looked at it and lashed out with it into Judas's mouth, splitting his top lip and causing a scarlet welt to rise across his cheek.

"Is that more to your liking?" he said in a whisper. "Return him to his cell!"

Chapter 21
Politics and Law

James sat on the floor leaning against the wall, his hand throbbing, bruised and swollen. The iron collar around his neck was secured to the wall with just six inches of chain, and his feet were clamped between two heavy pieces of wood bolted to the floor. His hands were manacled together and chained to his collar. He could barely move, for he was regarded as a dangerous and violent criminal. There were five other men down there in the pit with him, chained loosely to the walls of this 25 by 30 feet underground chamber which stank of piss, shit and sweat. The only way in or out was through the hole in the ceiling, guarded on the outside by two Roman soldiers. Well, at least he knew he would not be here long, as Roman justice under Pilate's authority was notoriously quick and often fatal. James knew he was doomed. To be imprisoned here was surely the first step on his road to either death or slavery. Whichever it was to be, he knew he would be sentenced within a couple of days. The others in the pit were curious and had asked him why he was there, but he had just glared at them without answering. He had no interest in why they were here. All he hoped for was a quick death, for he knew he was now beyond help. He closed his eyes and thought of his brothers.

Caiaphas sat at his desk and looked at the two shamed guards who stood before him. "So there were the two of you, armed to the teeth, and you allowed a man who was tied to escape. Not really a good thing to have allowed to happen, is it?"

The guards said nothing but stared fixedly at the space above the High Priest's head.

"Very well, you shall be handed over to the Roman Prefect to be dealt with under Roman law. You do, of course, realise that under Roman law, for a soldier to allow a prisoner to escape carries the death penalty? Enjoy being throttled, won't you? Take them away."

The two guards were seized by the six others who had been stood in a row close behind them and led from the room. Caiaphas sat back in his chair, twiddling his pudgy thumbs. He was happy with the timing of events, for Pilate was in Jerusalem staying at the Roman Palace. He had an appointment with him at noon, which gave him a couple of hours to dress, eat and make his way there. Now he had to persuade Pilate to execute his prisoner. It would be nice to have this affair all sorted out with as much speed as possible.

***

Pilate stood in the courtyard, impressive in his cavalry armour. His chain mail was painted white to reflect the heat of the sun, his red undershirt new and unfaded – seemingly glowing with colour. At his left hip hung his pugio – the foot-long leaf-bladed dagger, and at his right hung his spatha or long sword.

Under his left arm, he held his Attic helmet, old fashioned but stylish with its beautifully decorated metalwork and horsehair plume. He wore a leopard skin over his shoulders and stood chest out and shoulders back. Facing him stood Caiaphas in all his priestly regalia, and the two peacocks eyed each other suspiciously; each weighing up the other.

Pilate smiled graciously and gestured Caiaphas to a couch. "Please be seated," he said, "I am sure your faith does not prevent an old man from relaxing while important matters are at hand." Caiaphas nodded and sat, ignoring the barb in Pilate's comment about his age.

"Lord Prefect," he said, "there are disturbing events unfolding which threaten the security of Rome and the happy status quo to which we have become accustomed."

Pilate nodded – *happy for you perhaps* – he thought; for him, Caiaphas and his cronies were an unavoidable pain in the arse. "Please tell," he said.

Caiaphas drew a measured breath. "You face an insurrection. We, that is the Sanhedrin, have managed to uncover this plot and have done all we can to put an end to it, but our powers are limited and the final responsibility for the outcome of events lies in your hands. I wish merely to advise you in my humble capacity as a priest, on the way forward. Think of me as a cultural go-between, for this could be a delicate situation."

Pilate sat, wondering how this game of diplomatic chess was to play out. It was obvious from the priest's fake humility that whatever it was that was causing him concern was more to do with his own worries than that of Rome's. "Go on. Explain to me the events, please," he said, face showing no emotion.

Caiaphas sighed. "We have become aware of a rebel. A very popular one. He has for many years been preaching a new and subversive set of ethics which stand at odds with both our laws and yours – it threatens the governance of Rome, as much as it threatens the temple. And as you know, we the temple, are allied with Rome. This rebel is a man called Jesus – he is of the cast of Jews known as the Essenes; a holy order rumoured to be in alliance with the fanatical Zealots. He teaches blasphemy; which is our concern, not yours, but this blasphemy incites sedition. That I am afraid, is where it becomes your issue. He is a witch and claims to be the son of God. He thinks himself all-powerful, which is not a major problem, but sadly, a lot of the local populace think him to be so too. We seem to have averted a major rebellion by capturing this man but cannot deal with him in the manner required. So I must hand him to you for execution. He is dangerous, mark my words, and very cunning. He threatens Roman rule. Death is the only solution. During his arrest, two others were taken as they tried to prevent the seizure of the rebel. One lies in the jail in your barracks charged with rioting and attempted murder – we recommend he also is executed as a warning to others. I do not know his name, other than he is sometimes called Bar-Abbas; the chosen son. That is the only name he gave when questioned. The other managed to escape. In his place, I will hand over the two guards who allowed it, to face Roman justice and punishment. As a cultural advisor, I would suggest that these two be executed too, as a warning to other military men under both your command and mine. We must be obeyed, and we cannot afford to do the wrong thing here."

Pilate sat and thought about what Caiaphas had said. He didn't know quite what to make of the priest's accusations regarding this man, this Jesus. He would need to interrogate him. If he found him to have done no harm, then it would question the legality of his arrest. And as this Barabbas fellow was lying in jail as a result of it, then his fate also hinged upon the guilt of this Jesus. If Jesus was innocent, then by rights so was he. The two guards were not a problem – they had shown incompetence and allowed an escape. However, if this Jesus was guilty, then he would have to admit that he owed Caiaphas a debt of thanks and that galled him. But at the same time, he could not afford to make an enemy of the Sanhedrin – they had already got him in trouble with Rome, and he dare not invite more. He looked at Caiaphas and nodded.

"I need you to write a report on these events immediately. Once that is done, I will have the two guards dealt with straight away. Where are they?"

"They are outside under escort, Your Honour," Caiaphas replied.

"In the meantime, whilst you write your report, have this Jesus fellow brought here for my personal interrogation. The man taking his ease in my jail I will deal with later." Pilate clicked his fingers and a soldier appeared instantly. "Fetch the necessary items for the High Priest here to write a document and replace the temple guards outside with our own. Then have their prisoners escorted to the barracks and strangled to death. Then their bodies are to be taken to the temple to be dealt with." He turned to Caiaphas. "Does that meet with your satisfaction?" he asked.

Caiaphas nodded. "Gratitude," he said humbly.

Mary was distraught, sat with the still-unconscious Jesus, his face badly battered and bruised, with his wife holding his hand and crying. What had happened to her sons? One lying beaten senseless, one vanished from the face of the earth, and the other held hostage in the Great Temple. She did not know whether there was a hunt on for Jesus, but she thought him safe enough for now here in Qumran. His friends had all gone into hiding, except Simon who was being treated in the infirmary for broken ribs, exhaustion and the delirium of heatstroke, and Peter who had gone back to Jerusalem to find out what was happening with James and Jude. Peter was exhausted too, but she knew he would not rest until he had brought back news to her regarding the fate of her two sons. In need of fresh air, she stood and walked outside into the sunshine. It was impossible for her to stay here idle and unknowing; she had to go to Jerusalem herself; it was not far and perhaps attempt an audience with the prefect. Beg for their freedom and some semblance of mercy if that was what was required. Whatever had happened, she was sure that it was not according to plan but had no idea what the plan was. What had gone wrong?

Jude stood with his hands retied in front of Pontius Pilate, Roman prefect of Judea, a Knight of Rome and a war hero. Jude; shabby, smelly, unwashed and wondering what to do next. Pilate, knowing this interrogation could be vitally important to his career.

Jude studied the Roman as he waited for him to speak. The seconds went by as Pilate thought of the consequences of acting incorrectly. Finally, he took a couple of paces towards Jude.

"There are serious allegations made against you," he said. Jude nodded.

"Are you aware of them? In any detail?" Pilate asked.

"I am not too sure, Lord Prefect," Jude replied.

"That does not surprise me. Tell me, do you disapprove of those in power in the Great Temple? You may answer honestly, for having an unsavoury view of them is no offence under Roman law."

Jude nodded. "I think they are fat self-serving parasites," he said.

Pilate laughed. "Well, that is two of us of a like opinion. Tell me, do many of the population feel this way?"

Jude felt like he was standing on thin ice, and it was cracking a little. He knew he had to give guarded answers. "If they do, then it is because of the actions of those running the temple. If they upset the people, then they have only themselves to blame."

"And are you yourself one who points out the nature of those running the Great Temple and stirs ill-feeling towards them?"

"No, I am not," Jude replied.

Pilate sighed. "Have you ever claimed to be a god?"

Jude shook his head. "Never, and it would be a ridiculous claim. Look at me. Do gods look and smell like this?"

Pilate wrinkled his nose. "Mine certainly don't," he said. "Have you ever claimed to be the son of a god?"

"As I said in the Temple when questioned there, in our faith we are taught that our God is our Father. So, therefore, I must be. As are all men. But logic seemed to be blasphemy in their eyes. What man is not his father's son?"

Pilate smiled, thinking that what was said held no fault. He had a point.

"Have you ever claimed to be King of the Jews?" he asked.

"No," said Jude.

"*Are* you the King of the Jews?"

"I do not look like a god. I look even less like a king."

"So you are not a king," Pilate asked, to reaffirm the answer he had received.

"A man is only a king in the kingdom of his own making. I have made no kingdom. Therefore, I am no king. Unless others mistakenly think me such and then I am only a king in their eyes. If you thought me your king, then it would be so."

"So you are not a god, not a king, so perhaps you can do magic?"

"There is no such thing as magic. Just deceit."

"And do you possess a great army?" Pilate inquired.

Jude looked him in the eye and smiled. "I do not look like a god or a Jewish king, and I am certain I do not look like a general. I have no army."

Pilate turned and took a few paces, head bowed in thought. "The Sanhedrin want you dead," he said.

"I am sure they want lots of things," Jude replied. Pilate could not argue that comment.

"I think the only thing they have to fear from you is your disapproval. Your views on religion are hardly a matter for the Roman State to be concerned with. This is a matter of theology and not a matter of rebellion. I wash my hands of this matter. You are not my problem, and as far as I am concerned, from the Roman perspective, you have done nothing to break any law. However, I am not an expert on the laws of your Moses, so I will send you before somebody who has authority regarding your own law." Pilate turned to address the Roman officer stood in the doorway. "Have this man taken before King Herod Antipas, along with the report made by the high priest. In fact, take the damned high priest too, get him out of the bloody way for a while. Tell Antipas of my findings with this man, and let him judge him according to his own customs and laws."

***

Mary sat on a couch, eyes red with crying, and felt the touch on her shoulder of Claudia's hand. She had been unable to gain an appointment with Pilate but chance had it that as she was turning to walk away from Pilate's clerk, his wife had walked past and was taken with Mary's tears. She led Mary to a private ante-room, full of busts and sculptures.

"I understand your worry," Claudia said. "I have lost two sons. The first at two weeks old and the second just before his first birthday. It is a horrific stain on a mother's heart to lose a son. So I see your pain and your cares. My husband, the prefect, was knocked down badly by our loss. I shall speak to him. Please wait here." Claudia stood and swept from the room, leaving Mary alone with the stone-faced soldier at the door and the dozens of marble Romans on their plinths around the walls.

Half an hour had passed, feeling more like a week to Mary, when Claudia returned. "I have news," she said. "There is nobody of the name of James bar Yusef in Roman custody but a man of the name of Jesus was before my husband earlier."

Mary recoiled with surprise and confusion. Before she could speak, Claudia continued. "This man Jesus, my husband found innocent of all charges laid against him under Roman law, and he has been sent to King Antipas in Tiberias up north to be judged by him, with a report containing my husband's findings. It does not seem you have too much to fear."

Mary stood, confused. Jesus was in Qumran – so who was it going for trial with Antipas? James or Jude? "Thank you," she said quietly, "I will waste no more of your time."

"It was no waste," Claudia said. "A mother has a mother's worries. I am glad I have been able to help even though it was no great thing. Please feel free to speak with me again if the need arises."

It was six in the morning when Caiaphas, the Roman horsemen and their prisoner arrived at the palace of Antipas. It had taken 16 hours of rough terrain and pitted roads to travel the one hundred miles from Jerusalem by horse and cart, and Caiaphas was in a foul mood. Pilate had not executed this damned witch like he should have, and now he, the High Priest, had had to endure this awful journey to plead his case with King Antipas. He was tired, thirsty, hungry and ached. This was a waste of his time – thanks to that damned prefect.

He strode into the palace full of his own bluff and bluster and swept into the king's throne room upon hearing name being called for the audience. He strode up to the king and bowed deeply.

"Your Majesty…" he began but was cut short by the king.

"Quiet for now. I am reading," Antipas said.

Caiaphas was affronted but did not dare speak. This king had power and was bound only by his own rules.

The king read on, occasionally frowning. After a short while, he looked up from the document in his hand and glared at Caiaphas. "I have read your report. I have also read the report from the Roman Prefect; Pilate. I have a feeling there is a lot of time-wasting going on here."

"Yes, Majesty," Caiaphas said. "Had the prefect done his job as he should, I would not have had to journey here, and you…"

"QUIET!" the king shouted. "From what I read here, it is you that is the cause of time being wasted! You arrest a man for thinking differently to yourselves and making you look foolish. That seems to be the height of his crimes. If making you look a fool is a crime, have you considered arresting yourself?"

Caiaphas bowed, shocked by the king's words. Furious that he was not getting what he wanted.

Antipas stood. "I think it is high time I went to Jerusalem," he said. "I think my Roman friend needs counsel and support." He looked at Caiaphas. "Do not get comfortable," the king said, "We leave in an hour."

***

Pontius Pilate and King Herod Antipas lounged on the couches in the huge central courtyard of the Roman Palace. Small birds twittered in the branches of the lemon trees, and the water gurgled and splashed from the fountain in the middle of the mosaic floored pool, making the images of the Roman gods shimmer and ripple in the sunshine. On the table before them were spread dishes of figs, nuts and fresh fruits. In each corner of the courtyard, armed infantrymen stood at their ease in the shade of the overhanging roof and two half-naked slave girls stood beside the two rulers, waiting to attend their wishes. Both men clutched large goblets of wine in their ringed fingers and enjoyed the small breeze from the two large fans operated from behind them by a pair of young black slave boys; naked but for their deerskin loincloths.

Pilate and Antipas felt fresh and clean in their loose-fitting Indian silk togas, having just come from an hour spent in the bathhouse.

"What think you of Caiaphas?" Antipas asked.

Pilate grunted disapprovingly, "I would trust him no further than I could spit him. He has an opinion of himself far greater than the reality, and I feel he would sell his own testicles to further his own ends."

Antipas nodded. "Yes, he is a repulsive fellow, is he not? A manipulator and a greedy little shit, if my judgement is correct."

Pilate nodded and took a sip from his goblet.

"And this situation with this Jesus fellow. A lot of fuss over nothing at all really, wouldn't you agree?" Antipas asked, reaching for a fig.

Pilate sighed. "It could still cause problems, even though the man is plainly innocent. A missive from Caiaphas to the right person could stir all sorts of shit. Depending on how far he bends the truth of things and who reads it."

Antipas nodded in agreement. "Please, tell me your thoughts on the matter."

Pilate rubbed his eyes and then shook his head. "I confess I am at a loss," he said.

"If I release Jesus, I make an enemy of Caiaphas. Then I am in a sticky situation. If I execute him, I risk upsetting the population and could have a revolt on my hands. Especially, as he has done nothing deserving of execution. The last thing I need is to make a martyr of him; that would not go down too well with my overlords. I would be staring at my own balls sitting on a plate in no time. Either way, Jesus is a problem."

Antipas stretched. "He is a problem to me too," he said.

Pilate looked from the table to the king. "How so?" he asked.

"The temple is a thorn in my side also. Often meddling and interfering in affairs of state. Nothing serious as yet, but incredibly annoying. I do not wish for it to get worse. It was the Sanhedrin that had my half-brother Archelaus deposed by their shit-stirring and complaining. I do not desire the same fate. And this Jesus is a cousin of a very popular preacher I regretfully had beheaded a few years ago; some of the followers of Jesus were faithful to this preacher beforehand. I agree that we cannot risk executing an innocent man for fear of public backlash. But I would rather like to see this Jesus somehow made an example of. At the same time, I would rather not have the public think I had anything to do with it, especially as I killed his kinsman. And as you say, it would be unwise for either of us to make a martyr of him. Perhaps there is some middle ground that would keep everyone happy."

Pilate furrowed his eyebrows. "What have you in mind?"

"Perhaps just a public flogging? He does not have to be dead at the end of it, but you could leave him in a state where he won't preach or cause trouble for quite a time. He could be charged with something irrelevant under Roman law, I am sure. I don't know, showing disrespect to umm…the Roman state…or something. Being a cocky bastard to the prefect, is that an offence? Lewd behaviour, or causing a breach of the peace. Something like that."

Pilate nodded. "A flogging for Breach of the Peace does not sound unreasonable."

"Will you flog the man arrested with him too? For the same offence?" Antipas asked.

Pilate shook his head. "No, I think I shall make a public show of setting him free. It might sweeten the sour taste of having to flog his companion in the eyes of the public. I will get this unsavoury business dealt with at dawn. Until then, this Jesus fellow will remain in chains and in custody here, and I will send a letter to that damned High Priest informing him of my decision. I just hope it will appease the bastard."

Antipas was silent for a minute or so, then sighed. "Can you ensure that my involvement in this decision remains secret?" he asked.

Pilate nodded, realising he may actually have the advantage in this uncomfortable situation. "I will do a deal with you. A mutually beneficial one. I have this Jesus punished for some imaginary crime and keep you out of it. In return, we have an alliance; you give me any support I need if the high priest causes me trouble in Rome. Also, if this unlikely story about rebellion has any element of truth and there are any seditious repercussions regarding the fate of this Jesus, you place your troops at my disposal and write to Rome saying it is the fault of the temple, and I am doing everything in my power to deal with it and that my actions have been exemplary. The advantage for you in this is twofold; Jesus will be out of your hair and you can rub Caiaphas' nose into a big puddle of moral piss. He can take responsibility for the ill fate of Jesus. If the Sanhedrin are left discredited in the eyes of the populace that leaves a power vacuum for Rome and yourself to fill. And if there occurs any rebellion in your lands, I will come to your aid. Does that sound fair?"

Antipas smiled. "Perfectly – let us drink to the pact – to friendship and the status quo."

Chapter 22

Blood and Water

The Sun rose into a patchy blue sky. On the western horizon loomed ominous black storm clouds and the smell of rain still hung in the air as it had done for the last two days. Cheerful birdsong greeted the dawn, oblivious to the human suffering that the morning would bring.

Caiaphas sat at his desk staring at the letter that had awaited his attention since before he had woken. The letter stated that King Antipas had decreed that, in his eyes, Jesus was entirely innocent and that Pilate was only aiming the lowly charge of 'breach of the peace' at him – for which he had been found guilty under Roman law and was to receive a flogging.

Caiaphas ground his teeth and shook his head. A few lashes of the Roman whip would be nothing like a pleasant experience, but it was nowhere near enough. There was no way he was going to let this matter drop. He couldn't now even if he wanted to, for Pilate and Antipas had made him look a fool; an ineffective one at that. His authority had been completely undermined, and he had to reassert himself. No – he was not going to let this matter drop.

Jude was woken from his fitful sleep by a shout and a kick to his thigh. "Up! Up, your highness! Stand back against the wall, you stinky fuck!"

Jude stood stiffly and was pushed back against the wall behind him by a soldier with a hard and heavy-looking wooden baton. Pilate approached looking tired and dispassionate, wearing what looked like very well used lightweight armour. It was hard to see in the half light of dawn.

Jude gave him an affable smile. "Good morning, Lord Prefect," he said with a voice husky from the thirst he felt. His tongue felt like the sole of a sandal, his lips were cracked, and there was a foul taste in his mouth. The nasty split in his top lip that Caiaphas had given him had painfully stuck to his teeth and the bruises on his body were a tender reminder that he was subject to the authority of the land and was not on its good side.

Pilate looked at him, stone-faced. "No, it is not a good morning." He folded his arms across his chest and studied Jude for a few moments, as Jude's stomach started to twist with anxiety. What did he mean by that?

Pilate drew breath and finally spoke, "You are charged with breach of the peace, fighting with the temple authorities in the municipal and public park known as the Garden of Gethsemene and found guilty. This is a minor charge, much less than that of seditious behaviour which I could have charged you with. So you should be grateful. I could have had you killed. Instead, you are to be taken under armed escort to the barrack's gates and flogged in public. After that, I am done with you, and you will be free to go. However, if you find yourself before me again, I will have to consider whether or not you have been taught a lesson." Pilate turned. "Prisoner Escort! Take him away! Guard Commander! A word!"

Jude was grabbed roughly by the arms and led away, heart pounding with the thought of the pain he would soon suffer. He bowed his head with despair and thought of his training at the hands of the Sicarii years before, hoping he could detach his mind from his body and endure his fate.

As he was led away, Pilate turned to the guard commander and spoke quietly, "Do not kill him. But leave him close to the afterlife, and wishing he had made it all the way there. Make sure it is messy and isn't pleasant to look at. And if the poor bastard passes out, don't awaken him. It is a small mercy, but a mercy nonetheless." He handed the guard a small clay tablet. "And make sure you read this aloud to the spectators before commencing his punishment. Next free the man named Bar-Abbas. There is a thief to deal with this morning too…deal with him first of all. It is his second offence, so he has only the left hand – he can lose that one at the elbow. Use a knife this time, not an axe. Ten blows across the arse first with the rod to wake him up, is that clear?" Longinus, the guard commander nodded, saluted and turned to follow his captive and escort.

Jude sat with his back against the stone wall of the barrack's courtyard, the guarded heavy wooden gates open to his right, and watched as two soldiers struggled to carry the big solidly built workbench from a shed over to the gateway. One half of the bench was stained black with old blood, and there were four hefty iron rings bolted to the sides of it near the corners. One of the soldiers caught Jude's eye and grinned evilly at him. The man chained and sat to his left

177

sobbed. Jude turned his head to look at him, sat shaking and sweating with fear, eyes glassy and staring as tears ran down his cheeks. "Oh, shit. Oh, shit. Oh, fuck. Shit. That table is for me. Oh, fuck." The man kept repeating between his little gasps for air. Jude felt the same fear, and his heart was pounding in his chest as his own sweat poured from his body. He looked at his hands as they shook. How had things come to this? Had his brother planned this all along? If so, why? Was he just an expendable pawn in his brother's plans? Did Jesus want him to suffer this? Or was it just an unfortunate turn of events? He closed his eyes and rested his head back against the wall, feeling the early morning sunshine kiss his eyelids. He tried to focus his mind on the perspective of the whole situation. It was a whipping, that's all. No castration or amputation. Just a whipping. Then he was free again. He would heal. It could be much worse. Jude took a deep breath and opened his eyes. The soldiers who had carried the bench across the courtyard were stood in front of him, one holding a ring of woven twigs in his left hand.

"Ah, isn't that nice, His Lordship is taking a wee nap. I made you something. It isn't much, but I thought a man who claimed to be a king should wear a crown for his public. Couldn't find any gold, so I hope this bit of local foliage will do," the soldier said as he knelt in front of him. The soldier pushed two long daggers into the sides of the makeshift crown, and Jude saw the vicious four-inch thorns for the first time as the soldier raised it above his head, holding it by the dagger handles. The soldier laughed as he forced the ring of thorns down on Jude's head. For Jude, the sudden pain was unbelievable, as the iron-like spines ripped into his scalp. He gritted his teeth as he felt his skin tear, and one thorn tore through his right eyebrow just as another lanced through the top of his left ear. Hot blood ran down his face and neck, mixing with his sweat and stinging his eyes.

"You there!" a voice rang out. "Stop that and leave that man be!"

Longinus strode over. "This is not part of his punishment. Now take hold of the man beside him and tie him to the bench face down!"

The man sat beside Jude screamed like a child as he was lifted bodily from the ground, and Jude heard him begging for mercy as he was dragged over to the gateway. Jude started to shiver, the pain around his head starting to subside as his skin began to go numb. He would try to concentrate on the feeling as he was whipped, maybe it would help. He had no idea how long the whipping would last, but he knew that it was unlikely he would be conscious for much more than a half-hour. It would seem like a lifetime, but half an hour wasn't much to suffer until he awoke to the stings when the punishment was over.

The two soldiers had strapped the upper half of the hapless thief across the bench with his ankles tied to the legs of it, and the man was crying, still pleading to let him go and swearing he would never steal anything again in his life. Longinus stepped forward to him. "Do not fear. I know you will never steal again. We are going to make sure of it." He stepped back and motioned one of the soldiers forward. This soldier was dressed differently to the others; wearing only a light tunic, thin loose-fitting knee-length trousers and sandals. He also wore a belt, from which hung a small axe and what looked like a butcher's knife. He was a huge individual with horrific burn scars over his left arm and over the left side of his face and head. His left ear was a mangled mess, and in his right hand, he held a five-feet-long metal bar, about double the thickness of a man's thumb. A wooden handle had been crudely fashioned and wrapped with a leather thong. He looked up at Longinus, who held up both his hands, fingers spread to indicate that ten blows were required. The soldier nodded, stood to one side of the thief and lashed out with the metal rod, catching the thief square across the back of both thighs, just below the buttocks. The thief screamed with the unexpected pain. The soldier lashed out again, this time aiming his blow an inch above the last, and parallel to it. The thief screamed again, and before he could draw breath, the third blow came another inch higher. The thief gasped in agony as the fourth blow followed. There was a pause as the soldier adjusted his stance and took half a pace backwards, then he lashed out again, the tip of the rod smashing his victim's tailbone. The next blow, the sixth, landed in exactly the same place, and the thief vomited. Blow seven landed in the same place as the first, and the last three landed just above. The man was coughing and crying, howling like a child. Longinus stepped forward again and knelt beside the man to see if he was still aware of what was happening. He still seemed to have his wits, so Longinus stood, stepped back, indicated to the soldier that he should continue with the punishment. Longinus held his left arm out and drew his forefinger across the inside of his elbow, showing the soldier where the arm should be removed. "With the knife," he said simply. The thief looked about him in panic and screamed when he saw the scarred soldier approach with his knife held meaningfully in his clenched right fist. His wrist was grabbed and his arm twisted palm uppermost, then the soldier stabbed down into the crook of his arm. This time there was no scream. Two minutes later, the soldier stepped back and

179

held the detached forearm and hand aloft for the crowd to see. Longinus stepped forward, grabbed the thief by the hair and bent to look into his eyes. He had seen death before many times and recognised the lifeless gaze on the face of the thief. He turned and motioned the other two soldiers over. "This piece of shit died on us, get rid of the carcass. Then fetch the next one."

The two soldiers untied the corpse, which flopped to the ground, and they dragged the dead man into the courtyard by his feet, dumping him unceremoniously in a corner. They then walked over to Jude, hoisted him to his feet and led him to the table. Once Jude was stripped and tied face down and full length on the bloody bench, Longinus stepped forward, raised his right hand and shouted.

"Silence! This man is to be flayed as punishment for 'Breach of the Emperor's Peace' upon the insistence of the leaders of the Temple of Jerusalem. But first, his companion, the man named Bar – Abbas, is to be given his freedom upon the direct order of the Prefect of Judea, Pontius Pilate of Bisenti." He turned to the soldiers who had tied Jude. "Fetch the man and have him away through the gates," he said.

James looked up as the ladder was lowered through the hole in the roof of his cell. He felt nervous as two soldiers climbed down it one after the other and the first looked at him and said, "Barrabas?"

James nodded in affirmation, thinking he would be the next, his screams to go echoing around the walls of the courtyard. The soldier bent and undid his chains. "Out, you are a free man," he said brusquely.

James struggled to his feet, legs and backside numb from his many hours of tightly restrained captivity. The climb up the ladder was sheer torture, but he wanted out as quickly as he could make it before someone changed their minds. Once out through the hole, he was blinded by the bright light, but dear God the air felt and smelled beautiful. One of the soldiers took him by the arm and led him to the gates, where he saw the large wooden bench with a naked man lying strapped down on it. *Poor bastard*, he thought. Beside the bench a heavily built man stood holding a many-tailed whip, parts of which glinted in the sun and, as James drew closer, he could see the shiny bits were vicious metal barbs, blades and hooks which had been wound into the leather. As he walked past, the man turned his head, and James's heart leapt into his mouth. "Jude!" he cried out and made to go to him, but the soldier pulled him to one side and shoved him forcefully through the gateway. James turned, but the two sentries stood at the gateway lowered and crossed their spears, barring his path. "Don't even consider it," one said in a low and threatening tone. Jude looked up from where he was laid and called to him. "Go! Just Go! Fetch Mother! I will need…"

"Silence!" shouted Longinus. He looked at James. "Do as he says. He will need help when this is over. Away with you."

James turned and shoved his way through the crowd and ran as fast as he could bear.

Longinus cleared his throat. "Commence punishment! From bottom to top, both back and front!" he shouted. The scarred soldier dipped the tails of the whip into the bucket of salted water beside him, raised his whip and lashed out at the soles of Jude's feet. Jude screamed out in agony as he felt the unbelievable sting of the whip. He had never felt anything like it in his life. Immediately, the whip struck him again over the back of his ankles. Three more followed up his calves, and another three up the back of his thighs. Jude prayed he would lose consciousness, his head dizzy and swimming with pain. The next lash came across the lower half of his buttocks, and tears poured from Jude's eyes, and then came an unreal feeling as something wrenched across his backside, for one of the metal hooks had lanced into him and stuck. The soldier yanked the whip free, ripping out a strip of flesh and a chunk of the muscle beneath.

Jude screamed again.

Caiaphas stood in the grand villa of the Roman prefect with the other six High Priests, all of them dressed in their official regalia. "A mere whipping?" Caiaphas said. "He is a damned rebel! He could be the cause of the downfall of all we have worked for!"

Pilate gritted his teeth in anger and spoke as calmly as he could. "I think it would be pertinent to watch your tone. I find myself losing patience with this entire matter. I would remind you of your station and encourage you to think hard about how it relates to mine. The man Jesus may or may not be innocent, but the evidence points to the fact that he has done no more than proposing an alternative set of ethics to your own. And actually, I have to admit, I quite liked him."

Caiaphas deflated a little. "I apologise, Lord Prefect. We, that is, the Temple council, all think you may have underestimated the situation. I mean no offence to you when I say this. You see our country through Roman eyes, but we see things a little differently. It is a cultural difference, and I beg of you, please trust in us. For the good of everyone, take his life."

Pilate turned away, his annoyance getting the better of him. "I have had enough of this," he said. "If it is your wish he dies, then so be it. But I tell you this; I do not do this for anyone's benefit but your own. And I will make sure I make it plain that he be executed on your insistence. You shall also remember you will owe me an enormous debt of gratitude, and I will ensure you never forget it. It is not a debt that you will ever be able to repay either. If I execute your so-called rebel, you may think of it as a binding contract. Once he dies, I own you. Is that clear?"

Caiaphas drew breath to argue the point but then changed his mind and said simply, "Thank you." *Own me indeed,* he thought. *I think not – but that is a political battle to be fought at a later date.*

"You are dismissed," Pilate said. "I now have things to attend to."

The seven priests turned and left the grand room and King Antipas appeared from a doorway. "Well played," he said. "Now perhaps we have the Sanhedrin just where we want them."

"Enough! Turn him over!" Longinus commanded. He was not enjoying this. The man the bench still had not slipped into unconsciousness but was in a strange delirium. His body was a bloody mess, and the flesh on his back and buttock was no more than a disgusting pulp. Strips of skin hung in tatters from his upper arms, but still, he breathed strongly and in great gasps. Longinus had decided that the moment the man closed his eyes to slip to the land of dreams he would call a halt to the punishment. This all seemed far too much in his eyes for a mere act of fighting in a park. Jude was untied, lifted and placed on his back. He cried out weakly in pain and Longinus told the soldier with the whip that there was no longer any need to restrain him. "And just the thighs and chest this time," he said. The soldier nodded, exhausted and streaming with sweat. He drew his arm back and lashed out with the whip, and the skin on Jude's right leg opened cleanly, showing the muscle beneath. The next blow landed across his ribs, and one of the barbs hooked into his left nipple. Longinus stepped forward and unhooked it and looked at Jude's face. His eyes were closed and he had a strange smile on his face. Longinus looked up at the soldier and shook his head. "I think that will do for today," he said. He looked at the crowd. "Is anyone here kin to this man?" he asked loudly. There was a general murmuring from the crowd, but no one stepped forward so he turned to the soldier with the whip. "Fetch the medicus, tell him to patch this poor bastard up as best as he can." He looked down at Jude. "After what we have done to him and the way he has braved it, it is only right to treat him. I have seen seasoned soldiers succumb to less."

**

Jude lay face down on a cloth-covered wooden pallet in the cool of the barracks. The medicus had neatly stitched Jude's thigh and had washed his back with clean cold water infused with a mixture of herbs and was now busy bandaging his back and shoulders having laid the torn pieces of skin back in place as best as he could. "And he suffered all this before, he slipped into sleep?" he asked, amazed at the resilience of his patient. Longinus nodded.

"Many would have died in this condition, but he breaths well, and his heart beats firmly and steadily in his chest. His biggest challenge now is fighting infection. He will never walk properly again, and he has lost his right eye. I doubt he will ever have the proper use of the fingers of his left hand and he will never be pretty, but if he fights off the pus and fevers, he will live," the medicus said. Longinus was about to reply when he heard a call for the guard commander from the courtyard. He turned and stepped out into the blistering early afternoon sun and saw one of Pilate's messengers shielding his eyes from the glare, panting from his sprint from the Prefect's villa and carrying a clay tablet in his hand. "I am here!" Longinus called and the messenger walked over to him.

"The man Jesus that you flayed this morning, you have not let him go, have you?" he asked.

"No, he is with the medicus in there," Longinus replied, pointing his thumb over his shoulder to the building behind.

"Oh good," the messenger said. "This is for you; it is urgent and is to be acted upon without delay on the orders of the Prefect."

Longinus took the clay tablet and read the message gauged into its surface. "The Hebrew Jesus is now charged with sedition and found guilty by the Great Temple of Jerusalem. Punishment is the crucifixion, decided upon also by the Great Temple of Jerusalem. Sentence to be carried out without delay. The breaking of the accused's legs to hasten death is forbidden. Charge, judging authority and sentencing authority to be read aloud upon commencement of execution."

Longinus sighed and handed the message back. "Tell the Prefect the order has been received and understood, and I carry out his order immediately," he said. He shook his head and called for the blacksmith and carpenter. He needed nails, a big hammer, rope, and the cross-member for the crucifixion post.

Jude opened his eyes and bit his bottom lip as the pain washed over him. He saw he was in sunlight and twisted his head to look around, wondering where he was and what was happening. He saw he was being carried on a litter by four Roman soldiers and beside him walked the Guard Commander. He tried to sit and realised he had been tied securely to his stretcher.

"What's going on?" he asked, surprised at how weak his own voice sounded.

Longinus looked down at him. "It transpires you are a dangerous man and a rebel. I have to see you executed; crucify you," he replied, not unkindly.

Jude's head flopped back onto the litter, and he felt total despair, loneliness and helplessness wash over him. He said nothing but closed his eyes as tears ran down his cheeks.

"James! Where have you been? I…"

"Hush, Mother, there is no time. I cannot find the others, and Jude needs help." James interrupted. "Hurry, we must go now! To Jerusalem."

"Slow down, dear son," Mary said, "what is it that has happened? I have been worried sick…You look exhausted…"

"Just come now. I will explain on the road. It is a story of disaster I have to tell you. Everything has gone wrong…have you seen Jesus? Do you know where he has gone?"

Jude was untied from the litter and was laid on the ground with a spear at his throat. The spear was not really necessary as Jude could barely move for the pain he was suffering. A crowd had gathered, drawn by the sight of what was evidently a crucifixion party proceeding through the city – an all too familiar event these past few years. As commanded, Longinus declared the reasons for the execution, but there was no response from the crowd who just watched in silence. And then the order came. "Crucifixion troop; pin him and hoist him up!" Jude squeezed his eyes shut so he would not witness what was to be done to him and bit his bottom lip hard against the impending agony. His already sore wrists were grasped firmly as he was dragged a few short feet across the rough gravelly ground and then dumped unceremoniously onto a thick beam of wood, which ran across his already painful shoulders. His arms were stretched out and tied to the beam in the centre of his forearms, and after a short pause, he felt a thumb dig into his left wrist, searching for the gap between the two bones that joined to his hand. There was a sharp blow, and an unbelievable pain shot through his arm, repeated six or seven times as the four-and-a-half-inch-long iron nail was hammered home, skewering his arm to the beam. Tears of pain and hopelessness streamed from his tightly closed eyes as his right wrist was gripped and pulled taught. This time he knew what to expect, as again he felt the probing thumb and the heavy blow as the second nail was driven through his wrist. He felt more pain in his mouth as he realised he had clenched his jaw so tightly that he had broken a back tooth and bitten a large chunk of his tongue off. The blows to the nail stopped, and Jude gasped for air but found his chest was now stretched tightly and he could not fill his lungs. Jude started to pant shallowly and started to feel the beginnings of panic setting in. He felt a tugging and heard the ripping of cloth as his bandages were cut and torn from his body, his garish wounds on display for the world to see. The cloth was then pulled from his waist which served to cover his genitals, leaving him shamefully naked. A soldier grasped each end of the beam and lifted, the nails grinding and grating against his bones. Jude could bear the pain no more and he started to cry like a lost child. His sobs came from the pit of his stomach and left him gasping for breath. The only words the soldiers heard where his pitiful pleas for his mother as the cross-member to which he was affixed was hoisted eight feet into the air and lowered onto the big upright post which stood in the centre of a row of nine; a permanent landmark on the ridge above the dusty road into the city. There was a clunk as Jude was dropped the last two inches into place; the post top fitting neatly into the square hole chiselled through the centre of the beam. Again an unbelievable pain shot through his arms, shoulders and chest as his body jarred. Immediately, his left ankle was grabbed and placed against the upright. The agony as the next nail was pummelled through his heel bone and into the wood seared up his leg, and Jude screamed. There was a strange white light in his vision, and suddenly, he was a small boy again, laughing as his brothers played on the riverbank throwing sloppy mud clods at each other. James fell onto his backside having lost his footing, rear end splatting into the thick oozing mud. Jude laughed hysterically at the sight of his oldest brother, as his right ankle was gripped, and this heel was nailed to the wood opposite the other. Jude giggled as Jesus grabbed him in a loving embrace, and then fell backwards onto the water and mud, entwining him in the safety of his arms.

Longinus looked up at the cross. The poor wretch had been up there for two hours and he did not think there was much life left in the man; he was in a terrible state even before he had been nailed up. The insane laughing and crying had only

185

lasted for a short while, and then the man had slid into a delirium, murmuring and mumbling about who knows what. Occasionally, as his breathing became laboured, he would try to push himself upwards to relieve the stress on his chest, but the agony this caused in his ankles drew moans of distress from the man's lips. This caused him to cough, and Longinus could tell he was fading fast as his struggles to push against the nails through his heels became weaker and less often, whilst his coughs sounded more and more bubbly with the build-up of liquids in his lungs.

The sky had grown dark in the last hour and huge black clouds had rolled in. Eventually, Longinus noticed a fat drop of rain plop into the dust at his feet, followed by a distant rumble of thunder. Rain would be welcome. He felt like it had been years since he had seen it last and decided to stay out in the impending deluge and watch the man on the crucifix die. For some obscure reason, he felt he had some form of duty to watch his journey to the afterlife, although he could not explain why. The raindrops started to fall more often, although they had become smaller and within ten minutes had turned into a downpour. In no time, the road had turned into a fast-running stream, and there was a faint flash of lightning and a distant rumble of thunder. A few minutes later, Jude suddenly stiffened and shouted. His remaining eye was wide open and he had a manic grimace on his face. He stared at Longinus with a look that made him feel as if he was looking at his very soul. Longinus shuddered and Jude's lips turned dark blue; seconds later, his features softened and he smiled, then went limp. Longinus walked over to the foot of the cross. Rainwater washed over his feet, marbled with the blood that dribbled from the body of the man nailed up in front of him. He saw that the crucified man's eyes stared lifelessly at the ground. There was a bright flash of lightning and a huge crash as the sound of thunder ripped the air apart and rolled away into the distance, echoing back from the hills. The rain grew heavier. Longinus sighed; now soaked to the skin, gripped the shaft of his spear and to make double sure the man was dead, stabbed it deep into the man's ribcage. Satisfied the execution was now complete he trudged back to the city through the pouring rain to report the death to the prefect. The memory of that one-eyed man hanging bloody and flayed from the wooden cross; staring at him with his one beautiful blue eye would haunt him for the rest of his life.

Chapter 23
The Lie

"Please, can you help? What happened to him?" Mary asked.

The sentry finally looked her in the eye. "Who? What are you talking about woman?"

"The man you had whipped this morning, we just said, do you know where he is?" James asked.

"Oh, him. Yes, I know where he is. Up, on one of the posts on the Hill of the Skull. Crucified. Now go away."

Mary fell to her knees. "My Jude!" she wailed, tears pouring down her face and mixing with the rainwater as it tipped from the skies. James stood speechless for a few moments, then pulled his mother to her feet. He took her by the arm and led her away as fast he could, his mother sobbing and stumbling beside him. James knew exactly where the Hill of the Skull was and steered Mary through the streets and out of the city gates. It was only a short walk till they saw the pathetic lone body hanging lifeless from the cross standing on the ridge to the left of the road. A cloaked figure was standing motionless gazing up at the corpse, oblivious to the lashing rain.

Mary cried out and fell to her knees again as tears rolled from James's eyes. He helped his mother to her feet and together they walked up the ridge, slipping in the mud. The cloaked figure turned and spoke.

"He is gone. His soul has fled," he said sorrowfully as he pulled back the hood of his cloak.

"Joseph, why did this happen?" James said.

Joseph of Aramathea shook his head. "Jesus was just too much for the Sanhedrin. He was put on trial for blasphemy and sedition and found guilty. Then Caiaphas connived with Pilate to have him put to death. Sadly, I was away during the trial, but from what I hear, my presence would have made no difference."

"But that is not Jesus, it is Jude!" said Mary, choking back her tears.

"What? But…oh. I am afraid I could not tell the difference. Oh Lord, if only I had been there, I could have told them…"

"What is to happen to him? To my son?" Mary asked, stroking Jude's foot tenderly. She looked up at her son's mutilated face and fresh tears streamed down her cheeks.

"We shall take him down. There are no guards around, so there will be no objections, I am sure," replied Joseph. "My family's tomb lies not too far away from here; we can place him in there overnight and organise a burial later."

"Thank you," said James. "Now how do we get my brother down?"

**

"You were in league with them, weren't you?" Caiaphas said with a look of disgust.

"What do you mean?" asked Joseph. It was the early hours of the morning and Joseph had only just returned from his family tomb. Removing Jude from the cross had been an arduous task and had required tools to pull the iron nails out of the wood. It was a brutal and undignified affair. He and James were exhausted by the time they had laid Jude on the large stone slab in the crypt.

"Well, you old fool, why do you think you were summoned here? I knew there was something odd going on with you, so I have had you watched. That Jesus fellow, you and he were friends, were you not? Why do you think you were sent away during his trial? Because I did not want you interfering. And thankfully, now he is gone." Caiaphas grinned, a look of triumph spreading across his face. "And you are next – you were seen helping take his body from his cross. Now, why would you do that? When you leave here, you will do so under arrest and you too can be put before the prefect as another heretic and rebel. I have evidence against you, and do not think I am unaware of your little trips to Qumran to visit Simon the Magus. A nasty little spy you are; selling little snippets of information about the machinations of the Sanhedrin, were you? Or did you do it as an idealist, and for free?"

Joseph glared at Caiaphas. "Do you honestly think your games are over? Do you honestly think you have won? Do you honestly think you will last more than a week when it becomes clear what you have done, you fool? Go ahead, have me before Pilate, do it now and by dusk tomorrow I will see you nailed up on a cross too. You have finally gone too far and made a huge error. You did not have Jesus executed. And I am sure Pilate will be none too happy with you when he finds out!"

Caiaphas swelled with rage. "HOW DARE YOU SPEAK TO ME IN THAT TONE, YOU OLD FART!"

Joseph grinned. "You arrested the wrong man. I have heard that at the trial you asked him if he was Jesus, and he said he wasn't. You ignored his answer. That is your downfall because it was *not* Jesus but his brother. You pompous fool, so full of the premature happiness of victory that you overlooked a basic error. You now are guilty of providing false witness, and as a result, are guilty of murder. I would be happy to stand witness against you – against all of you. Jesus was right, you are not *holy*."

Caiaphas stood still for a moment, utterly shocked at the news, then leapt forward with a speed that belied his size. He thrust the thin dagger deep into Joseph's eye as hard as he could, and the two men fell to the ground, with Caiaphas on top of his victim. He pulled the dagger from Joseph's face and stabbed him in the chest again and again in a frenzy of rage, shouting, "No, no, no, no!"

After a few seconds, he suddenly stopped and stood up, hands shaking with the enormity of all he had done. "Guards! Help!" he shouted.

Two armoured men rushed into the grand stateroom, swords at the ready, and they stopped dead in their tracks when they saw the bloodied body of Joseph on the floor with the blood-spattered High Priest stood shaking beside him. Before either man could speak, Caiaphas pointed an accusing finger at the body.

"He…he…he tried to kill me!" he said in a shaky voice. "He tried to stab me…with this!"

Caiaphas held out the dagger. "I don't know what happened…we were talking, and suddenly, he lunged at me…I don't think I am hurt, but it is all a blur; the next thing I know I am stood here calling for help…"

One of the guards knelt beside Joseph and put a hand at his neck, checking for a pulse. He shook his head and stood.

"He is dead; you defended yourself well," he said. "These are treacherous times; of that, there is no doubt. You may trust us to keep our silence; do you wish us to dispose of the body?"

Caiaphas nodded, and the two guards bent to lift the corpse.

"And get someone in here to clean up this mess," Caiaphas muttered. Then an idea struck him. "Guards, are you able to make a second body disappear?"

"It is not impossible," one of the two men replied.

Caiaphas nodded, a wry smile slowly crossing his lips. If there is no dead body, then there is no murder and no martyr.

***

Just before dawn, Jesus opened his eyes and the faces of his wife and Simon swam into view. A look of confusion slid across his face as he looked from one to the other. His left eye was badly swollen and blackened with bruising and his bottom lip was crusted with a thick scab from where it had been split against his teeth. He tried to sit upright, but pain stabbed him in the ribs, and Mary gently laid a hand upon his shoulder and shook her head, then she bent and kissed him on the forehead.

"I love you," she whispered into his ear and left the room leaving him alone in the lamp-lit room with Simon.

"I...I do not understand – Simon?" Jesus croaked.

"Rest easy, friend. I will explain," Simon replied quietly, passing him a cup of water. "have a few sips of this whilst I talk," he said.

Simon pulled a chair over beside Jesus and sat.

"Everyone was caught out – it was all so very unexpected. One moment all was calm, and the next, there were soldiers all over the place. You and Jude were overwhelmed, and I can remember Jude shouting for everyone to run away. Your brother James and I could not leave you both, and so we tried to help the pair of you. We had no chance, and we were arrested. You were knocked out, and in the confusion, Peter managed to drag you away – and, from some feat of amazing strength, managed to bring you here. I somehow managed to escape. James and Jude did not. James was released for some reason, and Jude was sentenced to be beaten. James and your mother have returned to Jerusalem to collect him, for he will need nursing. Roman beatings are thorough, and I fear for him."

Jesus sighed, and a huge wave of guilt and despair washed over him.

"This is all my fault," he whispered. "All my fault. What have I done to my brother?"

"Of course, it isn't," Simon said. "It was just unfortunate, an unpleasant set of circumstances. I do not know why, but Jude seemed to be the target of the attack. What has he done?"

Jesus shook his head slowly. "He has done something on my behalf and paid the price. I have let him down. Is he all right?"

"I have no idea; there is no word yet. You must take things slowly; you have had quite a roughing up."

Jesus furrowed his brow. "And you haven't? Look at the state of you; all battered and bruised. No. I must get up, find out how my beloved brother fares. Help me up, will you?"

Jesus stood, with Simon keeping him steady on his feet as he was hit by a wave of dizziness.

"And where do you think you are going?" Mary asked from the doorway.

"I must journey to Jerusalem; I need to see Jude; to see if he is all right. Please do not think of trying to persuade me otherwise."

Mary tilted her head and smiled. "I understand. But please be careful; you are not really fit to travel, and Jerusalem could be a dangerous place for you."

James and his mother arrived at the family tomb of Joseph of Aramathea just as the sun rose, flooding the city with warm orange light and casting long distorted shadows. All signs of the previous rain had disappeared other than a light mist which hugged the ground. Mary had stared at her feet as she walked, heartbroken, and her eyes moist with grief. James had guided her through the city from the lodging house where they had stayed overnight and the unhappy pair were exhausted from the previous day's events and a lack of sleep.

It was James who noticed that the stone slab that served as a doorway to the crypt was ajar, and he whispered to his mother to stay where she was whilst he cautiously approached the entrance, wondering who was inside. He suspected it might be Joseph, but he thought it best not to assume. James sidled up to the gap in the doorway and slowly poked his head inside. The low-angled rays of the Sun illuminated the emptiness inside, casting a shadow of James's head on the far wall. He stepped inside and looked at the stone slab where he had left the body of his brother a few hours before. There was nothing there, but Jude's shroud. James called for his mother to enter.

Together James and his mother stared silently at the stone slab for a few minutes, not knowing what to do next. James knew he had no way of getting a message to Joseph to ask if he had any idea where Jude had gone. The only way of passing a message to him was through his brother who was lying senseless in Qumran 25 miles away. And he had no idea where Jesus' other followers had gone to; they had just vanished, and he had heard nothing from them. Peter had gone into hiding too. The only one he knew the whereabouts of, was Simon who was with Jesus. Everything had fallen to pieces, their entire band had become scattered and all was confusion.

Finally, his mother spoke, "James, go to Qumran. Wake Jesus. I do not care how. Tell him of events. Fetch Simon the Zealot. And Simon the Magus too. We need to find Jude. Go. Go now. I will wait here. I do not care how long it takes; I want my son found."

James kissed his mother on the forehead and walked out of the crypt and into the sunshine.

***

It was late morning when James saw the ox cart on the road ahead, making its way slowly towards him. As they approached, he saw the two men on the cart were his brother and Simon, and he gave them a wave and quickened his pace.

"James!" Jesus cried out as he gingerly lowered himself from the cart. James ran up to him and threw his arms around him.

"How is Jude?" Jesus asked desperately.

James took a step back and held his brother by the shoulders.

"Brother, there is no easy way to say this. He is dead. Executed. The bastards crucified him. And if that is not bad enough, his body has gone missing."

"Dead? Missing? Why was he killed? Where has he gone missing from?" Jesus asked, shocked by the news of the fate of his dear brother.

"I do not know why he was killed. Your friend Joseph and I placed his body in a tomb late last night…Joseph's family tomb it was…and when Mother and I went there early this morning, it was empty. He has been taken. Jesus, I do not know what to do; I don't know where our friends have gone; I don't know how to find out where Jude has gone. Mother wants Simon the Magus to help, but I don't know what he can do."

"Where is Mother now?" Jesus asked.

"She waits in the tomb for my return…but…"

"Fetch the Magus. I know where the tomb is. I will go to Mother."

Two days passed; confusion and denials abounded as regards the whereabouts of Jude's body. The Romans had no idea what had happened to it, and representatives of the temple just shrugged their shoulders and said it was nothing to do with them.

James and his mother eventually managed to gain an audience with Claudia, whilst Jesus returned to Qumran. Simon Zealote stayed in Jerusalem to hunt down their friends and send them to see Jesus, but of Joseph the Aramathean, there was no trace. He had simply vanished, just as had the body of Jude.

James and Mary were left with a dilemma; did they mention to Claudia that it was Jude that had been executed and risk the Romans carrying out a manhunt for Jesus; resulting in his crucifixion too? Or was it best to say nothing? They considered that if they told Claudia the truth, it may well mean that Caiaphas would be put on trial, but they had no idea if justice would be done; unaware of the uneasy relationship between the High Priest and the Roman Prefect.

In the end, they decided that caution was the safest option, for they had no wish to stir up a potential hornet's nest and make things worse. They would leave that decision to Jesus in the coming days.

Claudia made enquiries on their behalf, but the news was disappointing. Nobody knew anything. Longinus was summoned, but he could only account for the period of time ending in the death of the crucified man. Eventually, Pilate himself spoke to James and Mary, stating that he had carried his duties as far as required, and that the fate of the body was neither any of his responsibility or interest. He made it plain that Roman involvement in the affair was over and that brother and mother would be well advised to drop the matter before he lost patience with them. Claudia could do no more, for her husband had spoken and she sadly bade them good fortune in finding the body. They decided they had done all they could and sadly returned to Qumran.

"WHERE IS HE?" Caiaphas bellowed.

Simon Magus slowly shook his head. His hands were numb from the ropes that bound his hands, a blessed relief from the pain of his broken fingers.

He had been trying to find out where the Aramathean was; making discreet enquiries at the nearby synagogue when he had been roughly seized, a coarse rough bag pulled over his head and dragged away. He now found himself in a dark stone room tied hand and foot to a rough wooden frame with the high priest and two guards for company.

Caiaphas lifted Simon's chin and spat in his face.

"Tell me where Jesus is, and I will make it a quick death," he said.

Simon looked him in the eye. "You had him murdered by the Romans, didn't you?" he whispered.

Caiaphas turned to a guard. "Cut a nipple off...he pretends to be a man, so he has no need of them."

The guard stepped forward with a pair of sheep-shears in his hand, tugged Simons left nipple, stretching the skin, and snipped. Simon screamed.

"Tell me where Jesus is hiding. Now. Or you lose the other."

"I do not know!" said Simon.

Caiaphas looked at the guard again and nodded. The guard repeated his action with Simon's other nipple, and he screamed again.

"Answer me...remember you have a cock and pair of bollocks to go yet...my man could get four more cuts out of them I'll wager, so tell me where he is."

Simon raised his head. "He is in Qumran!" he blurted out, sobbing. "Please, no more..."

Caiaphas smiled. "My two guards here have quite unpleasant tastes and talents; the reason I employ them. Are you sure you are telling the truth? Swear to me you do not lie, and I will get them to kill you quickly. Or I could let them cut you into little pieces. It could go on for hours, especially as you are a chubby fellow."

"I swear! I swear! Please, just kill me." Simon begged.

Caiaphas nodded. "I believe you," he said and walked to the cell door. He looked at the two guards and smiled. "Cut his throat, make it a quick death. But before you do, you are both welcome to fuck his fat arse. Be as rough as you like."

Caiaphas turned, opened the door and walked out and down the tunnel, whistling, as he heard Simon start to scream again; ignorant of the fact that Jesus had only an hour before – along with some of his closest friends, packed up his family and started his last journey to Gallilee – out of Caiaphas's jurisdiction and reach.

Chapter 24

The End of the Dream

It was on the road to Galilee that the arguments started. Peter and Simon Zealote felt that the others had let Jesus and his brothers down by running away and that they should not have listened to Jude as he shouted for them to go. Andrew and his brother pointed out that they were powerless to help, Phillip remained silent, but Bartholomew and his brother James stood alongside and defended Andrew. Jesus himself tried to calm the situation; keeping the guilt he felt for his brother's death hidden, but Simon Zealote's anger at the loss of his friend refused to die and his temper kept boiling over.

By the third day of their four-day journey, the atmosphere within the group had grown almost unbearable, and there had become a palpable air of ill-feeling amongst them. They had become split into two groups who walked a hundred yards or so apart; Jesus and Simon at the rear. They even camped around separate fires.

As the mid-afternoon sun threw a shimmering heat haze over the beautiful but harsh landscape, Bartholomew, in the leading group, suddenly stopped and turned, eyebrows twisted as he pondered a question that had nagged his normally slow mind. The rest of his group stopped and gathered around him, Andrew asking what was wrong. Bartholomew remained silent until Jesus caught up.

"Jesus, something has been bothering me; a memory…I am sure it is real and I did not dream it. I need to ask you something," Bartholomew said quietly.

"What memory is this?" Jesus asked.

"In Gethsemane…I heard a shout before those guards burst out of the bushes…someone shouted, 'That's the kiss…I am sure of it.' I am confused…what did he mean by that?"

Simon Zealote turned to face Jesus. "Now Bart mentions it…I am sure I remember something like that too," he said.

Jesus felt the blood rush to his face, unprepared for the awkward question. He shook his head. His first instinct was to deny all knowledge, but the guilt he felt for his brother's death washed over him, and he knew he could not lie. His eyes welled with tears, and he had the overwhelming urge to fulfil a need to tell of the secret he and Jude had shared. He could keep the secret no longer, for it was burning away at his conscience. "Please…may we sit?" he said.

Jesus led the group 20 yards or so from the road and sat on the rough and dusty ground; the rest sat around him.

"I do not know where to start," he said.

Andrew coughed and spat the dust from his mouth, took a swig from his water-skin and said, "You can start by telling us what has really been going on. I think there is far more to this whole thing than you have told us."

Jesus nodded and looked down at his sandaled feet. "You are right…I have deceived you all," he said. He took a couple of sips from his own water-skin and looked directly at Bartholomew – all could see the tears now running down Jesus' face. He took a deep breath. "My brother is dead because of me. He did something I asked of him…and died as a result. I…I did not intend it."

"What?" asked Simon.

"I sent him to the Sanhedrin…to plot my arrest…so I could stand in front of their court and make fools of them…as the start of the rebellion. But something went wrong. In Gethsemane…I realised it was an idiotic idea…I was afraid…and I went to speak to Jude to tell him we should run. He was to identify me by a kiss on the cheek…and all I can think is the guards mistook my quiet words with him for that kiss…it was dark…it was confusing for everyone…I was scared…and I did not try hard enough to help my brother…"

Simon Zealot stood; furious, and kicked at a stone as hard as he could. "How could you have done this to my friend?" he shouted. "What a bloody stupid idea! And after all you have told us about the nobility of man! You come up with a hare-brained plan like that…and then your own brother gets killed as a result of your stupidity and cowardice! And what do you do to help? Fuck all but cry about a pathetic bang on the head! You are a prick! Oh so fucking wise with all your big talk and grand ideas, and then you prove to be no man worthy of them! All of you! You all ran away…nobody helped…Just James and myself…full of fucking talk – the lot of you! Grand words and wise thoughts…but lacking in balls to live by them." Simon pointed at Jesus. "You fooled your brothers…but you don't fool me. They were the only real men amongst you. They lived by your philosophy, and Jude died by it. He lived in honour, I thought you did too. I am done with you. I can remain loyal to your ideals, but not to you. You failed your own brother. You failed my best friend."

Simon glared at the group, then sneered at Jesus and walked off. Thaddeus jumped to his feet, muttered something which sounded like it was meant to represent some form of apology and rushed after Simon.

Jesus and the rest sat in silence for a minute or two and then Andrew stood up, looking down on the seated Jesus.

"Simon speaks the truth," Andrew said. "We are all guilty of fear. I am full of shame. And I for one will never feel this way again; that I swear to all present. Jesus, everything you taught is the truth…and I see you have tested us. We all failed. Even you. You sent Jude to speak against you in secret, and he was hung by his own words. And every one of us then failed him in his hour of need."

Bartholomew stood and placed his hand on Andrew's shoulder. He stared at Jesus and slowly shook his head. "Jesus, I am sorry," he said. "I can no longer recognise you as the man I thought you were. But I will be the man you taught me to be."

Bartholomew turned and started walking back towards the road, Andrew trailing behind whilst the rest watched. Once on the road, Bartholomew looked back at them and then resumed his walk to Galilee. Slowly the rest stood, and one by one followed him.

As Jesus sat alone, seeing everything he had planned and worked for throughout his life unravel before his eyes. His wife and children gathered around him and put their arms around his dejected form.

"It is over," he said quietly.

"It cannot be over, dear husband," Mary said. "This is just a setback; remember what you yourself said? That our lives are a test to mankind? This is just such a test."

Jesus remained silent for a while then sighed heavily. "The men will never forgive what I have done and what I have failed to do. They are better off without me now. I am finished. Perhaps this was my real destiny. To fail. To set an example of how not to be."

Mary held her husband tighter. "Perhaps, and perhaps not…Nobody knows what the future has in store."

"I think I do…I can see it clearly," Jesus replied. "You know, it is written that God created Man in his own image. But that is not true. It is the other way around. Men create gods. Humanity is the supreme being…for we pass judgement upon each other and ourselves, sometimes unwisely, I admit, but we then choose freely whether to punish and damn for eternity or be merciful and forgive, or to find innocent. My brother Judas Iscariot and I will be judged too. He will be known for all time as the man who died for a noble cause, trying to help me teach about the nobility of humanity. A true martyr. And I will be cursed as the man who failed him; a traitor…the one who ultimately betrayed him."

Jesus stood and looked at his wife. "Let us forget Galilee…let us just head east towards India and see where the road of life takes us."

Chapter 25

Aftermath

Israel was never an irrelevant isolated place during the time of the great Egyptian and Roman empires. The Jewish people had influence everywhere and the events in this book occurred in a global theatre. Herod the Great himself was no minor character in history. He was a shrewd king who ruled for 34 years, not averse to a bit of harsh cruelty if he regarded it necessary – in fact, somewhat renowned for his brutality. He dragged his country into the then-modern age. He instigated, oversaw and financed huge building projects, his most famous being the Great Temple in Jerusalem – of which only the western wall remains; known now as the Wailing Wall. Herod developed an efficient water supply system for the city of Jerusalem and built huge fortresses such as Herodium and Masada and founded new cities too. As a reward for his support of Caesar Augustus, he was given huge tracts of land in Gaul – what is now France – and saw his country trade in a global market. Although Herod had a reputation for cruelty and undoubtedly suffered from paranoia and depression for most of his life, he was not all bad. After a serious drought in 29 BC, he spent a fortune importing grain from Egypt to feed his people, and knowing how badly his country's economy was affected by this, he even waived taxes for a few years. As for the Massacre of the Innocents; there is no historical proof for this whatsoever. A latter-day comparison would be Saddam Hussein – loved by some, hated by others, a friend of powerful states and happy to torture and kill to maintain the status quo.

Herod ensured that Israel remained an important country in the Roman Empire, just as the Jewish peoples were an important factor in its economy. The Jews were a widespread people, living throughout the empire and heavily populating the Middle East. Forms of their religion were taken on by most – for the faith of Islam was still 500 years in the future.

The life of Jesus, Yehoshua Ben Yusef, took place during chaotic times in a country of great importance. Israel was torn by three great leaderships – Rome, the Herodian kings, and the Church. As a consequence, leadership was a balancing act of subtle politics, secret alliances, lies and deceit. Jesus wanted this to change, and he himself became an influence that Rome and the church saw as a threat. After the crucifixion of Judas Iscariot, and the disappearance of Jesus, there came a religious revolution – instigated by many of Jesus' followers and supporters. The status quo was threatened, as was the power of the church, and this coincided with a run of mentally unstable Caesars – for after the death of the weak and incompetent Tiberius came Caligula, Claudius and the insane Nero.

The Gospels were written during this period, and as there was a cultural and religious revolution in the air, anyone who taught this new belief system was in danger. The 'Pesher' technique was, therefore, used in these writings; a system of passing information not so much in code but in disguise using language full of ambiguity. Causing further confusion is the fact that many key people in the story of Jesus' life had more than one name. Thomas was in actual fact Herod Phillip, Simon was renamed Peter, whilst John, Mark, Bartholomew and Nathaniel were all the same person. Judas Iscariot was known as 'The Beast' and 'Satan' because of his fervent nationalist beliefs, whilst Simon Magus was also known as Zebidee, Lazarus, Ananius, Demetrius the Silversmith, Leper, and Lightning. Thaddeus and Jude were Theudas – the then leader of the Egyptian church, also known as Alexander and 'Earthquake'. The literal translation of the Gospels has, therefore, created the confusion and apparent contradictory nature of these documents and along with the many mistranslations which have occurred, one sees that nothing in the current biblical account of Jesus' life is to be taken as the absolute truth. Further to this, events previously attributed to other characters in the ancient world such as Horus raising El Azarus from the dead, have been transferred to Jesus.

Tiberius died in AD 37, having spent most of his time living on the island of Capri – avoiding as much responsibility as he could. Rumours abounded regarding the goings-on in his palace with tales of sexual perversion and so on. Caligula became leader, and three years later, Saul was 'converted' on the road to Damascus. Saul became known as Paul, but to the original disciples of Jesus, he was known as the 'Spouter of Lies'. The disciples disapproved of his translation of the teachings of Jesus and his depiction of the events in his life.

Some of this may have stemmed from jealousy that Paul seemed more devout than them, but this we shall never know.

It was around this time, that Mary Magdalene is documented as divorcing Jesus in records found at Qumran – indicating that he did not die on the cross at Calvary.

A year later, in AD 41, Caligula was assassinated, and Claudius took charge. Three years after that is the first recorded use of the word 'Christian'. That same year – AD 44 saw James son of Zebidee decapitated by Herod Agrippa 1. He was allegedly buried in Santiago de Compostela, Spain. Another three years later, Andrew was crucified in Patrae, Achaea, (Greece) on a diagonal or Saltire cross.

In AD 54, Nero became Caesar with his grandiose ideas of remodelling Rome and becoming the greatest leader Rome had ever seen. Rome was lucky – they now had a leader who was a god.

It is thought that it was during Nero's rule that Phillip, his sister Mariamme and Nathaniel were arrested in Hierapolis. All three were tortured, and the two men were then crucified. Phillip allegedly preached from his cross, extolling the virtues of Nathaniel. According to legend, the crowd then released Nathaniel, but Phillip insisted he should himself be left to die, which he did.

AD 62 and Jesus' brother James was stoned to death on the orders of the high priest of the Senhedrin, Ananus the Younger. Stoning was a popular method of carrying out the death penalty. It could take hours to die from stoning, and the cause of death was mostly from brain damage caused by skull fractures. In modern Iran, this practice is still carried out – the victim being tightly wrapped in a sheet and then being buried up to the waist, exposing only the upper half of the body to the projectiles thrown at him or her. That same year, James the Less was arrested and crucified in Ostrakane, Lower Egypt. After his death, his body was taken and sawn to pieces. Two years later, in AD 64, Nero swung into action his grand plan to redesign his capital city. Flames roared and thousands died and were made homeless as Rome became an inferno. Nero blamed the new religion of Christianity for the fire and had Christians rounded up throughout the remains of the city. Among those arrested were Paul and Simon Peter, and both were crucified.

The following year, Simon the Zealot and Thaddeus – having spent years preaching the teachings of Jesus in places as far as Syria, Samaria, Idumaea, Mesopotamia, and Libya, were arrested in Suanir, Persia. Thaddeus was executed by dismemberment – hacked to pieces by an axe. Simon Zealot was sawn in half. The method for this was terrible; the victim would be sandwiched between two large planks of wood which were held together by being staked together vertically into the ground – the hapless victim usually upside down. A large two-man saw much like those used in tree-felling was then used to saw through both the condemned and the wood – starting at the victim's crotch. The pain suffered by the victim during an event of execution in this manner cannot be imagined. The only survivors of Jesus' original band of disciples were Mary Magdalene, whose name was blighted after her divorce and her role as an early disciple played down, Matthew who preached until old age, and Thomas who left Middle East and made his way to southern India. Jesus himself was discredited by his own men – the bible records the disciples failing to recognise him as their teacher after the crucifixion. It is unlikely that this means anything other than they were disgusted at first, that he had allowed his brother to be killed on his behalf. It is possible that Jesus went to India years before Thomas, or even fled to Africa, where it is thought the Holy Grail was taken also.

By AD 70, there had been serious rioting and rebellion by the Zealots and Rome answered with a heavy hand. Jerusalem was almost razed to the ground and Herod's great temple was destroyed during the process. War was waged upon the Zealots. After a four-year campaign, the last of the Zealots were trapped at Masada, where the survivors committed mass suicide.

In the meantime, Christians used the sign of the fish to identify themselves, and it was many years before the 'Crucifix' was used as a Christian symbol – adopted as a sign of religious enlightenment and freedom. Christianity had spread like wildfire through the Roman slaves who already used the cross as a symbol of unity and the hope of freedom from the aftermath of the Spartacus rebellion which saw thousands of rebel slaves crucified along the entire length of the Appian Way. For them, Christianity promised something better than the fate which had befallen them on Earth. When Christianity first arrived in the British isles, it was regarded by the Celtic natives as a pathetic religion – unmanly and unlikely to ever become popular. A Celt would as soon kill an elitist Christian than speak to him. Without eventual Roman support and the desire for the empire to have one unifying religion, it is unlikely that Christianity would have ever become popular in western Europe.

Since then, Christianity has hijacked many aspects of other religions as a way of overcoming them. December 25 is one holiday seized by the church and a walk around Ireland shows how holy Pagan sites were built upon by Christians – for many chapels have Druidic stone circles or Neolithic burial mounds close by. Another prime example of this is the adoption of Brigit as a Christian saint when in fact, she was a Celtic witch-goddess. In the name of Christianity and in honour of Brigit, people still make corn-dollies in the shape of a Swastika, mistaking the traditional pagan sign of good luck for a Christian cross.

In the two millennia since Jesus lived, thousands have been killed and countless hundreds have been horribly tortured. The church has seen people dismembered, disembowelled, roasted alive, boiled, hung, flayed, raped and enslaved. No organisation in the world has ever been responsible for as much brutality and conflict through its history – not even Hitler's Nazi party or Stalin's Communists; there have been wars aimed at the accumulation of vast wealth and the seizure of land instigated by, and for the benefit of the church. That same church has covered up murders, rape and prevented many of its members from facing public justice for crimes such as paedophilia and child slavery, even until these modern times. They have even done their utmost to prevent people from thinking for themselves – for up until the mid-twentieth century the Office of the Holy Inquisition was responsible for education.

And all in the name of Jesus.

The Cast

Andrew

Lives with his older brother Simon **Peter,** and his wife, Andrew works as a fisherman on his brother's boat and is a former follower of **John the Baptist.** Peter and his wife have a great feeling for Andrew since his wife died in childbirth. Andrews's grief had turned into general anger at the world and had asked himself similar questions to Jesus when his father died – there is therefore a link between the two men. Andrew recognises this and is as a consequence drawn to him. They have more in common than they originally thought.

Augustus/Gaius Julius Caesar Octavianus

Caesar Augustus was the founder of the Roman Empire. Born in 63 BC, he ruled from 27 BC until his death in AD 14. He was born into the extremely wealthy Equestrian order – or order of knights. The life of Augustus was filled with major achievements; too many to list here but suffice to say he achieved true greatness for Rome. Although he is thought to have died of natural causes, it was rumoured at the time that he may have been poisoned by his wife.

Bartholomew (also known as John/Mark/Nathaniel)

Brother of **James the Greater**, he is a very honest man. Bartholomew bears an ugly scar along the left side of his head where he was struck by a shield as a youth by a Roman soldier during a fracas in a market place; he suffered a fractured skull, which left him generally as a placid individual, but with severe bouts of temper at times – usually over something minor. He is thought of by some a bit of a simpleton. Sometimes, he suffers delusions and has a tendency to get his facts mixed up, finding it difficult at times to grasp basic concepts which he finds very frustrating. He is at times a victim of severe and debilitating headaches.

Through his own experiences, he has become a very kindly and sympathetic man, with a fondness for stories. Bartholomew can appear quite childlike at times as he maintains an air of innocence, and would be regarded as one who, if he becomes your friend, is a friend for life, and is known for his generous and caring nature. He sees Jesus as a man who he can relate to as Jesus gives the impression of caring and generosity too.

In modern times, he would be considered as being 'vulnerable'.

Caiaphas

Power-hungry, pompous, overbearing, bad-tempered, greedy, selfish and overweight, Caiaphas is an archetype; he represents everything a high priest should not be but stereotypically is. Caiaphas has no interest in any form of spirituality and sees the hierarchy of the temple and his religion as purely a means for power and wealth. Utterly ruthless, Caiaphas is an empire-builder by nature and uses the law for his own gain. Also known as Yoseph Bar Kayafa, he was not only the high priest but also chairman of the high court.

Claudia

The wife of **Pontius Pilate**, Claudia is the daughter of a very wealthy merchant. Regarded as being beneath Pilate's class by some, she has proved to be very good at diplomacy and is entirely supportive of her husband's career.

Drusus

Drusus Julius Caesar was born the son of Emperor **Tiberius** in 13 BC and showed great potential as both a military man and as a politician. In AD 4, he married Livilla, who began an affair with his arch-rival **Sejanus** around the year AD 19. After years of positioning and power struggles, it was generally accepted by AD 23 that Drusus would succeed Tiberius as the Roman emperor. Then in AD 23, he suddenly died, although the circumstances were not suspicious at the time. The fact that he was murdered did not surface until AD 31 when Sejanus' ex-wife committed suicide and made the claim that Sejanus and Livilla were behind his death.

Elizabeth

Cousin of **Mary** and mother of **John the Baptist**.

Germanicus

Born in 15 BC, Germanicus Julius Caesar was the nephew of Emperor **Tiberius** and the brother of **Livilla**. He was a successful military campaigner and something of a hero in Rome. He died in suspicious circumstances in AD 19, in Syria, and there was suspicion that **Sejanus** was somehow involved.

Herod Antipas

Antipas was installed to the throne of Perea and Galilee by Ceasar Augustus in 4 BC upon the death of **Herod the Great**, his father. It was this puppet king who ordered the death of John the Baptist, and who also found Judas (in the Bible – Jesus) not guilty of any capital offence. In AD 39, he fell afoul of Emperor Caligula with the accusation of treason against Rome after some territorial disputes and was exiled to Gaul. His date and place of death are unknown, as is the date of his birth, although it is known he was alive between the dates of 20 BC and AD 39. He was the half-brother of **Herod Philip**.

Herod the Great

Born in Jericho in 73 BC, Herod came to the throne with Roman support in 42 BC. He was overthrown two years later by Antigonus and fled to Rome. In 37 BC, Rome recaptured Judea and put Antigonus to death, restoring Herod to power. He ruled for about 34 years until his death in 3 or 4 BC. During his rule, Herod started a campaign of building, possibly inspired by what he had seen in Rome and founded the cities of Maritima and Caesarea. He also built the massive fortresses of Masada and Herodium, and involved himself in the business of shipbuilder's asphalt and the copper mining industry.

Herod is a man of ruthless intent, with psychopathic tendencies, and suffered paranoid episodes.

Hezekiah

The elderly tutor of Jesus, Hezekiah is a Magi, or wise man. He originates from Egypt and is knowledgeable of many religions, medicine, languages and folklore. He is also party to what may be called the secrets and knowledge of much older civilisations. Hezekiah has a mysterious past.

James/Barabbas

The older brother of **Jesus** and **Jude,** he feels jealous of Jesus. James loves his brothers but feels his role should be more important and often questions Jesus' principles and methodology as a way of exerting his position as oldest brother. After his father's death, he feels he became the man of the house but was underrated. James has a bit of an inferiority complex, and feels the need to prove himself at times; he, therefore, takes on the role as duty-bound protector.

James is a big man, who imagined himself as a warrior hero from a young age. He is prone to bouts of violence – mainly borne of deep-seated anger and frustration. He also has very strong ideals regarding family ties which causes inner conflict; he will always be there to try and protect his brothers regardless of his mood with them.

James actually feels cold towards his mother as he feels she loves Jesus more. He undergoes many emotions but does not understand them. James is actually a fairly simple man, and he wishes life were simple too; seeing things very much in black and white, this leads often to confusion, so he tends to try and avoid thinking about things too much that involve complex issues. James prefers to act on impulse.

James the Greater/James Niceta (also known as Yaakov Ben Zebdi)

Brother to **Bartholomew,** James has a natural tendency towards bigotry, being a hater of the Samaritans. He has a fiery temper and an underlying vein of anger running through his entire persona; he directs this towards the established religion and the Roman authorities. James tends to rant on occasion and has a very angry style of preaching. The idea of a god who is vengeful and warlike appeals to him. He is attracted to Jesus as he believes that religious reform is long overdue and wishes to aid in the overthrow of the establishment; James is quite a rebel.

207

James the Less/James the Just (also known as Yaakov Ben Alfas)

James the Less is known as such as he is a very short man and quite thin.

He smells, does not wash, shave or tend his hair, and does not drink ant form of alcohol; he is also vegetarian. James is a very nervous individual, quite highly strung, and a little paranoid at times.

James claims to be proud of his appearance, and at the same time has self-esteem issues, mainly to do with aspects of his personality, and always feels insecure and lacking in confidence. His appearance is a way of overcompensating for his personal issues; his public face being that of a man who says, "Here is me, and who cares who likes me?" which is at odds with his true nature. He is attracted to Jesus, as being in his presence gives him confidence, and he sees that being so close to him increases his sense of his own worth as a man – it makes him feel important.

Jesus

Born in 6 BC; the year of the census of Quirinus, Jesus is a man on a journey, although he does not realise it. His entire life has been overshadowed by his mother's expectations of him. As the middle son, he feels he must do everything in his power to fulfil these expectations, and deep down he feels he has something to prove to his mother, **Mary**. Jesus is a peculiar mix of emotions; unconsciously jealous of his older brother **James**, trying to be a hero to his younger brother **Jude**. He feels his father **Joseph** let him down by dying in a roof repairing accident. Jesus has deeply philosophical ideas about who or what God is, bordering on Atheism at times. Jesus ended up believing in a more earthly spirituality but finds it frustrating that people find the need to believe in a god as a mysterious being, whilst he himself starts to find the whole idea as silliness. He sees the temple for what it is and feels desperate to cause its downfall and unite his people.

He cannot always deal with his own thought processes, and often talks in riddles as a way of sorting his own thoughts out. Jesus also believes that to a degree, the end justifies the means, and is happy to deceive his followers to achieve his end goal. He lives in constant fear that he will not have the courage to face what he feels is his own destiny when the time comes but would never admit this to anybody…his big secret is his fear of being a coward.

Jesus Justus

The son of **Jesus** and **Mary Magdalene**, and brother to **Tamar**, Jesus Justus was born in AD 21. He fled to what is now known as Southern France with his mother and older sister sometime after the Crucifixion but in his early teens returned to Judea against the wishes of his mother. He was in Rome preaching with Paul when Paul was arrested and executed in AD 64.

John, the Baptist

John is the only child of **Elizabeth** and is a cousin of **Jesus**. He was raised in the shadow of Jesus and had very mixed feelings about him. John was a jealous child, and prone to tantrums and spiteful behaviour. As he grew he became fanatical about his religion and was almost psychotic in his beliefs, and he thought himself above and beyond the law. He was openly critical of **Herod Antipas**, and for this, he was eventually beheaded. As an adult he was quite unstable mentally, suffering more and more from personality disorders which started in early childhood.

Joseph

Father of **Jesus, James** and **Judas** and husband of **Mary,** the Joseph of popular culture is a carpenter; however, this is merely due to mistranslation. In the earliest Greek literature, Joseph is described as being a Tekton, which is actually an architect and stonemason. This was regarded as being a very important job, and Tektons were very well respected. They were attributed with great knowledge, and even know this holds true regarding the mythology and secrecy surrounding the Masonic Order.

Jude/Judas Iscariot

Judas is a character every bit as interesting as Jesus, his older brother. He is a trained Assassin, and totally dedicated to Jesus; they look very much alike and have often been mistaken for one another. Judas looks upon Jesus with absolute loving trust, and as something of a father figure. He regards Jesus' opinions and views as far beyond his own simple understanding and without question.

Judas is not traumatised by his father's death as he barely remembers it.

Trained by the Sicarii, he is sometimes called upon by his order to carry out the odd 'hit' or assassination. He became known as 'The Beast' with the Qumran

Temple number of 666; referred to in Revelations, he is a religious policeman with a fanaticism born of dedication to his brother.

Judas feels he has a lot to prove as the youngest of three brothers, but with loyalty due to his desire to be loved by Jesus. He has feelings of destiny.

He endured great hardship during his training for the Sicarii, and as a consequence has a strong feeling of duty regardless of personal consequences. He is generally able to suppress his own emotions in order to get the job done.

Mary

Mother of **Jesus, James** and **Judas,** wife of **Joseph,** and cousin of **Elizabeth**, Mary is no ordinary woman. In modern religion she is quite a powerful and enigmatic character, however, she is not as popular culture would portray. There are many accounts of various Marys, and this due to the fact that Mary is not a name but a reference – such as 'sister' refers to a nun. The title 'Virgin' is also misleading, and does not mean she was actually a virgin but means she was actually a holy woman – possibly at some point even being a priestess (much like the title of Vestal Virgin). With the claim that Jesus was of the line of David, it is unlikely that this followed the line of his father, but more likely; given Mary's religious title – the line of David runs through her. Mary is a caring woman, although not exceptionally so, and because of her upbringing has an interest in educating her son Jesus in the best way possible. Because of her bloodline, she feels that her sons have a destiny to fulfil. Mary has high ranking relatives throughout the Diaspora, and especially in Egypt.

Mary Magdalene/Mary of Magdala

The wife of **Jesus**, and mother to **Tamar** and **Jesus Justus**, Mary met Jesus at just 16 years of age; he was 23. Spellbound by his enigmatic manner, she decided to dedicate her life to him. Mary was a spiritual woman, already in training to be a holy woman (hence the name of Mary), she turned her back on her order and education in favour of Jesus' new philosophy.

Philip

Originally from Bethsaida, he was a previous disciple of **John the Baptist.**

Philip is a teacher, an academic, fluent in Greek and a fan of geometry and mathematics. Something of a philosopher, he is searching for the meaning of life and is unhappy with the current reasoning. He is drawn to Jesus as he likes the new ideas he preaches. Philip is a true humanitarian, born with a wealthy background. As a child he was involved in a fight with another boy; Philip beat the boy severely and left him blind in one eye and with a facial disfigurement. He carries the guilt of this with him and is always trying to atone for his actions. Even now he is wracked with sorrow for what he did. This drives him on to be prepared to die in the name of good as he feels this will absolve him; as a result, this may lead to a clouding of his judgement.

Pontius Pilate

Prefect of the Roman province of Judea from AD 26 to AD 36, Pilate was of the Equestrian Order. More a soldier than a diplomat, his governance of Judea was watched closely by Rome as there was an awareness that Judea had to be handled carefully. Pilate's job was mainly military, but he was also responsible for the collection of taxes. Along with this, he had a minor role in law and order; being both chief constable, judge and jury. Pilate had a reputation for cruelty, although in actual fact he was not needlessly so, and certainly not by Roman standards. He was a very fair man, and a good judge, however, he did believe in harsh punishments. Pilate was very aware of his own limitations and had every respect for the opinions of his wife **Claudia,** in whom he relied heavily for advice on matters social and diplomatic. There were times when he was known to be quite heavy-handed; especially when dealing with rebellion, and it was just such an event that ended his duties as Prefect of Judea when he brutally put down a Samaritan uprising. He arrived in Rome, faced the displeasure of the new emperor, Caligula, and vanished into myth and legend. The is an early account that he was exiled, and eventually committed suicide in Gaul around AD 41.

Sejanus

Lucius Aelius Sejanus was born an Equestrian in 20 BC. He was a highly ambitious man, and utterly ruthless. When Tiberius retired to Capri, Sejanus acted as emperor in his absence and started a period of purges; killing as many who could cause a threat to his power base as possible. One of the very few to survive was the infamous Caligula. He was involved in the deaths of **Germanicus** and **Drusus,** both of whom probably died from poisoning. In AD 31, and without warning Tiberius had him arrested and executed by strangulation. His body was thrown to a hostile crowd who dismembered his corpse and promptly went on the rampage; rooting out and murdering anybody they could get their hands on who had allied themselves to him. Later on that year all his children were executed (his daughter Junilla was raped first), statues to Sejanus were pulled down, and his name was stuck from all official documentation and state records.

Simon Peter

A fisherman from Bethsaida, he is brother to **Andrew** and a married man who owns his own boat. Peter was named by Jesus as the next great teacher of the new way of thinking – the new order of spirituality which he is trying to form. He is a family man and is torn between his desire to follow Jesus and his duties to his family. He does not want power, and for this reason, Jesus chooses him to be the man to lead his new belief system. Peter finds the thought quite intimidating; however, he is very honourable and takes any trust placed in him very seriously.

Simon Zealote

Trained Sicarii, he shares a bond of brotherhood with **Judas Iscariot.** Simon is something of a lost soul, entering the Sicarii at a very young age. Simon is a mysterious and shadowy figure, with psychopathic tendencies born of a very traumatic childhood. He is an orphan from birth without any close family and seeks kinship and a feeling of belonging – being in the order of the Sicarii helped with this, but after his training, he joined the Zealots as he felt the need to bond with other men through further hardship. In time he left the Zealots as he felt they were not as hard-line as he thought, and is therefore happy to join Jesus as he thinks that action is just around the corner. Although he has moved from one group or organisation to another, he is incredibly loyal to his friends.

The aspect of his desire for kinship with other men is due to the fact that he is bisexual, however, he does not acknowledge this for some time as he does not understand his feelings. Eventually, he falls in love with **Thaddeus.**

Tamar

The daughter and oldest child of **Jesus** and **Mary Magdalene,** she was born in AD 19. After Jesus' failed rebellion in AD 27, she fled to what is now known as Southern France with her mother and younger brother.

Thaddeus (also known as Jude)

A priest in reality but known as 'the Farmer', he is a cousin to Jesus; their mothers being sisters. His mother is known as Mary too, being of the Holy Order of Qumran (an Essene Jew). His father Clopas is murdered for his belief in Jesus' new spirituality.

Thaddeus is a homosexual, and eventually has a relationship with **Simon Zealot.** He feels like an outcast of society, and is a bit feminine in character; he can relate to the teachings of Jesus as Jesus is not judgemental of his sexuality. He is quite noble in character, a very quiet man, thoughtful, and with a playful sense of humour.

Thomas/Thomas Didymus/Thomas the Twin/Herod Phillip/Herod II

Thomas is actually only a cover name for Herod Philip, son of the infamous **Herod the Great.** He is related to **Herod Antipas** (half-brother) who had **John the Baptist** beheaded. The beheading of John was the incident which leads to Thomas seeking out Jesus, as he was a supporter of John. Father Salome, he was also known as Thomas the Twin as he looked identical to Herod Antipas. As Herod Philip, he was exiled to Lugdunum in Gaul in AD 39 but returned to the Middle East in secret under the identity of Thomas – eventually ending up in India where he met his death.

Thomas would have had a very traumatic upbringing as a son of the megalomaniac and paranoid Herod the Great. He has great wealth and his own small but effective army, the generals of which he would not trust as he fears Herod Antipas would have spies within their ranks. Thomas was originally heir to Herod the Great, therefore Antipas would regard him as a potential threat to his own security; hence his association with Jesus under an assumed name.

Thomas actually has no desire for power as he has seen first-hand how it can corrupt and induce paranoia and cruelty.

Thomas feels the desire for forgiveness although it is not through anything he has done himself but the guilt of the actions of his family.